CATACOMBS

CATACOMBS

Paul McCusker

Tyndale House Publishers, Inc.
Wheaton, Illinois

JL BT

Visit Tyndale's exciting Web site at www.tyndale.com

Cover photograpy by Brian Eterno

Catacombs is based on the play *Catacombs* by Paul McCusker, published by Lillenas Publishing Company (1985, 1995).

Published in association with the literary agency of Alive Communications, Inc., 1465 Kelly Johnson Blvd., Suite 320, Colorado Springs, CO 80920.

Scripture quotations are taken from the *Holy Bible,* New Living Translation, copyright © 1996. Used by permission of Tyndale House Publishers, Inc., Wheaton, Illinois 60189. All rights reserved.

Library of Congress Cataloging-in-Publication Data

McCusker, Paul, date
  Catacombs / Paul McCusker.
    p. cm.
  ISBN 0-8423-0378-2
  I. Title.
PS3563.C3533C38 1997
813'.54—dc21   96-40211

Printed in the United States of America

03	02	01	00	99	98	97		
9	8	7	6	5	4	3	2	1

PART

ONE

The Escape

CHAPTER 1

THE gray dusk bled through the bars on the high, narrow windows. It poured over the prison cafeteria and filtered out all the color. The cold stone walls, the men in drab prison overalls with their trays, the metallic tables—it could have been a scene from one of the black-and-white movies Murphy loved so much. Back when they first gave him the shock treatments, those old films seemed like the only reality he could wrap his hands around. They were his life.

"Who am I?" Murphy asked himself as he stepped into the cafeteria. He hitched up his trousers in a losing battle against his round belly. "Am I George Raft or Jimmy Cagney?" He glanced to his right to make sure Fennis was keeping the guard occupied, then to his left and upward to where the surveillance camera hung limp in the corner, the victim of a wayward basketball earlier that morning. "Maybe I'm Humphrey Bogart. This is a Bogie scene." He moved across the cafeteria, weaving his way through the tables like Rick in *Casablanca*. He had his eye on Mr. Smith, who was hunched over his tin plate like a question mark. Smith was new, but he wasn't just anybody.

Murphy cleared his throat and sat his huge body down next to Smith. Smith's fork scraped the bottom of his tin plate like fingernails across a blackboard. Glancing again at Fennis and the guard, Murphy leaned on his elbows, his back to the table, so he faced away from Smith. He didn't want it to look like he was there to actually talk to Smith. Unfortunately, he *felt* as if he looked exactly like a man who was trying not to look the way he was looking.

Smith lifted his head wearily but didn't speak. Not with his voice, at least; his eyes spoke volumes. Murphy was certain that in those eyes he saw the blank despair of every prisoner he'd ever known in the rehabilitation facility center. It was as if somebody gathered every ounce of pain soaked in by these walls and squeezed it like a sponge into Smith's eyes. It broke Murphy's facade. He turned to look at Smith as if Smith had said something to him. It was a silent misunderstanding.

Murphy's voice was soft, gravelly, and full of nicotine. "Glenda, in the office . . ."

Smith absentmindedly jabbed at his leatherlike meat loaf and congealing gravy. "Glenda," he repeated mechanically.

"She overheard a call between Chapman—he's the warden—and that captain. You know who I mean. Slater. He knows you're here."

Smith didn't act surprised. He only shrugged as if to say that somehow "they" knew everything. Sometimes they knew sooner and sometimes later, but they always knew everything eventually.

"I guess they got your fingerprints back to Central, and somebody made a match." Murphy coughed in a thick, congested way. "Slater will come for you tomorrow, but he doesn't want anyone to know he's coming—even the guards. He's afraid they'll blab. Wants to surprise you, I guess."

Smith nodded indifferently as he gently put down his fork and pushed the tray away. Then he quickly looked up as if he felt eyes on him. Murphy stole a glance over his shoulder to

4

see what caught Smith's attention. A wizened old man sat at the far end of the table. The two men stared at each other, their faces blank.

"Who's he?" Smith asked quietly.

"We call him Preacher. He used to be one." Murphy circled a finger near his forehead. "Too many shock treatments. They're letting him out tomorrow."

Smith scratched at his curly brown hair, then rubbed the day's growth of stubble on his face. He looked as if he might say something, then simply sighed.

"We have a plan to get you out," Murphy said.

"*Just* me?" Smith asked.

Murphy smiled gallantly, like Bogie to Ingrid Bergman. "Passage for one."

Smith pressed his palms against the top of the scarred table as if holding down the lid of an exploding box. His voice was low. "Anyone who helps me escape . . . they'll kill."

"What makes you think they won't kill us anyway?" Murphy said. "But *you* have to get out of here. You're too important."

The words hung in the air, then dropped like cement between them.

Smith's eyes—those wounded eyes—settled on Murphy again. "Forget about it. I don't want the responsibility."

"You've got it whether you want it or not," Murphy said in a cavalier way. Bogie to Edgar G. Robinson in *Key Largo*.

Smith studied his hands, still pressed against the table. That was all.

Murphy felt disconcerted and disappointed. Smith was supposed to be upbeat and brave. He was supposed to be Errol Flynn in *The Sea Hawk*. What was he up to? Was he simply putting on an act to keep the guards from getting suspicious? That had to be it. Smith was being noble. He was being chivalrous: a man like Smith would hate for others to have to sacrifice for him. He wanted to carry the burden himself. "This is something me and the boys are proud to do. What else is there in this place? They might knock us around for it—maybe they'll kill us—even that's a morale builder. It sure breaks the tedium of the sweatshops."

"You have no idea . . . ," Smith said, then let his voice fade away to nothing.

When Murphy was sure that Smith had nothing else to say, he leaned forward and whispered, "The plan begins at lights-out. . . ."

Smith wouldn't look at Murphy. His whole demeanor, the way he stared straight ahead with those eyes, made it look as if he didn't want to know about the plan. Murphy felt agitated. It was a clever plan. Far more clever even than the time Murphy smuggled out another prisoner in the refrigerator truck. He got a beating and thirty days in solitary confinement for that stunt. He wouldn't have gotten off so easily if the prisoner hadn't suffocated en route.

But today he was Bogie, and Bogie didn't care about the risks.

". . . from there, you'll follow Riva Creek to Winoga Falls. Someone will meet you. Then you can get on with your work," Murphy concluded in his grizzled voice.

Smith turned his gaze to Murphy as if a curse had just been placed on him. "I'll do what has to be done."

It was a simple proclamation that Murphy didn't know how to interpret. What role was this man really supposed to play in this black-and-white movie? Was he affirming his duty like Jimmy Stewart? Or was he playing it like Gary Cooper in *High Noon?* Maybe he was being the steely Sean Connery to keep from betraying the seriousness of their plan. Murphy couldn't sort it out. Did Bogie make any movies with

Jimmy Stewart, Gary Cooper, or Sean Connery? He didn't think so.

Murphy heard Fennis cough, their signal that the guard was watching them. He stood up. He wished he could get a better sense of what Smith was thinking at that moment. The slender, pleasant face with the martyr's eyes didn't give him a clue.

As he worked his way through the cafeteria tables again— oh, if only he had a white tuxedo—he couldn't shake the feeling that Smith's words weren't really a proclamation of duty but an announcement of resignation. Murphy caught a quick glimpse of the scene one last time before he rounded the corner out of the cafeteria.

The old man at the end of the table stood up. Smith watched him.

Their mouths didn't move, but Murphy got the feeling that something was said between them.

CHAPTER 2

CAPTAIN Robert Slater, director of the government's Special Forces division, rode the last five miles to State Rehabilitation Facility with impatient glee. He watched the speedometer inch past seventy miles per hour, then turned to Officer Williams, his assistant. "Can't you go any faster than that?"

Williams, bemused, glanced at him out of the corner of his eye. "I assumed you wanted to get there alive. These back roads can be—"

"Never mind the roads," Slater said. "You have no sense of adventure."

They raced past the dead cornfields and skeletal trees that pierced the morning horizon. It had been a cold autumn; the leaves were long gone. Barbed wire, normally hidden by vegetation, sat thorny and exposed. On the horizon some unidentified camp barracks stretched out like round gray ships on a brown ocean.

Slater fidgeted in his seat. First he clenched and unclenched his fists. Then he ran his fingers through his wavy red hair.

"You're antsy," Williams said. He'd noticed that Slater had been like that the entire flight and subsequent two-hour drive.

Slater pushed himself against the cheap vinyl seat to stretch his legs and dug a hand into his pocket. "We're so close. You want a breath mint?"

"How long has it been in your pocket?"

"A week. I don't know."

"No thanks."

Slater popped the mint into his mouth. "Every second counts. If those yokels had processed his fingerprints right away, I'd have been on the first flight up. How long have they had him—*two* days? I don't have the patience for that kind of incompetence."

Williams knew it well. "Maybe you should've had the guards put him in solitary. Just to be on the safe side. They have solitary in the rehab facilities, right?"

"You're joking. Solitary there is a slap on the hand and getting sent to bed without milk and cookies. It's not like the maximum security centers," Slater explained. "Uh-uh. No special attention. Then he would've known I was coming, and his roaches would've come out of the woodwork to steal him away."

Williams allowed a flicker of a smile to cross his face. "*Roaches?* That's a new one."

"That's what they are," his boss said. "They're roaches—sneaking around in the night, behind the walls, across your face while you sleep. And just when you think you've squashed them all—shocked or blasted the life out of them—another batch shows up. Their tenacity is infuriating."

They drove on in silence. Williams remembered how, as a child, he had been taught about Christians. Back then they were regarded as cult members following a misguided philosophy. No one in his right mind would ever want to *be* one. They were pathetic creatures. Ignore them and they'll eventually go away was the general attitude. He now wondered how they had turned into roaches to be stamped out. He wished he knew his history better.

He watched as his boss opened and closed the glove box for no particular reason. Slater's agitation was unusual. This prisoner was important. This was a big day for Slater.

"Do you think they'll promote you?" Williams asked.

Slater shrugged. "Who cares?" He punched the button to engage the mobile phone, checked a number on his pocket pad, and dialed. "Let's let them know we're coming, shall we?"

The internal car speaker ran through the tones and then connected. It rang in the lodgings of Bernard Chapman, the warden. Williams had met Bernard Chapman two years before on a different assignment and remembered him as being a round, Dickensian fellow with long sideburns. The face appeared on the dashboard monitor and proved Williams's memory correct.

Predictably, Chapman was instantly in a flap when he heard who it was. "Sir, if only I'd known," he sputtered. He wiped a bit of egg from the corner of his mouth; they'd interrupted his breakfast.

"If only you'd known *what?*" Slater asked casually.

"You weren't due for another six or seven hours!" Chapman complained.

"My watch must be off," Slater lied. It was part of his makeup to be painstakingly punctual. You could tell it to look at him. His face was wound tight like a spring.

"Yes, sir. I was told specifically that—"

"I'm sorry. You were misinformed. Please prepare the prisoner for transfer," Slater said.

"But this is unusual . . . irregular . . . to facilitate a transfer at this hour," Chapman stammered on. "The staff that handles it won't come on until nine."

Slater leaned toward the monitor and spoke in low, measured tones. "Chapman, I'm going to be there in five minutes. It's a matter of national security that you have him ready."

Chapman's jowls flapped as he nodded briskly. "Yes, sir, I'll see what—"

Suddenly the speaker was filled with a shrill siren. Williams winced. "What in the world—"

"It's the alarm!" Chapman shouted as he turned from the screen. The line crackled, then went dead.

Slater pushed the button to disengage the phone. "Step on it."

✻

Slater and Williams arrived at the rehabilitation center amidst screaming sirens and general chaos. At Slater's urging, Williams nearly rammed the front gate as he sped to the main building. Slater leapt out of the car before it had stopped and grabbed the first guard he could get his hands on.

"What happened?"

"A riot!" the officer said, then rushed off helter-skelter with the other guards.

Slater found Chapman in his office barking orders alternately into a phone and a walkie-talkie. Williams looked smugly at the half-eaten breakfast plate on the desk.

Chapman stiffened when he saw Slater enter the room. "The perimeter has been sealed; the guards have everything under control," he dutifully reported.

"What happened?"

Chapman brushed the back of his hand across his glistening forehead. "Some of the prisoners were out for their morning exercise and started fighting. It got out of hand. It's OK now."

"Is it?" Slater asked with restrained impatience. "Do your prisoners often fight?"

"No—never," Chapman replied. "Most of the inmates are—er, *were*—insurrectionists."

"You mean Christians."

12

Chapman nodded. "But they've all had shock treatments. They're generally compliant."

Slater glanced at Williams, then asked Chapman, "Was my prisoner part of the fight?"

"No. He's in his cell."

"Are you sure?"

The blood drained from Chapman's already pale face. "The guards reported that all the cells were full. But in the confusion—"

"I suggest we check *now*," Slater said.

Chapman led the small entourage from his office to a closet-sized security room across the hall. In it was a wall of at least a dozen surveillance monitors watched over by a scarecrow-looking guard with thick glasses and a constipated expression on his face. He leapt to his feet when they entered.

"Sector C," Chapman barked.

"Yes, sir." The guard swung around to the archaic control panel and poked at one of the dimly lit buttons. He looked up at one of the monitors and gestured as if to say that they were looking at Sector C.

"Move down to Cell 47," Chapman said.

Using a toggle, the guard sent the camera down a track that ran in front of the cells, their numbers clicking away in blue on the bottom left-hand corner of the screen—52, 51, 50. But at 49 the camera suddenly stopped and refused to go any farther.

"It won't budge," the guard said nervously. "Something must be blocking the track."

"Call the sergeant in that sector," Chapman commanded.

The guard reached for the phone, but Slater snapped impatiently, "Forget it. Let's go see for ourselves."

✳

The old man with the wild white hair and beard clutched his gym bag as he was led down the corridor by Patowski, one of the new recruits.

Patowski had once hoped to be a police officer or, better yet, a member of the secret services. But to his everlasting annoyance, he'd had an infection in his left ear when he was a teenager, and the loss of hearing negated his ability to serve in anything other than the lower security services. Guard work was the lowest of the low. With a wife and two children at home, he was grateful for a regular paycheck—even if it came from a rehabilitation center.

The old man faltered, and Patowski gently tugged at his arm. He was being released today. Patowski looked at the rubbery wrinkles and vacant eyes. Preacher they called him. This one could have been let out a long time ago. He'd had enough shock treatments to be sure that any semblance of belief was deep-fried away like yesterday's onion rings. Patowski wanted to ask him how he felt about being released, what his plans were, whether he had any family left. But the old man would have quoted a Bible verse at him or talked about one of the few memories that played again and again in the fool's brain. Even new recruits like Patowski knew not to try and converse with Preacher.

They passed the front offices just as a group of men exploded out of Chapman's door. Patowski pulled the old man aside to let the men go by. They had stern faces, particularly the redheaded man in the expensive suit. Chapman looked stricken.

"I wonder what that's all about?" Patowski said to no one.

The old man didn't answer. A flickering fluorescent light

above seemed to catch his attention. "Am I working in the laundry room today?"

Patowski shook his head and guided Preacher on toward the exit area. *What's a big shot in a nice suit doing here?* he wondered. Things were already winding down since the altercation in the exercise yard. The prisoners were in the infirmary or their cells; the guards were back at their posts. Maybe there was something else going on. Patowski would have to check into it. The right word, the right action might draw the big shot's attention to Patowski. He could get better work than this, he just knew it. He was glad that his wife had just cleaned and pressed his shirt.

The process to release Preacher took no time at all. Frank O'Connor, the bushy-eyed man behind the desk, had the paperwork ready to go.

"Anybody know what started that ruckus this morning?" Frank asked.

"No idea," Patowski answered.

The old man hardly seemed to recognize the old watch, empty key ring, and worn wallet handed to him from the large personal possessions envelope. Frank checked them off. "You want them in that gym bag?"

He didn't wait for an answer, but unzipped the top and put the meager inventory inside next to a spare pair of trousers, a shirt, and a shaving kit. There were books, too, but Patowski couldn't see the titles.

"I can't imagine what got into them," Frank said, still talking about the fight. He counted out the obligatory release money—enough to get Preacher started in proper conditions of poverty—and handed it over. Preacher took it but didn't seem to know what to do with it.

"Put it in your pocket," Frank said.

Preacher obeyed and tucked it in the one on his shirt.

"Take care, Preacher," Frank said. "Do you know where you're going? To the end of the courtyard. Got it? Turn left and walk about a quarter of a mile. That'll take you to Beeson's Grocery and Gas. A bus'll come by there within the hour. Do you understand?"

Preacher nodded and, clinging to his gym bag as if it harbored jewels, stepped up to the large, mesh-covered door. Frank hit the buzzer, and the latch clicked free. Patowski opened the door for the old man.

"See ya, Preacher," Patowski said.

Preacher stepped into the light, shielded his eyes, then hobbled through the courtyard to the larger gate in a mindless way. The wind caught his white hair and beard and blew it around in wild waves.

"I don't know why they bother," Patowski said.

"Makes them feel just, I think," Frank commented.

A black sedan pulled up at the gate, and a fragile old woman got out. She wept as she held Preacher first at arm's length, then pulled him close for a hug.

"Wife, do you think?" Frank asked.

Patowski didn't answer. What little training he'd had in observational work told him that something wasn't quite right. The old woman guided Preacher to the passenger side of the car and then lightly stepped around to the driver's side. She crawled in and started the engine.

Something didn't ring true. What was it?

The sedan pulled away and out of view.

Patowski frowned. "His daughter?"

"Too old for his daughter," Frank said.

"But . . . the way she walked around the car," Patowski began, but didn't know where he was going with the thought. "Didn't you see it?"

"No."

"She walked like a *young* woman."

Frank looked out the window as if looking would replay the scene for him. "I didn't notice."

Patowski shrugged it off and went to see if he could help the warden in any way.

❋

Williams wished Slater had simply called the guards in that area to check the cell. But he knew Slater didn't trust anyone enough to do that. The two of them—with Chapman and a growing host of nervous guards—barreled past the various security checkpoints and arrived in Sector C on the other side of the center.

"Stand clear!" a guard shouted.

The inquisitive inmates stepped away from the bars of their cells and sat on their beds.

Chapman reached Cell 47 first and looked like he might faint. Slater and Williams arrived a second later.

An old man with wild white hair and beard sat on the edge of the bed, his hands folded politely in his lap. He looked up at Slater and smiled like a child greeting a special friend.

❋

Williams drank lukewarm coffee at Chapman's desk and watched his boss pace the room. Searches for the escaped prisoner yielded no results. An all points bulletin was issued for the black sedan and its occupants, but Slater made it clear that he didn't believe they'd be found. "They'll find the car all right," Slater said. "And it'll have the wigs and makeup in it. But nothing I want."

Frank O'Connor, the guard in charge of the front desk, and a new recruit named Jeff Patowski stood red faced by the wall. Chapman lingered nearby unhappily.

Slater was incredulous. "How could this happen? You're telling me that you simply *look* at an exiting prisoner and let him go? Don't you have a scanning system?"

"I tried to put one in our budget, but the Council cut it," Chapman answered.

"Fingerprints? Identification tags?" Slater continued, this time to O'Connor.

O'Connor nervously shook his head. "No, sir. That isn't part of the protocol for low-security rehabilitation centers like ours."

Slater glared at Williams, who made a note to address protocol issues with Central when they got back.

Chapman said, "We're not a big-city operation like you're used to, Captain. We don't warrant all the bells and whistles. The inmates we have here—they're mostly harmless. It's not like they're hardened criminals."

Williams waited for his boss to blow a fuse. But Slater only stared at Chapman with a cold expression and asked quietly, "What do you consider a hardened criminal, Chapman? A murderer? A thief? A child enslaver?"

"Well, . . . yes."

"And what do you think *makes* a criminal hardened? I'll tell you what it is: The *idea* that killing or stealing or enslaving children is a good idea. Criminals are criminals first in their ideas. Do you understand? It's what they have *up here*—" he pointed to his temple—"that makes them hardened criminals. These Christians have an *idea* that leads to action against our state—against *us*. Ideas bring down a world, not guns."

Chapman persisted. "But these ideas are just the naive superstitions of the weak-minded. You don't seriously believe that they're a genuine threat."

"Oh, I believe it," Slater said in a clenched tone. "Quite

seriously. Now, if we can stop this moronic banter, I want to talk to the escaped prisoner's accomplices."

Chapman knocked on the door, and a guard brought two men into the office. They were manacled from head to foot.

"Roaches," Slater said softly to Williams.

"These are the two," the guard announced. "They say they don't know anything about it."

"Thank you," Slater replied before Chapman could. He leaned against the desk and eyed the two men over. One was a medium-sized bearded creature with a face that looked like a purple leather couch. The name Fennis was stitched to the breast of his overalls. The other was larger and more substantial in build—Murphy.

"So you don't have anything to tell me about the escape, Mr. Fennis?"

Fennis shook his head. "No, sir. I don't have anything to say about it."

"It's not Christian to lie," Slater said with a smile.

"It's not a lie to say that I don't have anything to tell you," Fennis countered.

Slater conceded the point with a slight tilt of his head. "Fennis, I saw in your file that you're up for parole in three months. Only three months after—how long has it been? Four years? Four years in here for what? Teaching the Bible to a bunch of bikers. Was that your crime? Turning Hell's Angels into Heaven's Angels?"

Fennis looked impassively at Slater.

"You're so close, Fennis. Why would you blow it by helping someone escape? I don't understand. Help me, will you?"

Fennis kept his eyes locked on Slater's. "I'm sorry, sir. I'm not sure you'll understand no matter what I say."

"I could release you in *one* month if you choose to cooperate," Slater said suddenly.

Fennis's face tightened at the offer. He pressed his lips together, then relaxed. "I still wouldn't have anything to say."

"Patowski," Slater said with a wave of his hand.

Patowski nearly leapt across the room. "Yes, sir?"

"I want you to take your nightstick and hit it as hard as you can across the bridge of Mr. Fennis's nose."

Fennis took a step back. Williams braced himself for anything to happen.

Patowski went pale. He asked, "What?" but it sounded more like a click from the back of his instantly dry throat.

"I want you to take your nightstick and—"

"I heard you, sir, but I . . ." Patowski didn't have the words.

"You don't want to do it, I know," Slater said sympathetically. "And I don't want you to do it either. But Mr. Fennis refuses to help and, frankly, I can't imagine that talking will persuade him."

"But . . . why me?" Patowski asked.

Slater looked at Patowski as if he'd turned into a small child. "Because you let our prisoner escape, and this will go a long way in making amends. You want to make amends, don't you? You don't want words like *incompetency* and *recommended for immediate dismissal* to show up on your record, right?"

"No, sir."

"I'll be asking Mr. O'Connor for a similar favor," Slater said casually.

Chapman was wringing his hands. "Captain, I don't think—"

Slater held up his hand. "Warden, I don't care what you think. Patowski, go on. You can do it."

Patowski slowly pulled out his nightstick and looked as if he might vomit. Fennis was wild-eyed as he backed away. The guard put a restraining hand on him. Williams kept his eye on

Murphy—he was large and strong looking. Though his expression didn't betray any emotion, Williams suspected that Murphy would be the one to take action.

"Well?" Slater asked impatiently.

Patowski held up his baton like a baseball bat.

Chapman said, "I'll file a report."

"You'll kindly be quiet. Do it, Patowski."

The new recruit in the clean and pressed shirt positioned himself in front of Fennis, who was still trying to look tough but squirmed against the guard.

"I don't have anything to tell you because I don't know anything," Fennis said, his knees trembling and his legs beginning to buckle.

"No good," Slater said and signaled Patowski.

With trembling hands, Patowski stood like a batter waiting for a pitch. He brought the baton back.

"Go," Slater prompted him.

Williams touched his fingertips to the butt of the pistol in his shoulder holster.

Patowski closed his eyes, his entire body taut.

"No!" Murphy shouted. "Stop! He's telling you the truth. I'm the one you want. I concocted the whole scheme. He was just a bit player."

Slater moved next to Murphy and looked into his grizzled, pock-marked face. "You're Murphy," Slater said.

"Yeah, I'm Murphy," the man replied in a raspy voice.

"Another biker who saw the light, huh? I'll bet you miss those roaring engines and the feel of leather." Slater smiled.

Murphy straightened up and lifted his chin. It was a weak gesture of defiance. It reminded Williams of a movie starring Jimmy Cagney he'd once seen.

"Tell me what you know about the escaped prisoner," Slater said, leaning against the desk again.

"You may as well go ahead and kill me," Murphy said. "I'm not afraid of death, and I won't tell you anything."

Slater smiled. "Death is going to be the least of your worries, Mr. Murphy." He nodded at Williams.

Williams didn't like inflicting pain on people or animals or even insects—like roaches. But it was never a matter of liking or disliking it. He'd been trained thoroughly by the Academy to use the art of physical violence to extract whatever information was needed from anyone, at any time, with any tools available. With a dispassionate approach that had given his classmates the chills, Williams was able to flip a switch and change from a charming and friendly fellow into a cold clinician. Slater had referred to the insurrectionists as roaches, but for Williams they were frogs under the dissector's scalpel. It was a job that had to be done. That was all. At least that's what he kept telling himself.

So when Slater gave Williams the sign to apply his training to Mr. Murphy, he stood up, carefully took off his jacket as if he didn't want to wrinkle it, removed his shoulder holster and gun, and said politely, "I'm sorry, Mr. Murphy. It's nothing personal."

Murphy didn't die that day, though Williams was sure that he wished he had.

CHAPTER 3

Sam Johnson's life changed with two events that happened on the same day: He was fired, and someone slipped a mysterious note under his apartment door.

He guessed that the note had been delivered to his one-bedroom efficiency even while he was across the college campus at the chancellor's office being dismissed. Burdened with a box of books and sundry belongings from his small office, Sam had trampled the note as he entered his apartment. If his paperback copy of *Candide* hadn't slipped from the top of the box, he might not have seen the plain white envelope until much later—perhaps when it was too late.

He absentmindedly shoved the note into the pocket of his tweed sports jacket while he put the boxes down. Pressing a hand against the side of his head, he tried to massage past his thick, sandy-colored hair to the headache beneath. He sat down on the worn-out, spring-bent sofa and tried to sort out what had happened. It was hard for him to believe that he'd been fired. Sixteen years of classes, seven years of tenure were quickly dismissed by a nervous administrator who wouldn't look him in the eyes.

His friendly, blue eyes creased in a frown, highlighting the freckles and laugh lines around them, as he conjured up the scene. It was an odd moment for two old friends to share. But

Sam shouldn't have been surprised. He was the one who always said that your enemies can't betray you, only your friends can.

Just three days before, he and Bill had gone fishing together. Then they weren't chancellor and professor; they were just two old pals standing hip-deep in the cool river, smoking their pipes and talking about nothing in particular. But it wasn't *nothing* talk, was it? Bill must've been making mental notes.

What had happened? That night, as the fire filled the air around the tent with the smell of smoke, bad coffee, and pine, Sam felt at ease, comfortable in their friendship. He said something he probably shouldn't have said: He admitted to a belief in the impossible, a search for God that had taken him into a great mystery called Jesus Christ. He hadn't meant it to sound so serious or profound. But it did. It was.

Now he remembered that uneasy expression on Bill's rounded, beleaguered face as he stoked the fire. It was an expression that asked, "Why did you have to tell me? Why couldn't you keep your mouth shut?"

In Bill's office, after his friend delivered the blow, Sam was too shocked to say anything except "Why?"

The chancellor shook his head and muttered something about the college's economic woes and "signs of the times."

They both knew, though. "The fishing trip," Sam stated.

"It has nothing to do with that," the chancellor said without conviction. "But, Sam, you were supposed to study that junk to poke holes in it, not *believe* it."

Signs of the times indeed, Sam thought as he straightened up to his full six-foot height and indignantly strode out of the chancellor's office.

Now, sitting on his apartment sofa surrounded by his boxes, he felt depressed—as if he'd broken up with his lover. And the college was Sam's lover: his girlfriend, wife, and mistress rolled into grade books, exams, and class syllabuses. The joy of standing in front of a class filled with open minds and eager faces ready to receive the world's great literature like some kind of communion gave him a sense of fulfillment no human could have provided. He needed little else. Even after the new government closed the minds and the faces became stonelike, he continued to teach with every ounce of passion he had—faithful to a lover who would reject him in the end.

He thought of all the things you say when you experience a breakup. He'd have more time for those writing projects. He could go out more often. He might finally get to cleaning out the spare closet.

He leaned back and put his hands over his thin face. Weariness lighted on his shoulder like a bird and pecked at his eyes. They ached and burned. What was he going to do now?

The mysterious envelope rustled in his pocket. Hopelessly he pulled it out, looked at the unmarked front, and tore open the back.

"They won't leave you alone," the word-processed note said. "Pack your warmest clothing and be at 11 Camden Court by ten o'clock tonight."

Sam smiled sadly. The bottom half of the typeface was faded: a telltale characteristic of the printer in his department. Was he being warned by one of his interns? A student? Or was it the ever-faithful, ever-diligent Dolores who had been the department secretary for as long as anyone could remember? He never spoke of his Christianity with her, but he had always suspected she was a believer.

He slumped into the sofa like someone had pulled the stopper on his body and let the air out. He had to concentrate. The timing of the note couldn't be coincidental with his firing. Someone for some reason was trying to help him. Or it might be some kind of trap. His conversion to Christianity didn't happen very long ago and, like many new believers, he was less than discreet in his discussions about it.

But why would the authorities go to all the trouble of trapping him? It was easy enough for them to simply show up and arrest him on some pretext. A few questions at headquarters, they'd say. And then, like so many others, he'd simply disappear. Which friend or neighbor would dare inquire?

Signs of the times, all right. He had a student in a class two semesters ago who had unwisely defended Christianity. It was hardly a defense, actually, just a couple of comments that had given everyone the impression she was in favor of some of the basic philosophies espoused by Christ. He remembered how she had stood so lithe and determined, her long blonde hair cascading halolike around her fresh face. She had spoken about Christ in a matter-of-fact tone, as if she hadn't grown up in a state where matter-of-fact tones invited betrayal. Doubt and fear were what the State liked.

A class monitor—they had been secretly posted in each class by then—must have reported her. Two days later, while Sam was teaching about the merits of state-sanctioned censorship, the girl had burst into the class, frantic, wild-eyed, begging for help. Two police officers had raced in, caught her in the gallery, and dragged her out. "Won't anyone help me? Won't anyone stop this?" she had screamed. Sam had felt a pang of conscience then—not because she had been arrested but because he and the class had merely watched with all the concern of a flock of grazing sheep. Once the doors had slammed shut, they had simply gone back to what they had been doing, as if nothing had happened. He never saw the girl again.

Signs of the times.

He remembered the night he had been abruptly awakened by a commotion one floor up. At first he had thought it was the young couple who'd just moved in having a fight. But then he had heard a third voice, then a fourth, talking in that dull procedural monotone the security forces often used to convey their emotional detachment. The girl had cried out; the boy had protested. A scuffle had followed, with the sound of furniture being knocked over and glass breaking. Sam had lain there listening, sweating. He had wanted to do something. His instinct for freedom had said that they had no right to barge in on people in the middle of the night like that—and that he should do something about it. He had wanted to step into the hallway to protest. But he hadn't moved. He had dug his claws into the blanket and waited. The silence would come—he knew it would. After the scuffle sounded a banging door, footsteps echoing in the hall, and the broomlike swish of someone being dragged out. Was it the girl or the boy? Maybe both. It wasn't Sam's business. And when silence had returned, Sam had felt the relief of anonymous safety.

Leon and Margaret Maxwell, the couple living with their two kids in the efficiency next door, predicted the same end for Sam if he didn't keep his mouth closed.

"You professors are all alike," Leon had said, waving a spoon at Sam during dinner the night after the couple had disappeared. "You can't keep your thoughts to yourself. Gotta think the whole world is your classroom. What happened to those kids will happen to you one day if you don't watch it."

Embarrassed, Sam had laughed—but not too loudly—and that night they had drunk wine together until Margaret chased Sam home and put Leon to bed.

When Sam accepted Christ, Leon was the first he told. Leon—liberal minded as he was—didn't like it and didn't approve. He furrowed his brow and lectured Sam for an hour about the dangers of such a decision, knowing full well it wouldn't change Sam's mind—or his heart. They saw little of each other after that. Just an occasional hello in the hallway if they happened to bump into each other. It was safer that way.

Sam wondered what Leon would think if Sam disappeared that night. Just another missing person? Another enemy of the State? Maybe Leon wouldn't think anything at all. It was safer that way, too.

He tucked the note back into the envelope. It must be from someone in the Underground—not that he knew much about them except what he got from the inflammatory rhetoric in the newspapers. A couple of revolutionaries named Moses and Elijah, along with a network of followers, helped the persecuted escape. *Their own version of the Underground Railroad,* Sam thought wryly.

But how did they know to contact him?

He thought of Dolores again and regretted that he didn't have a chance to say good-bye.

Maybe Angus McLeod told the Underground. Angus was another professor at the college who'd been Sam's nemesis for years. They didn't agree on anything. Ironically, Angus was responsible for Sam's becoming a Christian. It was one of their typical lunchtime debates—about the nature of Christ as expressed in medieval literature—that sent Sam home to find his mother's Bible buried in a box with other family heirlooms. He read it—and couldn't put it down. After two months of inner searching and battling, he yielded to the Spirit.

He told Angus, of course, who immediately disagreed with Sam's interpretation of salvation and then exclaimed, "Good heavens, man, I didn't expect you to take it seriously. I thought for certain you'd realize what a sham it is and help me teach it as such. You'd be wise to forget about it."

No, McLeod didn't contact the Underground.

Did it really matter who was responsible? The question now was whether or not to go. He looked around his apartment at all his worldly goods. There wasn't much to hold him. He went through a mental checklist and found himself even more depressed. Any reason to stay? No. Any family? No. Any friends, any place to call home, any attachments of any form? No, no, and no. What had he done with his life? He had spent it with a lover who'd rejected him. Even now she stretched across a bed of fallen leaves, still and indifferent to whether he stayed or left.

He thought of the girl who'd been dragged from his class—Leanne?—and then tried to imagine the indignity of being dragged from his apartment in the middle of the night or chased across campus or led handcuffed from the cafeteria in front of the students and faculty . . . in front of his disinterested lover.

He started to pack.

CHAPTER 4

ELEVEN Camden Court was a row house with chipped and faded paint, shutters barely clinging to their hinges, and trash spilling out of dented and overturned cans. *It's a mistake*, Sam thought. He considered strolling on past it. But the cracked gray sidewalk that limped to the road beyond offered him nowhere else to go. He had no alternatives.

He walked cautiously up to the door. In spite of the cool autumn air, he sweated. The handle to his overstuffed overnight bag tried to slip through his fingers. His knuckles went white as he adjusted it for a firmer grip.

The full moon's light varied as stark shadows drifted like ghosts across the brownstone's door. It touched some part of his heart, triggered something in his mind, and gave him the creeps. There was something uneasily familiar about this place. He shivered and remembered: his college fraternity initiation, when he had to spend the night in a house that was allegedly haunted. Of course he didn't believe in such things and had known that the only "ghosts" would be whatever pranks his schoolmates had contrived for him. He had decided to go along with it, forgoing his hatred of embarrassment in favor of being accepted by the club. . . .

❋

Sam stretches his sleeping bag out in the middle of what was once a living room. Dust balls shake loose and fly toward the lopsided fireplace. Suddenly apprehensive for agreeing to this silliness, he sits down to wait.

There are no haunted houses, he tells himself again and again as the seconds become minutes, and the minutes turn into the first hour. Then the second. Then the third. Anticipation turns into a deep irritation. Come on, guys, let's get this nonsense over with.

There's a loud crack behind him, and he turns, expecting something horrid. No one—nothing—is there. Sam is disappointed. He shouts to no one in particular, "If you're going to do something, hurry it up."

His echo is the only reply.

The shadows from the trees outside play on the decaying walls. Cobwebs shake as if they've been brushed by moving spirits. Another hour goes by. Then another. Sam is angry with his schoolmates. He'll make it a point to write an editorial about initiations for the school paper. He sees no proof of his character or courage by sitting up all night in an old, empty house. Another hour slips by, and he lays down. Ridiculous, he thinks as the shadows cascade past and fade. Dawn works its light into the sky.

Sam falls asleep.

He has no idea how much time has passed. Fifteen, maybe twenty minutes? He couldn't have been asleep very long. He didn't even have time to get into a good dream. Regardless, he awakens with a start, surprised at himself for falling asleep in the first place. He looks at the cracks in the ceiling. They remind him of . . . what? A road map? Veins? Rivers?

He notices the smell.

Something rotten in Denmark, he thinks and sits up. How juvenile. They hid a dead animal in here somewhere. But the corner of his eye tells him that whatever it is isn't hidden, and it isn't an animal. His entire being is poised to leave as he turns to get a full look at whatever lies next to him.

It is a corpse. Just inches away from his sleeping bag. The head is tilted in his direction, the eyes stare vacantly at a point beyond him, the mouth leers. The body is naked with green-blue skin and patches of purple. One arm reaches out to Sam, the hand clutching the edge of his sleeping bag. The other arm is folded sedately across its chest.

Sam screams and moves at the same time. He jumps up with the other end of the sleeping bag in his own hand. Even in fear he is too practical to leave his bag behind. He heads for the door, pulling the bag along. The body moves with him, as if alive, and won't let go. He pulls and yanks more, but the corpse can't be shaken loose. The image is comical. He knows his schoolmates are watching and laughing from somewhere. Finally, he figures he can't drag the sleeping bag and the corpse out to his car, so he gives up and runs out.

❋

He had passed the initiation but had refused to join the fraternity. He never forgave his schoolmates either. They had videotaped the entire event and passed it around the school. But that slight humiliation wasn't what bothered him. With their little prank, they had introduced Sam to a worse humiliation: the fear of death.

Swallowing hard, Sam gently knocked on the brownstone's door. His fist shook after he withdrew it; his nerves were strung tight. Everything seemed to go quiet. Even the breeze in the treetops stopped. He stood frozen, as if he expected the corpse itself to answer the door.

Then he heard a soft scraping noise from the other side. A pinpoint of light betrayed the peephole in the middle of the door. He was being checked out by someone.

Sam waited for an inordinate amount of time. Just as he started to think that it really was some sort of mistake and he should leave, he heard the slide of the bolt. The door opened slowly, and a middle-aged woman with sharp eyes and hair tied in a tight bun stood before him. She had the look of someone who could make you feel at home or like a complete stranger. As her gaze took him in from head to toe, he felt like a stranger.

"Yes?" she asked.

"My name is Sam Johnson—"

"So?"

Sam was bewildered. He thought his name alone would tell her what she needed to know. "I got a note saying to come here tonight."

"Did you? Then I suppose you should come in." She stepped aside so he could enter. By the time he closed the door behind him, she was walking briskly down the narrow, stale-smelling hallway. Sam followed.

From the hallway, they walked through a room barren of furniture, down a flight of creaking stairs, and into the back room of a damp, mildewed basement. A bare bulb hung above a small wooden table. Around the table sat a young girl—she must've been nineteen or twenty years old, Sam guessed—and an old man with shocking white hair and beard who Sam thought might have been her grandfather, but then again probably wasn't. Both looked extremely tired, but the girl looked especially frightened. The old man seemed completely detached. Sam sympathized with the girl and wanted to tell her that he felt frightened, too. Maybe they could share the emotion and somehow conjure up courage between them. But politeness constrained him. They managed only to mutter their first names to each other: she was Amy; the old man was Luke.

Sam suddenly realized that the woman who had brought him down had slipped out of the room.

"Welcome," a stocky man said as he stepped out of the shadows. He wore a plain white shirt and gray pants held up by black suspenders. He was bald and sported a large walrus mustache. In a smock, he would have looked like an old-fashioned village butcher or baker. "I'm Ben."

"I'm—"

He held up a thick hand with stubby fingers. "I know who you are. We don't have much time. Follow me." He walked out of the room.

The girl and old man obeyed, with Sam trailing hesitantly behind them. This was no place for a college professor to be, he thought. Ben opened a door, and cool air filled with the smell of gasoline, old grass, and garbage wafted in. It was a garage. A large van sat with its doors open. Except for the front cab, it was windowless. "I hope you brought warm clothes. Throw your bag in the back, Mr. Johnson." Sam did while Ben continued, "This van has a false floor, under which you three will hide until you're safely out of town. It won't be comfortable, but you'll survive. I'll be taking you to the next rendezvous point, where you will meet the rest of your group."

"Group? What group?" Sam asked. "Where are we going?"

"Please." Ben smiled patiently. "I can't tell you anything just in case. . . ." He faltered, glanced at the girl, and cleared his throat. "We're helping you escape. Remember that."

The three of them lay down under the false floor of the van like corpses in a mass grave. What little air came through the makeshift ventilator smelled of exhaust. Sam felt sick. Amy was at his side and, at one point, grabbed his hand. It gave him such a start that he jerked his hand, and she instantly withdrew it. He felt a sharp pang of regret: the loss of even that simplest of human touches welled up in him. He pushed it back with a greater feeling of embarrassment.

The van stopped and, through the side of his coffin, Sam could hear the low-toned authority of the police patrol. They must have reached the checkpoint at the edge of town. They barked at Ben, asked for his papers, and then sniffed around the van like bloodhounds. Ben said something about being on his way to pick up goods for a delivery. Sam held his breath, expecting the false floor to be thrown open at any moment. He heard a low growl and was alarmed to realize it was the old man snoring. Amy must have nudged him because he suddenly stopped. The doors slammed; Ben wrenched the truck into gear and jerked away.

Sam imagined the checkpoint: the pristine guards in a cold-white, fluorescent-lit box with their papers and stamps and metal desks and roller chairs. It was potent in a sterile way. The most innocent person felt intense guilt, as if the guards had an intuitive sense of all of one's sins, particularly when the checkpoint had the new scanner—a large machine that x-rayed every vehicle, every piece of merchandise, every heartbeat, even every soul, Sam supposed. These scanners were standard equipment for the checkpoints in the big cities; the outlying areas were just getting them installed. Sam guessed that within a year, transporting fugitives like this would be impossible.

Ben surprised them by laughing aloud and kicking his heel against the floor. "I'm surprised they haven't figured it out by now," he said and then told them it was safe to come up. As they pushed the panels up and away to crawl out, Ben explained that it would be two hours to the next rendezvous point. "Make yourselves as comfortable as possible. Just be ready to jump back under the floor if I say so."

They picked their spots around the floor and stretched out. Sam leaned against his bag of belongings and tried to relax. He couldn't. Amy and Luke both seemed to stare into the spotted blackness of the van, avoiding Sam's and each other's gazes.

Sam was certain now that the girl was no older than twenty. She was pretty in a wholesome, sweet way, with her brown hair tied back. She wore jeans and hiking boots, a thick ski jacket and, when she took that off because of the van's heat, Sam saw she wore a plaid flannel shirt. He thought she had the potential for a nice figure, but for now she looked thin and undernourished. Though she wore a constant expression of fear, he imagined that she'd be particularly beautiful when she smiled.

Luke was expressionless and didn't seem bothered by what was happening around him. Sam guessed he was in his late sixties, maybe seventy, by the wild uncombed white hair and Moses-like beard. In the scattered light that sprayed them through the windshield, Sam saw Luke's lips moving as if in prayer. Yet his eyes weren't closed; they were wide open. Too wide. Sam remembered eyes like that from a picture in a psychology textbook he had once read. They were the eyes of someone who had suffered a serious mental or emotional trauma.

Eventually Sam dozed, cast adrift on a rolling, empty sea. Not only was he a lover scorned, but he had now banished himself from her presence by taking this voyage to parts unknown. He had unfaithfully given his mind to another, and now his body followed this new love as well. In his half-sleep he prayed for grace he hadn't yet felt.

The lulling vibration of the van suddenly stopped. Sam jerked his head up.

"Our next pickup point," Ben announced. He climbed out of the van, leaving the door open. The burst of air was crisp and carried the distinct smell of hay and animals. Sam scooted forward to peek outside. A farmhouse and barn stood off in the distance like yellow-eyed specters.

Outside the van someone whispered. Someone else whispered back. Sam cocked his ear to listen more closely but couldn't make out any of the words. He knew one voice was Ben's. He could also hear—or feel—an urgency in their tones. Amy's head was slightly tilted as if she was also trying to hear. The sound seemed to worry her.

"Must be having an argument," Sam said.

Amy looked at him in dismay, as if he were a man on an elevator who broke the rule of silence, who looked at the faces of the passengers rather than at the numbers above the doors.

The rear doors clicked loudly, then swung open.

"Make room," Ben said. "We have five more people. But this isn't a party. No talking."

Silently and obediently they came in. First, a woman with a deer-in-the-headlights expression—Madonna eyes, red and bloodshot from shedding endless tears. She held onto—dragged, actually—a young boy of six. He looked around with wonder and excitement as if he were on a school field trip. The boy had many of the woman's features: dark wavy hair, oval face with a pale complexion, and deep dark eyes—without the redness. They were mother and son—Mary and Timothy.

"Can I ride up front with the man?" Timothy asked.

"No," his mother replied with a sharp jerk of his arm to sit him down.

Ruth entered next. She was a stout woman—of "pioneer stock," Sam's mother might have said—with a square build and a face deeply etched by laugh lines and too many days working in the sun. She glanced at Sam and smiled. It surprised him, and he smiled back in gratitude at this tiny spark of humanity.

A distinguished-looking gentleman poked his head in and looked the van over. He eyed the interior and the passengers as if he might disapprove of the accommodations and wait for something better. He retreated, and Sam could hear him talking to Ben. "This?" the well-bred voice asked with more than a hint of indignation. "You expect me to ride in this?"

Ben sighed, "Please, Mr. Beck, we don't have time."

The head peeked back in, and Sam noted the quick, darting eyes, the natural frown, and the thinning hair gone gray at the temples. Howard Beck sighed, sniffed, and pulled himself in.

Amused, Ruth smiled and shook her head.

Peter, who turned out to be Ruth's nephew, climbed in last. He was a handsome man in his early twenties, muscular and lithe. He moved with self-confidence and, as he made his way through the van to sit down, he patted backs and smiled reassuringly to everyone, looking like a high schooler running for student council president.

Peter winked at Sam, reached for his hand, and shook it vigorously. "Peter," he said simply.

"Sam."

"Quiet back there!" Ben snapped.

"OK, OK," Peter mumbled and slid down next to Ruth.

Ben threw some additional boxes of provisions into the back—to be placed wherever they could make room—then slammed the doors closed. A moment later he was back in the driver's seat. With a protesting groan, the van took them away.

❋

They drove on, up winding roads that took them to chillier air and the smell of snow. The farther they went, the less confident Sam felt about his decision to join them. It was possible

39

that he wouldn't have been arrested. He was a new believer, certainly no threat to anyone. Just the opposite, in fact: His faith was academic, not passionate. For all he knew, it was nothing more than a romantic interlude that he would have quickly ended if it came to the choice between it and time in a rehabilitation center. But if that were true, then he was an even greater fool for making this journey. To do this without heartfelt motivation was ridiculous. Was this just a reaction to being fired? What was he doing here?

The van hit a hard curve, and Sam slipped against Timothy. "My turn," Timothy said. They went into another hard curve in the opposite direction, and Timothy slid into Sam. "Your turn." Timothy giggled.

"Quiet," his mother said.

Sam looked into the shadows, catching the outlines and silhouettes of his fellow passengers. He wondered about their stories, their reasons for escaping. He sighed. They probably felt something deep and stirring, a furnace of belief that burned within their very souls. They had the sort of fire that the State would have to extinguish or be consumed by.

How he wished he felt that kind of passion—felt something other than an intellectual predestination about his choices. Those initial talks with Angus, reading his mother's Bible, pretending he wanted to study it just to disprove Christianity more effectively in the classroom . . . when did he ever feel like he had the choice to stop? But it was the intellectual stimulation that pushed him along. How could he be truly open-minded and not consider the mystery of Christ from an academic point of view? Or maybe it was simply an adolescent desire for the forbidden. In this modern government-induced paradise of jackboots and correct thinking, the State had said not to touch the fruit of that particular tree. "Touch it and you shall surely die." But another voice tempted him and, for intellectual reasons, he couldn't resist. He had accepted what Christ offered without tears. He merely gave assent. There should have been tears. He should have red eyes like Mary the Madonna. He had once read that the first-century Christians had bloodshot eyes from so much crying and knees like a camel's from so much praying. Sam had neither.

He shivered. The air was noticeably colder now, even in the overheated van. It was autumn in the towns and cities below, but early winter in the mountains. Had the first snow fallen yet? Which mountains were they driving into? Sam tried to create a mental picture of a map and find the You Are Here point on it. Had it been two hours or four since they left the farm? Where were they when they stopped to get gas behind the abandoned motel? He could've guessed for a million years and still not gotten it right. His life had been spent at the college, with weekend fishing excursions to nearby Silver Lake and Patuxent Point and nowhere else. He felt bile rise in his throat that tasted like remorse: What had he done with his life?

Ben slowed the van down and turned onto a dirt road. Rocks and gravel machine-gunned the chassis as they bounced along the pitted path. "This is intolerable!" Beck said after they'd hit a pothole and he had bumped his head. Tim giggled to see who'd bounce the highest.

Ben swung the van in a semicircle, then brought it to a stop.

"You can get out," Ben announced just before he climbed out of the front cab, "but don't go anywhere. It's dark."

A moment later the back doors clicked and swung open.

They filed out, leaping from the back like sky divers on a secret mission. Stepping onto the crunchy gravel, they stretched and groaned intermittently. The smell of pine filled the air. Somewhere a creek gurgled and splashed. The moon had ducked behind some clouds, leaving them in darkness for a moment; then it returned.

Sam tried to adjust his eyes. Slowly, he saw that they were in a clearing. A forest surrounded them like mourners at an interment, except for a small patch of clear ground that rose up onto a slight hill away from them. Sam saw stones of various shapes and sizes poking out of the ground in planned disarray. He squinted, not sure of what he was seeing. The clouds gave the moon's light a full berth, and Sam recognized the shapes. A chill went up and down his spine. He stood at the edge of a graveyard.

The rest of the group gathered around him. They saw what he saw.

"I don't believe it," Beck whispered.

Ben beckoned from the van. "Help me get these boxes out. We'll take them inside."

The group merely turned to him, speechless.

He didn't catch on. "This will be your home for the next couple of weeks until your contact comes. You have a little over three weeks' supply of food and, praise God, a furnace that works well in spite of its age. There are cots to sleep on in the rooms, a kitchen, and a freshwater creek over on the other side of the hill. It has everything you'll need, and you should be safe." He chuckled. "It's such an obvious hiding place that no one thinks to look here."

Sam glanced around. *"Where? What's* such an obvious hiding place?"

"This must be some kind of joke," Beck said. "We're staying in a graveyard?"

"What?" Ben asked, then saw what they had been looking at and laughed. It was an uncommonly jovial and hearty laugh. "Of course not," he said at the tail end of his amusement. "You'll be staying over *there.*" He produced a flashlight, turned it on, and pointed it in the opposite direction. The beam just barely illuminated a small structure buried in the darkness at the edge of the forest. Realizing it didn't answer their questions, Ben said, "Oh, you'll see. Help me with these boxes."

They each grabbed a box and followed Ben down a path into the trees. As they got closer, the beam of Ben's flashlight showed them what they couldn't see before: a building with boarded windows, decayed wood that splintered through broken paint, and a roof and walls covered with leaves and sticky pine needles. A small cross hung lopsidedly above the front door.

"A church," Luke said.

"You see?" Ben said. "Who would think to look for Christians in a church?"

"It's perfect," Peter whispered as they paraded up the rickety wooden steps into what must have once been a kitchen area.

"Wow!" Timothy cried out and started to run off, but Mary yanked him back. He yelped like a puppy.

"It's *not* perfect," Beck said, taking in the scene. "You don't really expect us to stay here."

"It's your home for now," Ben replied.

"I won't do it. I won't stay," Beck said.

"That's up to you," Ben countered. "But you're not going back with me."

"Why not?"

"You've seen one of our best hideouts. If you went back and got caught, you might tell where it is."

Beck put his hands on his hips defiantly. "You can't stop me from leaving."

"I can't," Ben said. "But if I were *them*—" he hooked a thumb at the rest of the fugitives—"I'd want to stop you."

Beck looked uneasily at his comrades and said no more.

Sam's stomach turned as the realization that he had cast his lot with this group settled on him with a sick finality. They had assembled at this abandoned church in the mountains and placed their lives in each other's hands—strangers who may or may not be trusted. Theoretically, the only thing that held them together was a shared faith. Was it enough? A full dose of reality washed through Sam's body like scalding water. This was no game, no field trip. It had life-changing consequences.

They finished unpacking the van, and Sam helplessly watched as Ben shook their hands, said a short prayer wishing them God's grace, then climbed into the van and drove away.

There was no turning back now.

CHAPTER 5

WILLIAMS was glad that he and Slater hadn't gone back to Central as planned. Unlike his boss, he enjoyed the small rural communities, the open land and endless woods. It was such a vast difference from the steel-and-cement-induced claustrophobia he had to endure back home. Apart from following Slater from town to town looking for leads and filing reports, it was like taking a vacation. He hadn't had one in years.

Slater, on the other hand, looked restless and annoyed. He stayed only because he was convinced that their prisoner was still in the area somewhere and counted on the slim chance that one of his informants might come up with something. He was vindicated when, a week later, one of them did. At ten in the morning he received word that the escaped prisoner had been seen in an abandoned building next to a long-forgotten train depot in Tannerville.

By eleven Slater and Williams had pulled together a strike force made up of the local police from several of the towns near Tannerville. Slater briefed the men, then warned them that any slipups would be construed by him as subversive action to aid the insurrectionists. In other words, mess up and you'll get thrown into a rehabilitation center yourself. "And I want him alive. Kill him, and you'll get the same yourself. Now, let's go roach hunting."

Williams listened to his boss with chagrin. After three days, Slater had reached his limit with the "incompetency of the local yokels" and given up diplomacy altogether. He spoke with all the tact of a clenched fist.

At 11:47 they hit the abandoned building from all directions with over fifty police officers. They came in police cars, on motorcycles—Slater would have brought in tanks if he thought he could get them there in time—and a single helicopter that monitored from above. It was a massive show of force. The 327 citizens of Tannerville pressed against their shop windows with mouths agape and eyes like saucers. It would keep them talking for weeks, Williams knew.

Williams, who drove the lead car, hit the brakes, coming to a sliding stop in front of the derelict building. A faded Victorian-style sign announced that it had once been the Imperial Hotel. Slater jumped out and made his way through the positioned officers to the boarded-up double doors. Inside, other officers with axes and picks broke through walls and wrenched away stubborn hinges, literally tearing the building apart.

"Nowhere to run, nowhere to hide," Slater shouted to Williams over the racket of shouts, crashes, and the helicopter beating the air overhead. The place smelled of dead animals and excrement.

Williams handed Slater a mug of coffee as they leaned against what must've been the front desk of the hotel. "I hope your informant knew what he was talking about."

"Billy's been ten for ten. He wouldn't let me down. H knows what would happen if he ever did."

Within minutes the report came from the captain of the

wrecking crew. "Unless he turned into a piece of wood, we can't find him."

Slater warned Williams with his eyes, then said to the captain, "You can't find *anything?*"

"There's a room—it looks like he *was* here, but—"

Suddenly the walkie-talkie crackled, and a voice from the helicopter shouted, "There's a woman running across the roof! On the south side! She's running for the fire escape!"

"Somebody get her," Slater commanded into the device. *"Alive!"*

Slater and Williams rushed back out to the open lot, navigating to the south side of the building. The woman had just hoisted a leg over the side when the officers grabbed her. From six floors down, they could hear her protests. They walked back to the car and waited.

Slater poured his coffee out.

"You don't like it?" Williams asked.

"It's good, but I hate the taste of it in a plastic mug."

"I didn't have time to pack the china," Williams said dryly.

The woman was feisty and still fighting with the three officers who half dragged, half carried her out the front door and across the lot to Slater. One of the officers had a large gash on his forehead, which Williams figured would need stitches later. Williams had to admire her determination, but knew that his boss wouldn't. Who admired determined roaches?

Held firmly in front of Slater, the girl stopped fighting and waited. He locked his gaze on her. "A little makeup and a wig . . . you're probably the old woman in front of the rehabilitation center. Far more attractive, though. That was a very clever stunt you pulled. But it ends here."

"I didn't do anything," she scowled, struggling again. "Tell these baboons to let go of me."

Slater leaned close to her slender face, now smudged with

dirt. Her black hair was disheveled, and the peasant dress she wore clung damply to her body. "OK, my little gypsy. I'll tell them to let go. But you should know that these marksmen are prepared to shoot you if you so much as blink in a questionable way."

She glanced around quickly as if to confirm the truth of his words. It was enough to calm her down.

"Good," Slater said. "Now let's get to business. I'm looking for an escaped prisoner, and you know where he is. Tell me, please."

She shook her head. "I don't know."

Slater rolled his eyes. "We're not going to play that game, are we?"

"No. I'm telling you the truth. I don't know where he is," she answered.

"Uh-huh," Slater said. "And you're also going to tell me that you're not a member of the Underground."

"I am," she admitted, "but each member of the Underground knows only enough to help with one part of the operation. That way, if we're caught, no one person can ruin it for everyone else."

"Clever," Slater said without taking his gaze from her.

Williams watched the girl, too, and felt like something was wrong. She had behaved predictably except . . . her eyes. They kept twitching, looking past Slater.

"So I don't know where he is now," she said abruptly.

"She's stalling," Williams said.

Both the girl and Slater snapped their heads to look at him.

"She's looking at something."

Williams turned to look behind them and, even in the din, they heard a motorcycle start up. A uniformed police officer revved the cycle's engine and then pulled quickly away.

"Him!" Slater shouted at the officers and pointed. "Stop that motorcycle!"

There was a massive scramble by the officers for their cars, as the motorcyclist zoomed into the distance, leaving a cloud of Tannerville dust behind. Williams dreaded how his boss would react to this *second* near miss with his prey.

As if answering Williams's unspoken question, Slater grabbed the woman's face in his hand. "You can't imagine all the things we'll do to find out how much you *don't* know."

He pushed her back toward the three who'd been holding her. With a signal to Williams, they jumped into the car and joined the chase.

❋

Slater took to calling the woman Gypsy, even after he'd learned that her name was Jennifer Walters. As usual, Williams did the actual interrogation and was surprised by her performance. Someone had trained her well. She knew how to answer just enough questions to give the impression that she was cooperating. Of course, the information she told them was useless. Slater was no closer to catching his man now than he was after the entire convoy of police and special agents lost the motorcycle outside of Tannerville.

Gypsy sat slumped in an unyielding metal chair. Her face, beautiful only a few hours before, was now pale, drawn, and haggard. She had no bruises or scars: Williams subscribed to a pain-without-blemishes technique. She had suffered a lot of pain.

Williams turned to his boss and said, "I think she's finally ready to talk."

Gypsy looked up helplessly at him. Her eyes told him everything. They were empty. The defiance was gone.

Slater leaned on the edge of the table next to her. "I believe you, Gypsy. I really do. When you say you know only part of the plan, I think you're telling the truth."

"I am," she croaked. "Please, . . . I'm so tired. No more questions. Why can't you leave me alone?"

"Because you helped him get away from me—not once, but twice—and I'm sorry, but I don't think I'll ever forgive you for that. Now," Slater continued, "let's talk about the man himself."

"I don't know anything about him."

Slater wagged a finger at her. "How can you tell me you don't know anything when I haven't even asked my question yet? You were with him. You must know a lot of things. Unless he had your ears covered and a blindfold over your eyes. Did he?"

"No," she answered weakly.

"So you *can* tell me what color his hair is, right?"

"Brown."

"Good for you." Slater smiled coldly. "Tell me about his frame of mind?"

"Frame of . . . ?"

"Mind, yes. Did he seem happy? Sad? Determined? Playful? Confident? Tired? Energetic? Just jump in here and grab a word. Depressed? Wild? Adventurous? Melan—"

"Sick . . . a fever . . . depressed," she answered. Her eyelids were half-closed. She looked drugged, though she wasn't.

"What makes you think he was depressed?"

She smacked her dry lips, then licked them slowly. "For one thing, he didn't go."

"Didn't go," Slater repeated.

"He wasn't supposed to stay with me as long as he did. He was supposed to go to the next rendezvous. He didn't seem to . . ." She faded for a moment.

"Gypsy."

She continued, "He didn't want to go on. It's like he . . . wanted to just hang around and . . ."

"Gypsy? Anything else?" Slater asked.

Gypsy's head slumped forward. "For troubles surround me—"

"What did you say?"

She mumbled, "I can't see my way out. They are more numerous than the hairs on my head. I have lost my courage. Please, Lord, rescue me! Come quickly, Lord, and help me."

"What is she saying?" Williams asked.

"Sounds to me like a psalm," Slater answered.

The girl was quiet.

Slater hit the table with his open hand. The sharp report didn't get a reaction from her.

"I think we've taken her as far as we can," Williams said as he unrolled his shirtsleeves.

Slater looked at her, disappointed.

Williams stepped forward and lifted her chin. Her breathing was shallow.

"I think we should take her to the hospital now." Williams picked up his jacket.

Slater waved his hand. "I don't care what you do with her."

Williams signaled the two officers by the door, and they carried her out.

"Sick and depressed," Slater said thoughtfully.

The phone buzzed, and Williams reached across the table to get it. He grunted twice, then handed the receiver to Slater. "The police captain at Tannerville," he said.

Slater cocked his eyebrow. "Yeah? Put him on the speakerphone."

Williams obligingly pushed the button. "Go ahead," he said.

"York here," the voice on the other end crackled. "We found the motorcycle. The one your man escaped on."

"Where?"

"Outside of—" He stopped, then asked someone, "What's the name of this village? Henley? Outside of Henley. It was up a path that leads deep into the woods. At the base of Providential Mountain."

"You're kidding."

"Nope," York said. "But you should know that the bike's a mess. I think he crashed."

Slater nodded. "Canvass the area and begin a search of every nook and cranny in every town and village. I'll get there as soon as I can." He hit the button to disconnect the line, then eyed Williams. "Are you up for the drive? You want a nap or anything?"

"Why? Should I be tired?" Williams asked.

Slater smiled. "What a man. Come on."

PART
TWO

The Church

CHAPTER 6

Death. I can't pinpoint what I think about it. Which is funny since we seem surrounded by it lately. When I think of death, I think in terms of literature. I was an English professor for a long time, so death comes to me in words. Poetry, mostly. It is noble, lofty, multisyllabic.

And it has a British accent.

I like to think I'm prepared for death now. I'm not. I don't think anyone really can be. How can one fully prepare oneself for something one experiences only the once?

Yet, it's a paradox because death is such an important part of living.

Don't ask me to explain that, because I can't.

—from *The Posthumous Papers of Samuel T. Johnson*

✳

S AM sat, pen in hand, at an old wooden table in the corner of what was once a sanctuary in a Protestant church.
Which specific denomination he didn't know. He hadn't been in a church since he was a child. The altar and preacher's

podium had been hacked to bits. The pews were upended and torn apart. Cobwebs haunted every corner, spiritlike. The place reeked of animal excrement and urine. And the windows—presumably stained glass at one time—were broken and boarded up. The day after they'd arrived, they had wrenched a few of the boards away to let some light in. It didn't help much. They replaced the shutters at night to keep their light from being seen by strangers—the opposite of Jesus' command.

He could guess when the desecration had happened: four years ago on the Night of the Purge, when citizens all over the country had been rallied by the government to ransack the churches as a show of loyalty and support to the Committee. It had been coming for years, of course, but that night was the culmination of the defiance everyone was expected to feel against organized religion. Sam remembered watching from his apartment window as the flames had licked the dark sky above the campus. The chapel had been vandalized and razed. He had been angry at the time, but only because he thought the building could have been used as a study center.

Glancing around this sanctuary now, he could imagine the frenzy of the local townspeople marching toward this little church, torches held high, as if they were out to destroy Frankenstein's monster. No doubt they had started here in the sanctuary, then made their way through the rest of the building.

Sam used this table here in the corner rather than the desk in his assigned room. His excuse was that it gave him more surface space on which to spread his books and papers. It was a half-truth. The full truth was that Sam's room had once been the pastor's office. It contained a visitor's couch that Sam alone seemed capable of sleeping soundly on. Of course, the windows were boarded up, and the many bookshelves had long since lost their contents to the bonfires. Any semblance of warmth or charm had been stripped away like those other old garments of faith and grace. But Sam could cope with all that. It was specifically the desk that bothered him. The bloodstains on the top, actually. It wasn't just one or two drops, as if the pastor had gotten a paper cut. This stain looked as if a modern artist had taken a large brush of dark red paint, flicked it suddenly and violently at the desk, then changed his mind and smeared it around instead.

Sam shivered every time he thought of it.

He had covered up the stain with a large piece of cardboard from a box in the cellar. That helped for appearance's sake, but Sam could never use the desk for reading or writing. How could he? Not while that stain made him wonder what had become of the pastor.

It took Sam back to the nagging questions that had plagued him since he'd become a Christian: How in the world did they get in this mess? What forces were at work to strip all elements of faith from their society? How was it possible that a pastor's modest office could become a chamber of unthinkable violence? It was a simple room where church bulletins were dictated, where words of counsel were whispered to a wife who wanted to leave her husband, where Scripture was read aloud to a college student who demanded answers, where a comforting hand was placed on the shoulder of a father who wept over his lost teenage son, where the story of Jesus walking on the water was told once more to a wide-eyed child, where marriage certificates were endorsed, funeral papers were signed, birth announcements were completed, obituaries were finalized—all aspects of life had passed through, sweetly oblivious to the ticking clock on the time bomb that would explode and . . . and . . . splash blood across a desk.

So Sam had adopted the old wooden table in the corner of the sanctuary. Everyone seemed to accept his half-truth as a whole truth and took to calling it "Sam's desk." Peter had carved Sam's name in the upper right-hand corner just to make it official.

Sam adjusted the flame on the kerosene lamp. He had been trying to concentrate on one particular thought for his journal entry, but found himself lost in all the thoughts surrounding it instead. It annoyed him since he considered himself capable of a reasonable amount of mental discipline. All he had to do was line his thoughts up like books on a shelf and pluck one off that suited him. But lately, it didn't work that way. As he had begun to write his journal, with the story of Ben and their escape in the van, the shelf's supports had given way and had spilled everything into a heap. While digging through the pile, Sam encountered feelings and memories he had hoped were sufficiently buried: feelings about death. That's why he had titled his journal *The Posthumous Papers of Samuel T. Johnson*.

Ruth thought it was a terrible title, a sick play on words. She was right. But that didn't make it any less appropriate. Death was but a whisper on the other side of a heartbeat, an inevitability that took away our illusions of dignity and pride. Where were the dignity and pride in a corpse comically clutching a sleeping bag? Death is the great equalizer—it leaves nothing behind but vague memories and fading shadows. Ashes to ashes, dust to dust. In the scheme of eternity, what we do and say here doesn't amount to much without us around to say it does.

Which was why Sam had started a journal. Writing was the only way to leave something behind.

The lamp flickered. Sam leaned forward to adjust the wick again. The flame steadied. He scrubbed his hands over his face wearily and wondered what time it was. He tapped his pen against the top paper—it was no longer blank. He had written the word *desk* across the top, but didn't remember doing it. The thoughts and memories were clogged somewhere between his brain and his fingers and couldn't seem to drain through his pen.

The group had been at the church for over three weeks. In that time they'd grown from being frightened strangers to unlikely friends. They initially established a practical routine: a rotation of chores and responsibilities that gave them the comfort of regimentation. Normality, even in the most abnormal circumstances, was a salve. They also went through a "let's get to know each other" period during their daily worship times when they told a little bit about themselves and their backgrounds. For the first two weeks, it was much as Sam imagined the first-century church as being: close-knit, compassionate, and generous. But a change had crept in over the last week and a half as they began to get on each other's nerves. Personalities clashed on a regular basis. Patience was as scarce as their food. And panic disguised itself as claustrophobia and wormed its way into their attitudes.

Sam's thoughts were interrupted as he heard Mary scold Timothy in another part of the church. "Look at you!" her voice echoed. "Lunch is almost ready and you're a mess! I thought I told you not to play in the cellar. It's dirty and dangerous down there. Something could happen to you, and we'd never know it until it was too late!"

"But I found cans of food down there," Tim said as if his find justified his disobedience.

Sam remembered the cans. Peter had found them the day after they had arrived, when they all had searched the church if only to get familiar with their temporary home. The cans were old and dented and, as Peter had put it, probably ripe for new undiscovered cultures of bacteria.

"Just leave them alone," Mary said firmly.

"But I was looking for Joshua," Tim said, continuing his defense. Joshua was a chipmunk he had befriended.

"I don't care. I wish you'd stay away from him. He might bite you."

Sam could hear the pout in Tim's voice. "But he's the only friend I have."

Mary wasn't moved. "I'm your friend," she said. "Now let's get cleaned up for lunch."

"I'm not hungry. My stomach hurts."

The voices stopped, and Sam heard their footsteps retreating down the hall.

Sam shook his head sympathetically. Poor Tim: six years old and forced to confine all his youthful energy in a boring old building. Which wasn't to say that he was never allowed outside to play; they had worked out a system so he could. But Mary's nerves were so tightly bundled up that her fears dictated everything she said and did. Every minute Tim was out of her sight, she wrung her hands and lamented his absence. Poor Mary. She was the kind of woman who lived for that inevitable disaster, real or imagined. After the group's second "let's get to know each other" meeting, Ruth observed that Mary could find a dark cloud behind every silver lining. Sam wondered if she had always been that way or if it was the result of losing her husband to the State's goon squads. Probably a combination of both.

"Sam?" a voice whispered.

He looked up to see Ruth peeking in at him from the doorway. "Hi," Sam whispered back and then wondered why they were whispering.

"Lunch is almost ready."

"Thanks. I'll be there in just a minute."

She hesitated but then walked up to him. "I hate to bother you, but we've got to talk about our food situation." She spoke quietly, seriously but without panic. Ruth would be the last one to panic in any crisis, Sam had learned quickly. It was one of the things he admired most about her.

"I know what you're going to say." He stood up and stretched. He had known it was only a matter of time before they would have this talk.

"They gave us enough food for three weeks. That was all. We're running out."

Sam nodded but didn't have an answer. "We have no way of knowing what's going on down there." Blind again, Sam thought, just like in the back of the van. Darkness, no answers, no sense of time or direction, just riding blind. But wasn't that what constitutes faith? Give God the steering wheel and relax in the back, right? "We have to wait. Have faith and wait." He spoke sincerely but knew he didn't sound convincing or convinced.

Ruth gazed at him patiently.

"Peter went to check his traps. Maybe he caught something," he offered as a token of hope.

Ruth fiddled with the makeshift apron tied around her waist. "Tomorrow we'll have to start rationing even more than we have already. Maybe half a meal a day."

Sam winced. After only a week with this group, he had known that rationing would cause a panic. Why shouldn't it? If someone from the Underground didn't come soon, what were they expected to do? He thought of the cans in the cellar. It could come to that.

"I wanted you to know," Ruth said.

"Thank you. Maybe we can put our heads together and come up with some alternatives." Sam wasn't sure what the alternatives might be, though. He added apologetically, "I have experience fishing, but that was usually under civilized

61

circumstances. Real wilderness survival isn't my forte. I read *Walden* once, but that only inspired me to speak profoundly."

"Profound speech isn't edible," Ruth said as she turned for the door.

"I don't know about that." Sam shrugged and followed her. "I've had to eat my words on many occasions."

CHAPTER 7

S MITH made it to the woods just as daylight began to fail. He ran as hard as his rubbery legs would allow, pushing forward, ignoring the branches that lashed out at his face, the nagging stitch in his side, and the rasping breath that only added to his pain. It didn't matter that he had lost track of who he was running from or where he was running to. He just had to keep moving. The mountain stood before him, and his instincts told him he must reach it. For some reason he imagined he'd find safety there.

Every muscle ached; every sinew begged his fevered brain to stop and rest. But his instinct for survival was a slave driver who cracked a whip across the back of his need to live.

So he rushed onward, though the forest conspired against him. Obstacles rose and fell in the shapes of decaying logs, thick bushes, and sharp briars. Finally, a large root grabbed his ankle. He stumbled, spun, whirled drunkenly like a puppet, then collapsed as if his strings had been cut. He landed facedown in a pile of leaves. The smell of old earth filled his nostrils. He heard only the sound of his own breathing.

The slave driver screamed for him to get up and run. His body refused. The most he could manage was to roll onto his back. With his eyes closed, he let the sounds of the forest give him an artificial peace. A faint mountain breeze rode through the naked treetops. A maverick leaf, dead and dry, slid across his cheek. The birds called out to one another, and he heard them. But it lasted only for a second before the slave driver twisted the sounds in his ears until they became a scream. The scream of one person, the echoes of a thousand as the boots of uniformed men crushed twigs like brittle bones, their guns cocked, dogs barking and chains rattling. He could smell their leather and sweat. He could taste blood filling his mouth.

His own blood.

His eyes opened, hoping reality would take away this nightmare. The branches above him reached out like jagged fingers and pointed accusingly at him. The darkening sky frowned in agreement with their condemnation.

Get up, you fool. The mountain waits for you. You will find safety and peace there. No one can touch you or harm you. It will be like returning to the warmth of the womb, like being swallowed up into . . . into what? A positive image failed him. He could think only of being swallowed up in the belly of the whale.

Hurry before you're caught. You can't just lie there. The mountain waits for you. There's no point in giving up now when you've come so far. So far . . . Now, run before it's too late. Run, and soon you won't have to run anymore. It will be very comfortable for you there . . . in the belly of the whale.

Just a few more miles . . . a few more miles . . . a few more . . .

Slowly, he got to his feet.

CHAPTER 8

IT'S pointless. Do you think the animals up here are morons? They'd never fall for your stupid traps," Howard Beck said from his position against the tree.

"Look, Howard, I never said I knew how to do this."

"Good thing, because you obviously don't."

Peter bit his tongue and started to count to ten, very slowly. It was something his mother had taught him to do when, as a child, he was on the verge of an outburst. He'd inherited his father's propensity for anger and, through the hard lessons of experience, clung to this one maxim like no other. He found it helped clear his mind and strengthen his resolve to keep from doing or saying something he would regret later. In this instance, it was his desire to punch Howard Beck in the mouth. That was number one on his top-ten list. Number two—and rising fast—was to tie Beck's tongue in a knot. Both appealed to Peter more and more as the group's month together dragged by. Both appealed to him now as he knelt next to the small crate he'd set up as a trap to catch game to eat.

"Why do we kid ourselves?" Beck asked. He dug at something under one of his fingernails. "No one's coming for us."

Peter continued to count. Four . . . five . . . He would be the first to admit that he could be hotheaded. But what he felt toward Beck was new and foreign. It was a dark red emotion.

At first, he figured it was simply a personality clash. After that, he blamed their situation—a touch of cabin fever, maybe, or the fear that no contact from the Underground would come, that they'd been left on the mountain with nobody to lead them on. Those would be enough reasons to make anyone edgy. And he accepted them as valid excuses for his impatience with Beck—the first week, even the second. By the third week they'd dispensed with their barely disguised mutual toleration and had moved to a more active dislike for one another. Beck called him cocky, egotistical, rude, brash, and even a delinquent. Peter called Beck an overstuffed, whining, lazy snob.

Today, as he hopelessly checked his traps and endured Beck's ongoing diatribe about all that was wrong with their situation, Peter had to admit that dark red feeling for what it really was: hatred. It stung Peter's conscience like one of the nettles he had removed from Timothy's hand. It made him feel deeply ashamed of himself. Even before he had become a Christian, he had honestly believed that he'd never hated anyone. Conflicts were merely problems to be diplomatically worked out. Then, as a Christian, he knew he *shouldn't* hate anyone: not his persecutors, not the brown-shirted guards who had taken his parents away, not Eddie Richie for giving him a dirty hit during football practice, and especially not a fellow Christian. "Love your enemies," Jesus had said. "Love one another as I have loved you." Peter knew the sayings well, and he thought he had lived them out as well as he could. And then Beck came along.

Beck continued as if he didn't care whether or not anyone was listening. "If you think I'm going to sit around while we starve to death, well you have another thing coming. . . ."

Peter hated Beck for being Beck—and for making him hate at all. It was a neat cycle of resentment. He didn't want to know how feeble his experience of love was; Beck brought it out. Beck showed him his hypocrisy. Beck showed him that his knowledge of love was childish. Sometimes the substance of love can't be known until it's pressed into service by hate. He prayed for God to forgive him for hating and to give him strength to love Howard with the heart of Jesus. Then he despaired that within the next few minutes he'd hate Howard all over again.

"We should send Luke down to the village. That way, if he's caught, we won't be missing anything."

"Howard!" Peter snapped. He'd lost count somewhere between six and eight, between the prayer to be forgiven and his appeal for strength.

"I don't know why they brought him along. The odds are against us to begin with, and we're lessening them by dragging around excess baggage—*crazy* baggage, at that!"

"Shut up, will you?" Peter marched into the woods to the next trap.

"I'm just trying to be practical," Beck said as he followed. "It's absurd for us to continue a charade of compassion when our lives are hanging by a thread. You know his story. They've put enough voltage through him to light the capital. He's useless."

Peter considered the pleasure he'd get from stuffing Beck into the next trap, then pushed the thought away. *Be calm, be reasonable: count to ten.* "He's here, Howard. He's one of us."

"But why? Why did they bring him along? What were they thinking?"

"Maybe they were thinking about the years he spent as a pastor. Maybe they remembered how he stood up for the gospel when nobody else would. Maybe they felt loyalty to him because he'd suffered so much. What do you think?"

"I think the contact should take him back to the village. He's oblivious anyway. What does he care whether he's with us or in a rehab center somewhere? Escaping doesn't mean a thing to him."

"And if they kill him?"

Beck smiled smugly. "Then he goes to heaven. It's his gain, right?"

They reached the edge of the woods where Peter had set up another crate, precariously balanced on a thin stick with a piece of carrot tied to it by a small string. The carrot was untouched.

"You might want to take that carrot back with us. I wager we'll be needing it before long," Beck said.

The woods opened up to a sprawling meadow. The sun, a stranger to them for the past few days, shone brightly. The crisp mountain chill was ever present—it was late November, after all—but Peter wanted to bask in the golden warmth for a few minutes.

"Well? What are we standing around here for?" Beck asked.

Peter gritted his teeth and hooked a thumb back toward the woods. "This way."

"Why this way? Did you think to put a trap in that field? It looks perfect for—"

"There's a farmhouse down there. We can't take a chance of them seeing us. Sam said it's best to stay clear."

"A farmhouse?" Beck's voice showed surprise, a tone he didn't often use. "What's a farmhouse doing way up here?"

"I don't know. Next time I stop by to visit, I'll ask." Peter picked up his pace. He figured they were about two miles from the church. "Come on."

"Where are we going now? Haven't you seen enough empty traps?"

"No," Peter replied. "I have three more up ahead." He

pushed through some branches to a thicker, darker collection of trees. "Why? Do you have a pressing engagement somewhere?"

Beck snorted. "I certainly have more important things to do than wander around in the woods with a smart-mouthed kid."

"Why don't you go back to the church?" Peter grunted as he plowed through the underbrush.

"And get lost on the way? You'd like that, I suppose."

"You should've left a trail of bread crumbs."

They fell into silence, except for their labored breathing and occasional grunts. Beck mumbled under his breath as the branches poked, prickers jabbed, and leaf-covered holes caused him to stumble. There was an easier way to go, Peter knew, but he was enjoying Beck's discomfort. Revenge tasted only slightly sweeter than anger, but the aftertaste was like poison.

Suddenly Beck dropped down on a log, gasping. "That's it. My side hurts. I can't go any farther."

Peter stopped long enough to give him a stern frown, then sighed. "The trap is just on the other side of that ridge. I'll check it and come back." He turned away with a smile that Beck couldn't see.

❋

Brat, Beck thought as he watched Peter work his way through the vegetation. There were few things more irritating to him than a know-it-all kid whose arrogance was unsupported by experience. Youthful, cocky, mindlessly energetic, ready to conquer entire worlds . . . all the things Beck himself was like when he was a young man. For that fact alone Beck had to admit that he and Peter had a lot in common. But he would never have said so aloud. It was something he recognized in that secret, rational place in the back of his mind—and nowhere else. He might even concede that their similarities were the cause of their conflict. But the thought bored him, and the acknowledgment that Peter was like his younger self generated no appreciation or respect. Peter was a nuisance, no more and no less.

Beck looked up at what he could see of the sky through the tangled web of branches and stubborn leaves. It was noon. He should be on the corner of First and Centennial trying to hail a taxi to Sarasota's. Once there, he would make his way among the tables that hummed with the latest deals, investments, and mergers—"Hello, Frank; hi, Bill. Did you hear the latest?"—then sit down with the world's best club sandwich and malt whiskey while watching the stocks rise and fall on the TV monitor. Closing his eyes, he savored the memory like a tender piece of filet mignon. It melted in his mouth and dissolved into dry mountain air.

What was he doing here?

He asked himself that question often: *more* often as the days rolled over them like a steamroller. Did he have a choice? It was the most practical and expedient thing to do, surely. It was one thing to take risks with other people's money. It was quite another to take risks with his own life.

A ray of sunlight hit the tops of the trees and fanned out like a garden sprayer. Beck caught part of it with his upturned face. A breeze moved through the forest with a gentle sound of waves on a beach. He thought of Louise and their last vacation at the beach. He could hear the water pulling at the shore, the gulls crying overhead, a radio playing somewhere, a blonde in a rather optimistic bathing suit, and children kicking sand on them as they ran past.

Brats.

He could see Louise turn to him from her blanket, her grief-stricken, cow-eyed expression making him feel both small and angry at the same time. He disliked children for their intrusiveness, for their assumption that all people liked them. Louise felt it was her duty to have children. She couldn't be fulfilled as a woman otherwise. Dear Louise. Sweet, sensitive, self-righteous Louise. He bought her a poodle as a placebo, and it seemed to work for a while. ChiChi became her baby. She pampered and coddled and spoiled it until Howard hated it as much as if it had been a child. When Louise became ill, he locked the dog in the cellar except when she asked to see it. When Louise died, he had the dog put down. It wasn't a malicious act; it was the practical and expedient thing to do. Not much different from authorizing the removal of Louise's life-support equipment.

Opening his eyes, he shivered and wondered why he was thinking about these things. He'd buried them a long time ago and left no marker. After Louise died, he had been resurrected. Why look back at the tomb? He had spent three years there— dutifully caring for her while she died. He had made his sacrifice; he had given life as much as he planned to give. In his resurrected state it was payback time. His plan was to structure his life to receive maximum pleasure with minimum pain. That had been his deal with God. And since his god was made in his image, agreeing was the least God could do.

With the sun still on his face, he regretted that the plan had gone awry. Hiding in a run-down church on the top of a mountain certainly wasn't part of the idea. God wasn't keeping his part of the deal. Howard shrugged it off. It was a momentary interruption. A small additional price to pay for being foolish enough to get caught with his hand in the wrong cookie jar. He would get out of this one way or another, with or without God's help.

Howard looked in the direction of the farm. He pondered it as the seed of an idea dropped into the fertile ground of his mind. This seed, carefully nurtured, might grow into a plan. He had to be practical—and this was one possible way to do it.

"Howard!" Peter called out. "Help me!"

The urgency was unmistakable and startled Beck enough to get him to his feet. He considered pretending he didn't hear Peter so he could run in the other direction. If it was trouble—if the police were wrestling Peter to the ground—he didn't want to be anywhere close by.

"Beck!"

He could see Peter now, stumbling towards him through the dense forest, waving frantically. *Maybe he caught a deer,* Howard thought hopefully.

He headed in Peter's direction. "What? What's wrong?"

"This way," Peter said breathlessly when they were closer. "You have to help me."

"Help you with what?"

Peter shook his head and tugged at Beck's sleeve. "Come on."

Annoyed, Beck followed Peter back through the woods. *It better be good,* Beck thought as a stitch formed in his side again.

"There," Peter said and pointed.

Beck's first thought was that Peter had indeed caught a deer somehow. It lay half-covered in leaves. As he got closer, he realized it was too small to be a deer. He focused on the object, squinting in a way he knew made him look foolish. He took a few more steps for the picture to come in clearer and then froze in his tracks. Peter had found a man's body.

CHAPTER 9

S AM finished helping Ruth and Amy clear up lunch. Even after a month the scene was awkwardly played out, as if behaving like a family and washing dishes in that mildewed, rotting kitchen were part of some ancient liturgy they'd newly discovered. Luke stared silently at a cross he'd made on the table with his fork and knife. Timothy fidgeted in his chair while Mary scolded him for playing with Joshua, his chipmunk friend. It was so domestic, so mundane that Sam felt quickened by it. These little things were the *true* stuff of life. He imagined it was a form of church that' he'd never been allowed to enjoy in his adulthood—in his Christianity.

"I'm going to wash some clothes this afternoon," Amy offered.

"Ah! You got your rock fixed," Sam said glibly. Amy looked at him as if she wasn't sure whether he was joking or not. He appreciated her expression and its fresh-faced innocence. She could have been one of his students; they had often looked at him that way when he made jokes in class.

Ruth wiped a dish with an old sponge. "I'll help you, Amy."

"No," Amy said. "I'd rather do it myself. I like doing it. It's therapeutic."

"Laundry is therapeutic?" Sam asked.

Amy nodded soberly. "Being alone in the woods, the sound of the creek—it gives me a chance to think and pray."

Luke said, "'Jesus awoke long before daybreak and went out alone into the wilderness to pray.' Mark, chapter one, verse thirty-five."

"Thank you, Luke." Ruth smiled as she grabbed his cutlery cross for cleaning.

What a collection of misfits we are, Sam thought. *Why are we together? Of all the runaways that could have been assembled, why these? Was it God's peculiar sense of humor? The same sense of humor that had assembled the twelve mismatched disciples, so different in personalities, so unlikely as saints? Maybe some other plan is at work that isn't humorous at all.*

A commotion suddenly erupted in the sanctuary. Peter's voice yelling for help echoed down the corridor into the kitchen.

"Good heavens!" Mary cried out and grabbed Tim before he could rush to investigate.

Sam instantly raced in the direction of the sound, with Ruth and Amy hot on his heels. His first thought was that they'd been caught, that the place was surrounded by the police. His second thought was that Peter or Howard had been hurt somehow. Neither thought was encouraging, and his mind shot immediately to a simple phrase: "Lord, have mercy on us." In the past three weeks it had become his automatic prayer when his mind didn't know what else to say or where else to go. He wasn't even sure where the phrase came from. His mother, perhaps, said it as he was growing up, and he'd hidden it away in the unattended rooms of his brain until he'd arrived at the church. Then it suddenly appeared like a jack-in-the-box from a lost toy chest.

Sam rounded the doorway into the sanctuary in time to see

Peter and Howard laboring down what was once the main aisle, carrying a man.

"Get blankets!" Peter shouted.

"I will," Amy said and raced back down the corridor to the other wing of the church.

Howard wheezed and puffed. "He's heavy."

Sam came alongside them to help with their load. "You were supposed to catch rabbits and deer, Peter, not people."

"Is he alive?" Ruth asked.

"We wouldn't have bothered to bring him back if he wasn't," Howard growled.

"You didn't want to bring him back at all," Peter spat.

Amy returned with the blankets and spread them out on the floor next to the radiator. "Here!"

They put the man down and then stepped back. An unspoken vote was instantly taken and Ruth, nominated and unanimously agreed upon, knelt next to the stranger to check his condition.

"We found him in the woods," Peter said, finally catching his breath.

"Who is he? Do you know who he is?" Amy asked. Sam noticed that her eyes were fixed—transfixed—on the stranger's face.

"No identification, no marks," Peter replied.

Howard pushed his disheveled hair away from his forehead. "We should have left him where he was. He may be one of *them*—sent to catch us."

"Or he might be one of us," Amy allowed. "Maybe he's our contact. Maybe Moses and Elijah sent him."

Howard shook his head; beads of perspiration dotted his face. "Wishful thinking. It's a big mistake bringing him here. Like I told the *whiz kid* when—"

"He might have died out there," Peter said defensively. "I thought—"

Sam put a hand on Peter's shoulder. "You did the right thing, Peter. Don't worry."

"Even these days we have a responsibility to help others, don't we?" Amy asked.

"See if you feel that way when he turns us in," Howard said.

"I checked him out for broken bones and wounds," Peter explained to Ruth. "I couldn't find anything wrong."

Ruth looked up. "He has a fever. It looks like he hasn't eaten in days."

"I wonder how he got so far up here?" Amy asked. She hadn't taken her eyes off the man.

"Help me get his coat off," Ruth said to Sam. As they wrestled his arms through the sleeves, she said, "Get a damp rag, will you, Amy?"

Amy nodded and ran off. Sam noticed Mary, Tim, and Luke lingering in the doorway like bystanders at a car accident. Mary kept a tight hold on Tim.

"Is it Moses or Elijah? Is he a secret agent?" Tim asked excitedly.

"We don't know," Mary said.

Luke brushed past them and drifted toward the stranger. "Let me see him," he said, his hands outstretched.

Peter, who Sam thought seemed more attuned to Luke than anyone, was on his feet to intercept the old wizard. "Hold on, Luke; you better stay back. He's sick."

Luke smiled. "I know—I can heal him. Let me lay my hands on him."

"Crazy old coot," Howard muttered.

Sam wondered what would happen if they actually let Luke try what he said. Would the stranger rise up and walk like so many characters from the New Testament? Or would the stranger lay as he was, with poor Luke looking even more like a fool. "Let's try some conventional approaches first," Sam said, knowing he lacked the faith to do otherwise.

"You have no faith . . .," Luke said as if he'd read Sam's mind. "No faith at all. I have power in these hands. But it's a mystery."

Amy returned with the damp cloth, which Ruth applied to the stranger's slender face, patchy beard, and matted brown hair. The stranger suddenly groaned and tossed his head from side to side.

"Take it easy," Ruth said.

His arms, tucked within the blankets, thrashed around. Deliriously, he mumbled something that sounded like "Moses."

"Did you hear that?" Peter exclaimed. "He said 'Moses'! He has to be one of us!"

Howard sneered at Peter. "You'll grab at any straw, won't you?"

"Moses," the stranger said louder and sat straight up, nearly knocking Ruth over. He looked without seeing, then his eyes rolled upward, and he sank back down. Amy knelt with Ruth to readjust the blankets and mop his brow.

"His mind is in turmoil. I can give him peace and rest," Luke said.

"Sit down before you hurt someone," Howard shouted.

"Not hurt, *heal*," Luke corrected him, then turned and walked away toward Sam's table. "You have no faith."

Howard frowned. "Why in the world did we bring that lunatic with us?"

Peter grabbed Howard's arm. "Look, Beck—"

Sam moved between them, his eyes on Peter. "Go find the first-aid kit. We'll need to dress some of his scratches."

Peter glared at Howard and, like a belligerent child, spun on his heels and left.

"Howard," Sam said wearily, "try to show some compassion."

"We're trying to survive here. What chance do we have if we take on every kook and runaway we come across?"

"Don't you remember your Bible?" Ruth lectured him. "We could be entertaining angels unaware."

"Angel's underwear?" Tim called from the door with a giggle. His mother hushed him.

"I'm just trying to be practical," Howard said. "I mean, am I the only one who finds this situation absurd? We're a group of fugitives trapped in a wet, leaky, abandoned church on some desolate mountain. The police are looking for us. We're running out of food. Winter's coming, and that broken-down furnace we've been using is more likely to blow us to smithereens than keep us warm—all while we wait for some mysterious contact from the Underground to come and lead us to the promised land! *Now* we've taken in a sick stranger and—" He seemed to lose his words in his red-faced apoplexy. "It's laughable! Why don't we just put up a flashing sign out front that says, 'Here we are, come and capture us'?"

"God has taken care of us so far," Amy said. "Why should we believe that he'll stop now?"

Howard laughed scornfully. "Taken care of us? You call this being taken care of? Didn't you hear anything I just said? Look around you! If this is being taken care of, then I've got some swampland in Switzerland I want to sell you."

"The prophets said it would be like this for believers. God said it." Amy rebuked him with her hands on her hips and her cheeks flushed. Then she said more softly, "His will be done."

Peter came back with the first-aid kit and added, "You were probably asleep when they taught it, Beck, but the Bible talks about the joy of being persecuted for Christ and the crown that awaits us if we die for our faith."

"If you're so hot to die and get a crown, why don't you turn yourself in? Then you can have all the joy of persecution you want."

Peter jabbed a finger at him. "And if you spent as much time praying as you did complaining, you wouldn't be worried about a thing."

"You should have more respect for your elders," Howard said.

"Respect is something elders have to earn."

Sam held up his hands. "If the two of you will stop arguing, maybe we can talk about this new turn in our predicament. Mary, you and Tim should come in here for this."

"If you think it's necessary," Mary said and guided her son forward.

"Is he one of the heathen police?" Tim asked as he drew closer to the sleeping stranger.

"Heathen police?" Sam asked, amused by the phrase. "No, I don't think so."

Tim dug in his pocket and produced a Swiss knife. "I can take care of him if you want. My knife has a bunch of neat attachments. One flick of this, and he's done for."

"Take it easy, Daniel Boone." Peter smiled at the boy and pulled him away.

"I'm not Daniel Boone," he protested. "I'm Moses—and Joshua is my assistant. Just like in the Bible story."

"Joshua? Your chipmunk?" Amy asked him.

He nodded earnestly. "He went away, but he came back this morning. I thought he would starve without me. But I think he was on the Mount getting the Ten Commandments."

Peter chuckled. "You have your stories mixed up, champ."

Howard grunted. "You've been feeding chipmunks? Terrific. Now we've taken in animals."

"It's just a few crumbs," Tim said.

Sam shook his head like he always did when the conversation spun away from his control, which it did most of the time when they were all together. "What about his condition, Ruth?"

Ruth shrugged. "I'm no nurse, but it looks to me like he's sick from exposure. He probably hasn't had anything to eat or drink in days. We should probably take him to a hospital."

"What?" Howard shouted.

"I know, I know," Ruth replied. "If we take him in, then we'll be caught."

Peter stood up. "I'll take him."

"You'll take him *alone*," Howard said.

"I'm not asking you to go," Peter said. "But if I—"

"Wait a minute," Sam interjected. "Nobody's taking him anywhere. For one thing, carrying him ten miles to the village might do him more harm than good. For another thing, we don't know that he's as sick as all that. Maybe we should try to take care of him for a day or so and, if he gets worse, then we'll come up with a plan."

"Plan? What kind of plan?" Howard asked. "Short of calling the police and asking them to come get him, there's no plan."

"Unless we took him to the farmhouse," Sam said.

Howard laughed. "And—what?—leave him on the doorstep in a basket with a note pinned to his diaper?"

"Maybe. Do you have any other suggestions?"

"I made my suggestion earlier to Peter," Howard said. "We should've left him where he was."

"You're impossible!" Amy cried out and turned away from him indignantly.

"Meanwhile," Sam went on, "what can we do to help him, Ruth?"

"Stay nearby and try to get liquid into him—water, maybe some broth later. We need to keep applying cold compresses to him to try to break that fever."

"All right. I'll stay nearby this afternoon. We can take shifts through the night, if anyone wants to volunteer." Sam looked at Peter, knowing he'd step forward. He did. Then Amy. Ruth agreed. Finally, Mary also said she'd help if she could. Luke announced that he would pray for the man. Howard kept any further comments to himself.

The group broke up, everyone returning to the afternoon's activities. Sam knelt next to the stranger as Ruth handed him the damp rag. She lingered, and Sam knew she had something on her mind.

"Well?" he asked.

"I want to know what you *really* think," she said.

He dabbed at the fevered forehead and said softly, "I don't *really* think anything right now. By helping to bring this man back to good health, he might rise up to bless us or turn us in. That's the gamble, isn't it?"

Ruth nodded. "I don't believe in gambling, but it's certainly a risk."

"A risk, then. But all we can do is wait to see what happens."

There was nothing else to be said, so she walked away. The soft heels of her shoes tapped against the floor and echoed throughout the sanctuary like a ticking clock in an old library. Amy stood in the doorway until Ruth passed her; then she followed as if she'd been pulled away by the slipstream.

Sam looked down at the sleeping stranger and sighed. "All we can do is wait for you—whoever you are."

CHAPTER 10

FROM Williams's vantage point on the sixteenth floor of Central, the people on the plaza below looked like punctuation marks. The rain had been falling nonstop since yesterday morning, and the standard black umbrellas, open against the depressing drizzle, turned the entire scene into a mass of ellipses moving across a gray page—with the occasional exclamation mark supplied by the stiff soldiers who appeared from or disappeared into doorways. They were everywhere, those soldiers, those exclamation marks, nestled conspicuously among the more functional dots and dashes in a meaningless order. From his lofty perch, Williams detected no rhyme or reason for all the activity. How easy it was to forget that those were people. This was the point of view the Committee wanted all good citizens to have: no individuals, just the collective mass.

He wondered if that's also how everything looked to God: small dots moving helter-skelter for no apparent reason. A sentence run amuck. An explosion in a typesetter's room. Did God forget the individuals, too? Who could know?

Williams didn't believe in God as an ongoing concern, but found the concept of some Giant over and above them all intriguing and even hopeful. It could be Zeus or Mother Goose for all he cared, but he liked to think that there was something or someone up there, if only to give the Committee who governed the State a run for their omnipotency. A little competition was healthy for everyone.

Fingers of lightning fractured what piece of sky Williams could see between the two high-rises across the street. Perhaps that was God. When it came to choosing between personalities—God or the Committee—there wasn't much difference between them. Both were unnamed and faceless and held fast with an iron fist. No icons or statues or photos on the office walls. Just slogans and catch phrases to inspire all good citizens everywhere. Williams was amused to realize that, for him, it took as much faith to believe in the Committee as he imagined it took to believe in God. And who was he to say that he wasn't also just a punctuation mark to someone above, just like the black umbrellas below him.

He self-consciously looked up, half expecting to see someone watching him from a window across the street. There were no human forms to speak of. Only a billboard on top reminding him in bold, authoritative neon to Do Your Duty! Otherwise, the buildings—nondescript offices for the government's countless clerks—merely winked at him with dull yellow eyes through the gray rain. Lights were being turned off; clocks were being punched; the clerks were going to join the ellipses heading home.

Home wasn't on the agenda for Williams tonight. It rarely was. Home for him was an efficiency apartment two blocks away with an unmade bed and a pile of dirty laundry in the corner. There was little point to it being otherwise. He knew when Slater hired him that he was taken on for one reason alone: because he was like Slater—unattached to hearth and kin, completely dedicated to his work at all hours of the day or night. That's what made their relationship work. They were kindred spirits in the same graveyard—or two parts of a semicolon.

He turned away from another flash of lightning, the dying day, and the mixed metaphors, and looked across the mess they'd made of the conference room. The long table was littered with reports, files, communiqués, and the Chinese takeout they'd had for lunch. Three weeks had gone by since they had heard anything at all about their escaped convict. Arrests had been made, suspects questioned, and informants paid off, but no one knew what had become of him. The tracks were getting cold, and Williams knew that Slater was worried about losing the scent. The fiascoes at the rehabilitation center and in Tannerville didn't put Slater in good graces with his supervisors either. They expected results and if he couldn't deliver, then he'd get moved to other assignments. And that was the rub. Slater didn't want other assignments. He wanted to catch the roaches.

Why Slater was so determined to catch the Christians was something Williams hadn't sorted out yet.

"Are you listening to me?" Slater asked. Williams hadn't noticed that he was standing in the doorway. "Do you want some coffee?"

"Sorry. I was just thinking."

"Good for you. About what?"

Williams sat down at the long table and began to sort through the day's papers. He wanted to ask but didn't know if this was the right time. He felt tired and reckless enough to try. "I was just wondering why, of all the things you could be doing with your time, you're so determined to catch the Christians."

Slater looked at him, surprised. "Why shouldn't I? Aren't you enjoying your work?"

"I wasn't wondering for my sake. I was just wondering."

"I do it because I'm a law enforcer and because they're breaking the law." Slater rolled up his sleeves and sat down on the opposite side of the table. The fluorescent light above his head crackled and flickered. "Did you say you wanted some coffee?"

"No thanks."

Slater poured himself a cup from the ancient coffeemaker while Williams flipped through a binder of police reports that had been passed on to them from other offices. *I should let the conversation go,* Williams thought. It was dangerous to be too inquisitive about a superior's private motivations.

"It's simple," Slater began, answering the question. "I want to round up these roaches for the sake of our children."

"You don't have any children," Williams said, trying to feign a disinterest in the topic by being lighthearted.

"For the sake of the next generation, then," Slater said impatiently. "Don't be so picky. I want them to have something we didn't have: the chance to grow up in a world without the kind of neurotic fears and crass manipulation the Christians use to get their way. They're roaches who breed and pass on their sick thinking like a disease. Have you ever read a Bible?"

"Not really, no."

"You should get one from Evidence. Then you'll see." Slater sipped his coffee, winced at it, then went on. "It's a collection of myths that, as ancient writings go, are mildly curious. But to twist them around into an oppressive belief system that threatens some kind of punishment in an afterlife, unrealistic expectations in *this* life, and forces children—*children*—to worship it, is—well, it's beyond reason. It takes young, innocent minds and fills them with nightmares and rotten images—eating flesh, drinking blood, burning in eternal fire, denying your natural impulses, crushing your pride underfoot, praying and praying and praying into what turns out to be nothing more than a great void and. . . ." He paused, swallowing as if the memories were a collection of phlegm in the back of his throat. "I think you get the idea."

Williams got the idea, all right. In some ways it was more than he wanted to know. He wanted to change the subject and hoped these reports might do it. His eye caught one from College Park, a university town in the North, that said something about a van driver who'd been questioned on suspicion of bootlegging, then released for lack of evidence. Bootleggers were a dime a dozen these days. He needed something else.

"My father was one of them, you know. A Christian, I mean. Don't deny that you've heard the rumors."

Williams had indeed heard them—and he nodded.

"I'm not exaggerating when I tell you that it literally killed my mother and very nearly ruined my life. If it hadn't been for the Party . . ."

"Most of us were rescued by the Party in one way or another," Williams said.

"*All* of us were. Make no mistake about that. The hope it gave, the clear thinking, the chance to break free from the chains of my background . . . it made all the difference in the world."

Williams glanced at his boss and wondered if he was being sincere. It wasn't like him to be emphatic about the State. In fact, Slater often came off as one who had no particular ideology and only the most practical allegiance to those in power.

"I've surprised you." Slater smiled. "Maintaining an air of detached objectivity keeps certain people—" here he pointed to the ceiling—"from taking you for granted. Give your heart to anyone or anything and let them *know* they have it, and you'll get used up. That's something they don't teach you in the schools, but take it from someone who knows. Now, aren't you glad you asked?"

"Asked what?" Williams said innocently.

Slater laughed. "Smart boy. Now pass those police reports over here. Time is wasting away."

It was after nine o'clock, and Williams had yawned for the twelfth time in as many minutes when Slater slapped the paper in his hand. "Did you see this?"

"Probably," Williams said, stifling another yawn. "What is it?"

"The report from College Park."

"The van driver who was questioned about bootlegging. Yeah, I saw that one."

Slater stood up. "But did you *read* it? This driver—what's his name? . . . Ben Greene—gets pulled over on a routine offense. One of his headlights is out. The officer decides to do a routine check of the van. Greene says it's empty. He made his delivery of dry goods earlier, which makes perfect sense, but the officer goes ahead with the check. Rather than flash his light around, this bright boy actually climbs *inside*. That's when he notices that the flooring has a peculiar sound—'hollow' he said. He looks down and sees a bit of clothing sticking out from what he discovers is a panel."

"The van had a false floor," Williams said. "That's why they questioned him about bootlegging."

Slater nodded. "Why else would a van have a false floor? Greene explains that it's not intended as a false floor, but it's simply another storage area that helps maximize space in the van. The sheriff doesn't have any proof of bootlegging—Greene's papers and identification are in order—so he lets him off."

Williams yawned again. "Sorry, Captain, but I don't get the significance of this."

"I wonder how big the so-called storage area under the false floor was?"

"Why?"

"Because it might be big enough to store *people*." Slater was pacing now. "It's such an old trick; why wouldn't they use it? I want you to call that sheriff, talk to the officer, and track down the driver of that van."

Williams glanced at his watch. "Right now?"

Slater smiled wryly. "Right now."

CHAPTER 11

WAS it a dream?

Peter rubbed his eyes and looked again.

It was gone.

He sat at Sam's table and shook his head in a feeble attempt to ward off the weariness that wanted to cover him like a soft blanket. It made his brain fuzzy, and he couldn't have that. Not on his shift, not while he was watching the stranger.

It must have been a dream. For a moment the church sanctuary seemed to return to its former glory. The stained-glass windows were intact once again, the pews polished, the parishioners standing with hymnbooks in hand singing a song that Peter didn't recognize but knew was old and traditional, the kind of song his mother sang around the house when she thought no one was listening. The congregation was radiant with its joy, unafraid, lifting its voice until it echoed up to the rafters, high above the glittering chandeliers. Peter panicked and ran down the aisle, screaming at them to be quiet. The police might hear, he shouted at them. Were they crazy? Did they want to die? He screamed frantically again and again, but they were unconcerned. They kept singing. It was as if they couldn't see him, as if he were nothing but a spirit moving in their midst. Finally, with indescribable terror, he saw soldiers burst through the doors with machine guns and mow the crowd down. They kept singing. Even as they danced and fell under the barrage of bullets, they sang. Peter stood frozen with fear until the soldiers pointed their guns at him. He couldn't move. He couldn't do anything but scream, as hard and as loud as was humanly possible.

It was a dream.

Peter jolted awake to a thick, nightly silence. The sanctuary was just as he had always known it: cold, desolate, no songs, no soldiers, not even the echo of his scream. Just silence. The stranger lay where he'd been all night, under the blankets by the radiator. Peter shook his head violently, as if that might shake loose the memory of the dream, and stood up. He stretched long and hard.

The hallway door opened slowly, and Peter fixed his eyes on it with a residue of fear, like Scrooge waiting for the appearance of Jacob Marley. Amy stepped into the uneven lamplight carrying a tray with a mug and a thermos of coffee. She showed no signs of having heard Peter scream or that anything could possibly be wrong. He took a deep breath and relaxed.

"Tired?" she asked quietly as she approached him.

"Just a little, I guess," he answered. She was dressed in her usual attire of jeans and hiking boots, but tonight she wore a turtleneck and cardigan sweater. It was his favorite of the three outfits she wore. He wondered if it was a sign of some sort, if she wore it for him.

Amy set the tray down on Sam's table and poured some coffee. "This is in case you get tired."

"Thank you." He sipped the coffee. It tasted stale and burnt. "It's perfect."

She gestured to the stranger. "It's nice of you to stay up with him tonight."

"Nice has nothing to do with it," Peter said, appreciating her attention. "I don't want to let him out of my sight."

He stared at her a moment while she stared at the stranger. There was something about her expression. What was it? Her face was normally radiant, so fresh and pure. He thought he could sit and look at it for hours. Her hazel eyes, too, haunted him no matter what he was doing. He knew them well. So what was it that he saw in them now? It was a light that glowed beyond the mere flame of curiosity they all felt about the stranger. She was looking at the stranger the way he had looked at her since they arrived at the church. Was it love? He'd wrestled with that question every night while saying his prayers. If it wasn't love, then it was something a lot like it. Was that what she felt for the stranger, for this man she didn't even know?

He took another sip of coffee, hoping it might wash down the jealousy rising in his throat. "I think his fever is falling," he said.

"Why is he here?" Amy asked without taking her eyes off the sleeping figure.

"Beats me." Peter looked into the shadowy darkness of the sanctuary. The memory of the dream came back to him, and he shuddered involuntarily as if someone had just stepped on his grave.

She drifted away from him and stopped a few feet from the stranger. "I keep praying that he's our contact. I want to get out of here."

"We all do."

She hugged the sweater to herself. Whatever her expression was before, it gave way to one of distinct sadness. "I hate this place."

Her tone—with that expression—gently but undeniably brushed against his heart. He wanted to say something hopeful and encouraging, but the desire eclipsed his ability. "Sure beats jail" was the best he could come up with. He hated himself for it.

"Sometimes I see little difference," she said, then hesitated as if she immediately regretted her honesty. "No, I'm sorry. I didn't mean that."

"Yes, you did." He put down his mug of coffee and took a few steps closer to her. "But it's OK."

"No, it isn't," she said firmly. "I don't ever want to sound ungrateful to God for what he's done. This *is* better than jail. I have to remember that. It's just that I've been feeling so homesick lately, remembering how it used to be . . . when my parents were alive. . . ."

"Don't, Amy." He didn't know why he wanted to stop her, but he felt like he should. One thing life in this world had taught him was that you couldn't go back. Dwelling on memories, on the losses, on moments and days that could never be recreated, was a particular kind of torture. Peter had blocked out as much as he dared. To do otherwise was to invite a mental breakdown.

A thin smile worked across her lips. "I know. Don't worry. I think it's the weather. It must be. Certain times of year always trigger memories for me. I've been tough until now. But today turned overcast; did you notice? Sunshine, then overcast. Do you know what it makes me think of? Walking home from school, stepping in the back door of my house, and smelling my mom's chocolate-chip cookies baking in the oven."

"You're only making it worse," he said, knowing that if she cried it would be all the excuse he needed to take her in his arms.

"I don't care. I'd rather have the memories with the pain than no memories at all." Her tone was defiant, and he felt rebuked. "Sometimes I'm afraid that if it weren't for the pain, I wouldn't feel anything at all. I'd be numb. A walking corpse."

"You're no corpse."

She nodded. "No, I'm not. That's what I realized today. But I *am* a corpse in a way; we all are if we bury the memories and even the pain. Do you know what I mean? You don't. I can tell by your expression that you don't."

Whatever his expression was, he tried to change it—but with little success. He *didn't* understand. It hadn't occurred to him that all his training to bury his feelings, his memories, would make him a walking corpse. He had thought it was a means to keep himself alive.

"That's the contradiction, isn't it?" she went on. "Coming here has made me feel alive again. And, in coming alive, I realized that I hate being here. I *felt* hatred, and I thought about how long it's been since I felt anything resembling an emotion. I felt other things, too."

The twinge of jealousy pricked at Peter's heart. Whatever else she felt, it wasn't for him. It was for the stranger.

"It's like spending a night in a tomb just to learn how much you love life," she concluded. But there was no happiness in her voice. It was a simple conclusion, a resolution.

He struggled valiantly to connect to what she was saying. "Look, Amy, all I know is that being alive . . . well, that's part of being a Christian, right? It's that memory verse I learned as a kid: 'You were dead because of your sins. Then God made you alive with Christ.' You wanna know who's dead?" He gestured to the darkness as if it contained the very people he was referring to. "The ones who are chasing us, the ones who want to lock us up. They're dead, and they're jealous because we're not. They want us to be like them, and that's why they want us out of the way. If they don't succeed, then—" He stopped, suddenly aware that she was looking at him like an older, wiser sister might look at an immature younger brother. He felt exposed and embarrassed. He'd overplayed his hand, tried too hard, and she noticed it the way girls do when guys are trying to impress them. It was like a sixth sense. "I'm sorry. I'm talking too much."

"You are sweet, Peter," she said gently. "Under normal circumstances, a girl would be very fortunate to have you."

His heart suddenly started to skip rope in his chest; his mouth went dry. "How about *you?*" There. It was out.

She smiled indulgently at him. "These aren't normal circumstances." With that, she walked to the doorway and disappeared into the darkness of the corridor.

He wanted to kick himself around the room. "Feelings? I'd like to tell you what I'm feeling right now," he said to the sleeping stranger.

※

Like Peter, Sam was visited by dreams. As he lay awake on his couch, he tried to piece together the various subconscious fragments to see if they would make any sense. First he dreamt he was a young boy again, playing hide-and-seek in the woods with some friends. He was *it* and, after counting to ten, began to search diligently, checking the usual places and the not-so-usual places. He couldn't even find Fast Freddie, who was named not for his speed but for his slowness caused by obesity. You knew you were in trouble when you couldn't even find Fast Freddie. Sam continued looking until boredom overtook his determination, and he decided it was time to quit. "Olly, Olly, in-come-free!" he shouted. No one responded. He shouted again. An upset bird caring for her young screamed back at him. Finally, he heard rustling in a thick overgrowth of bushes. Certain that he'd found at least one person, he raced into the bushes, scrambling hard and furious to catch whoever it was before they could get away. Pushing through, he stumbled out on the other side into a clearing. He was startled to see a large military tank under a netting of camouflage, waiting like a sleeping giant. The turret suddenly turned to him, training its sight on his heart.

This dream was part memory, Sam knew as he stared at the ceiling of the pastor's office. As a boy he had stumbled onto an arsenal of tanks—a base for the rebels who would later lead the country to revolution. It was what had happened afterwards—in the dream—that had him perplexed.

Afraid of the tank, Sam turned and ran back through the bushes. But, as happens in dreams, he was no longer a young boy but an adult, clawing frantically through the underbrush. He was lost and in a panic. He was aware only of some anonymous fear that made his heart pound and his legs move even though they were sore and numb. The woods broke open into a sunny clearing covered with tombstones and open graves with coffins scattered and disheveled. It was the graveyard behind the church, the same graveyard that had startled him when he had first arrived and had since become simply a passive neighbor. But the familiarity didn't calm him, and he ran, tripped, gashed his forehead against a marble cross, and fell in a heap onto the soft earth.

He heard gunshots and looked up toward the church. It was still and silent. Suddenly the ground beneath him shook, then cracked and split. A hand broke upward through the dark soil only inches from Sam's face. It was decayed, the flesh barely holding onto the bone as it reached upward from the green moss. He saw the maggots squirming between each finger and smelled the stench of death's visitation. He shouted and jumped up, the hand now reaching for his ankle. He ran for the church, dodging the headstones. Hands pushed up out of the ground all around him, like flesh-colored plants under a time-lapse camera. They strained for him as he ran past. One grabbed his pant leg; another caught his shoe. It slipped off, and he ran ahead without it, just like he had done with a sleeping bag in the hands of another corpse. He made it to the gravel parking lot as the sun disappeared behind fast-moving black clouds. Lightning flashed. Some part of Sam's mind told him not to worry because it was only a dream—he would wake up and all would be well. But he couldn't wake up. The rain fell, drenching him. He turned to run to the church door and was surprised to see that it was five times its normal size. It swung open, looking like a mouth waiting to devour him. He was pulled toward it, toward an inevitable end. A turret poked out of the shadows in the doorway—and fired with a deafening roar. Then he woke up.

He tucked his arm behind his head. Someone was walking down the hallway. It was Amy; he could tell by the walk. She had probably taken a snack or coffee to Peter. He wondered if she had run the errand out of thoughtfulness for Peter or desire to see the stranger.

Sam wondered about nightmares like the one he'd just had. Without the benefit of a proper clergyman or a theologian, he didn't know the Christian stance on the subject. There were dreams in the Bible, he remembered. Two Josephs had dreams; probably others did, too. The dreams were interpreted then for spiritual insight or prophecy. In the age of Freud dreams were interpreted for other insights. But what now? What about tanks and convulsing graveyards and a church that seemed to symbolize death? What was he supposed to make of that? He sat up and turned on the light. Where was his Bible? He'd lent it to Ruth. He wanted it now to read a psalm for comfort. He knew he wouldn't get any sleep until he could erase these images from his mind. Reprimanding himself for not memorizing more verses, he sat on the edge of the couch. He tried to find the words for an elaborate prayer, but they didn't come. So he simply asked God to show him the meaning of the dream or take it away. It didn't seem too much to ask, though dreams—even nightmares—weren't usually a cause for worry, and he hated to bother God with a silly request. But this was the sixth time he'd had this particular dream.

❋

Peter gently felt the stranger's forehead. It was still warm. He stood up and nearly jumped out of his skin when someone tapped him on the leg.

"Tim!"

"What're you doing, frisking him?" Tim asked.

"No," Peter replied, trying to relax. "What are you doing up?"

"I can't sleep."

"Why not?"

"Mom's snoring."

Peter placed his hands on Tim's shoulders and gently pushed him toward the door. "Moms don't snore; they just breathe hard."

"Then Mom's breathing *really* hard."

"Put some cotton in your ears. If your mom wakes up and finds you gone, she'll kill *both* of us."

"But my stomach hurts. I have to go to the bathroom."

"Then *go,*" Peter said. "You don't need me to help you."

Tim allowed Peter to guide him for a few steps, then stopped. Peter anticipated a stall. "Peter . . ."

"What?" A glass of water? A bedtime story? He wondered which tactic Tim would try. In the month they'd been together, Tim had tried every excuse imaginable. Peter didn't mind; he remembered doing the same thing to *his* father. And, just like his father, he'd fall for an excuse sometimes, while other times he wouldn't. Peter looked down at the boy and knew with certainty that Tim was the closest thing to a son he'd ever have. He couldn't account for this sudden revelation—he suspected it was linked to the failed conversation with Amy—but he knew that normal family relationships, marriage, and children wouldn't happen for him. He wouldn't live that long. A sense of loss and regret crowded in on him, and he vowed to spend more time with Tim as an appeasement. It wasn't too late, right? He could take Timothy out tomorrow and show him how to set the traps. It was a start.

"When I was little," Tim began, "my dad used to give me a hug before I went to sleep."

Peter smiled and knelt down. "You want a hug?"

Tim nodded.

Peter pulled the boy close for a hug and added to his previous vow: *We'll do something together not just tomorrow, but every day from now on. You can be the son I'll never have, and I'll be the father you lost. It's a game we'll play to keep from losing our minds with sadness.*

"And then he said a magic prayer to keep the monsters away," Tim said.

"You're pushing it, kid."

"He really did!" Tim insisted.

Peter looked at him warily, then placed his hand ceremoniously on his head. "OK, let me think about this." Peter wondered if Tim meant imaginary monsters or the ones that were real, the ones that were hunting them. Maybe there wasn't a difference. All the nightmares of his childhood had been fulfilled in the reality of his adulthood. The death and decay that he thought waited for him in the shadows of his bedroom closet now stood before him in the shadows of this church. Peter cleared his throat and spoke in a mock drone:

"Now I lay me down to sleep, I pray the Lord my soul to keep. And if I die—" He stopped and looked at Tim, who waited expectantly. "And till I wake this next good day, please keep the monsters far away."

"Amen," Tim whispered, satisfied. "Good night, Peter."

"Good night, champ."

Peter watched him disappear through the doorway, just as he had watched Amy a short while ago. He shook his head and went back to Sam's table to pour another cup of coffee. "Magic prayers," he chuckled.

He looked over at the stranger and decided to say a few of his own.

CHAPTER 12

BOBBY took his usual place at the edge of the alley and watched the deserted streets of Hopewell for any sign of the police. Just opposite, a blue-and-green neon light announced the name of a beer through a large window. A low thump of a muted bass beat through the tin siding. It was a slow-dance number, the dance he was supposed to share with Heather. Depressed, he shoved his hands deep into his coat pockets and glanced down the alley. The night air was cool and heavy with a vague promise of snow, but that didn't stop the two shadowy figures from taking their jackets off. It was a mere formality for the fight to come. No sense getting bloodstains on the leather.

One of the figures muttered obscenities, the condensation of his beer-drenched breath rising like smoke from a factory chimney. He kicked a bottle that rattled along the pavement. A rat squealed and scurried down the edge of the wall to some hiding place behind the stacks of garbage.

"Keep it down, Clay!" Bobby whispered harshly.

"Yeah, keep it down," a man with a body like an anvil said as he pushed at the sleeves on his flannel shirt. His tongue was thick with liquor.

"You too, Jake," Bobby said, then checked the street again.

The one called Clay—a lean, blond-haired teen with a chiseled face—said, "I'll keep it down after I put you down."

Jake snorted as he lifted his fists, stumbling on a wooden pallet as if the weight of his hands was too much to carry. Clay also held up his fists, rock steady.

Bobby watched the two lumber around each other like armor-burdened gladiators from another time. He knew how it would turn out; it always ended the same way. But he watched anyway. Clay was his best friend, and it seemed important for him to witness the details—if only to tell Clay what had happened tomorrow after the liquor wore off and the memory was unclear.

Jake threw a punch—and missed. He stumbled forward, and Clay sent out a hard right that connected with Jake's jaw. He staggered back and glared at Clay. "You—" Jake swore and threw himself at Clay.

From Bobby's vantage point it was a confusing mass of grunts, blows, and wrestling amidst the clattering trash cans, banging boxes, and breaking bottles. The noise would draw attention, Bobby knew. Somebody would call the police.

He tried to figure out his explanation if they were caught, but nothing sensible came to mind. This fight would be hard to justify. How could he tell them that Clay went to the bar with the intention of beating up Jake for threatening to turn off the utilities at his father's farm? Jake was only doing his job, after all. But that didn't matter to Clay, anymore than it mattered that they hadn't been able to pay the bill in two months. There simply wasn't enough money for it. Jake was supposed to understand that. In this town, you were expected to look after your own, not the interests of the big utility company. Jake wasn't homegrown but had lived there long enough to know better anyway. Clay intended to beat the idea into his head. Bobby doubted the police would be sympathetic in any case.

A light blinked in a window overhead, and Bobby looked up. Someone had peeked out to see what was going on. That means the police were probably on the way. Bobby turned in time to see Clay knock Jake to his knees. His fists flew wildly against his weakening opponent, who no longer even had the strength to raise his arms in defense. Jake's knees buckled and he fell heavily, pathetically sprawled out, limp and unconscious.

"Get up!" Clay demanded and started kicking the prostrate figure. "Get up!"

It was over. Bobby slipped from his position just as a siren wailed in the distance. "Let's go, Clay."

Clay kept kicking Jake. "Get up, you no good—"

"Cut it out! He's down, he's down! We have to get out of here!" Bobby grabbed Clay's arm and tugged at him.

"Go ahead! Try to turn off our power," Clay yelled as he delivered one last kick to Jake's head. He yielded to Bobby's pull, grabbed his jacket from the top of a trash-can lid, and they ran out of the alley together. They made it down the street and around the corner just as a police car pulled up to where Bobby had been standing.

"Are you all right?" Bobby asked.

Clay rubbed his jaw. "He got me once, but it didn't hurt. I paid him back ten times over."

"Are you satisfied? Can we go home now?"

"Satisfied?" Clay asked, as if the thought were an impossibility. He answered by pushing open the door to Hank's Place and stepping inside to the dark, smoke-filled room. Bobby groaned and followed him in.

CHAPTER 13

THE gray morning light filtered through a crack in a board and found Sam exactly as the moon had watched him most of the night: lying on his couch, his eyes glued to the ceiling. He thought about the small town where he used to visit his grandparents and how, on Sunday mornings, he would lie in their guest room and listen for the church bells to announce the start of services. It was such a long time ago. He couldn't remember the last time he heard bells of any kind ringing for any reason. Nowadays he heard only sirens and alarms. He wondered: At what point did the world decide it didn't need church anymore? What shift in the world's axis led the mass population to believe that mysteries of faith and their physical manifestations—like bells and steeples and statues and crosses—were no longer needed by humanity? And where was he when it happened? He knew. He was asleep in the arms of his lover. Now he may never be able to sleep again. Regret was like that, carrying with it a sharp vengeance of remembered things done and left undone.

He rose with the sluggishness of age beyond his years, took care of necessities, and padded quietly down the still hallway to see how Peter and the stranger were doing. He felt a sense of foreboding as he approached the doorway. He was afraid that he would find Peter unconscious or dead and the stranger gone. The cool, damp mustiness of the sanctuary reached him before he reached it and, with relief, he saw the stranger still on the floor buried under several blankets and Peter bent over the table asleep.

Sam gently nudged him.

Peter jumped. "It's probably just the water bottle," he said in his sleep.

"What?"

Peter blinked. "What?"

"Good morning," Sam said as he moved to the stranger and felt his forehead. He was drenched in sweat; the fever was gone.

"I wasn't sleeping," Peter said apologetically. "Well, not deeply."

Sam checked the stranger's pulse. "Of course not."

"Nothing happened last night. He slept like a baby," Peter said as he stood up and stretched.

"Did he mutter anything else in his sleep?" Sam asked.

"No. In fact, he was so quiet that I kept thinking he died or something. I must have checked him a dozen times."

Sam looked down at the sleeping stranger. He had to be the answer to their prayer, their way out. While the stranger slept, it could be true. The essence of any mystery was that you could project anything you wanted into it until your projections were proven otherwise. This mysterious stranger could embody hope or despair. Sam remembered a poem he'd once studied in school:

> *Oh, man of mystery!*
> *Be ye prophet or messenger of doom*
> *Keep still thy lips*
> *and hold fast your sickle of destruction*
> *For the wrath of God is found in death*

and not in life alone.
Cast a cold eye on life, on death.
Horsemen pass by.

The stranger might be a redeemer or an angel of death. But who was to say that he wasn't one and the same? Sam shook his head. This wasn't a good way to start the day.

"You should get some sleep," he said to Peter.

Peter nodded but didn't leave. He looked around the church and asked a question as if it had been on his mind all night. "I wonder how people could worship in a dark, cold church like this?"

Sam let his eyes trail up one of the modest arches, now cobwebbed and soot covered, to the gray shattered chandeliers above. Any semblance of beauty and grace was long gone. "One assumes it wasn't always like this. For one thing, I doubt it was always so dark and cold."

"It's hard to imagine it being anything else. It's like a big cave."

"This is appropriate for us, I think," Sam said, saying aloud what he'd been thinking for days. "When the early Christians were persecuted in the first century, they hid and worshiped in dark, cold passageways that made up the underbelly of Rome. I've seen pictures of them in archaeology books. They were called the catacombs. There are a lot of similarities between our Christian ancestors and what we're experiencing now. But then, that's true for any group that experiences persecution, I guess. Somehow, though, it's like time has gone full circle and—"

Peter yawned.

"I used to get the same reaction from my students." Sam smiled. "You better get some sleep. I'll keep an eye on our friend here."

Luke stepped through the doorway and announced, "I've been praying all night. God has been preparing me to heal this man. The Spirit is moving within me."

Sam and Peter exchanged a sad glance. "Go get the others, Luke," Sam said. "We'll meet in the kitchen this morning."

Luke frowned. "But we should meet here in the sanctuary. We should always study the Word in here. These old walls have heard many a sermon, many a hymn from people who loved Jesus." He paused and when he spoke again, there was an unmistakable strain in his voice and Sam thought he saw tears welled up in his eyes. "I preached here once."

"You did?" Peter asked, surprised. This was the first time Luke had said anything to indicate he remembered his life before the shock treatments.

"I was on my way through the village, and they asked me to preach. I preached in a lot of churches before . . ." Luke stopped and frowned, his face knotting up with concentration. "Before something happened."

Sam wondered how far Luke's memory would take him—if it could take him back to the pain he'd obviously endured.

"What happened?" Luke implored Sam. "What happened to me? Please, tell me. I don't remember."

Sam thought about the nature of mercy: when God allows us to forget our pain and when he allows us to remember it clearly. It wasn't the same for everyone. "Maybe I will tell you sometime, Luke. But first you need to get the others."

Luke's face cleared, like a child who'd been offered a candy bar to forget about his skinned knee. "Yes. And then I will call on the power of God to heal the stranger." He walked away, almost happy.

"It's heartbreaking," Peter said.

Sam shook his head. "It's better he doesn't remember."

"Is it?" Peter asked.

Sam shrugged. "What can the memories do for him now?"

Peter didn't answer, but walked out quietly. Sam turned to the front of the sanctuary and imagined Luke preaching there—and not only Luke but other preachers and other congregations. If the wooden walls could absorb sound, what would he hear if he could put a stethoscope on them? Songs of praise, Scripture being read, prayers of repentance and joy . . . screams of terror, blood spilled from the persecution, the rattle of death.

In death, though, there is peace. Sam willed himself to believe it.

※

At nine o'clock the fugitives left the stranger for a few minutes and gathered together, as they did every morning, for a time of prayer and Bible study, followed by a general discussion of whatever problems they were having. Sam figured it was the closest thing to a proper church he would ever experience. They even tried a form of Communion one morning with stale bread and powdered lemonade. It left him feeling forlorn, as if he'd missed the most important appointment of his life by a minute. He imagined it must have been even harder for Ruth and Mary, who had attended church throughout their lives. How does one feel when stripped of something so easily taken for granted? The closest he could come to a relative feeling was when the Political Censors had gone through the college library to remove "questionable" materials. He had considered access to the library's resources simply a fundamental human right. All that changed in the name of the common good, equality, fraternity, and all the other meaningless buzzwords the new society had used at the time. They took his favorite books.

Now, huddled together in the kitchen, the Church of the

Last Fugitives met in the name of the Father, Son, and Holy Ghost. Amen. They made it halfway through an old hymn Mary thought she remembered. The verses were elusive and jumbled, and the song eventually petered out to a comical standstill.

Sam's mother's Bible was brought out for reading and commentary. It was all guesswork to Sam, trying to be relevant with things like chronologies and Levitical laws, but the other passages spoke for themselves. "Whenever trouble comes your way, let it be an opportunity for joy," the apostle James said that morning. "For when your faith is tested, your endurance has a chance to grow."

Ruth chuckled and said, "Then I guess we should have an overabundance of endurance here."

They sang "Jesus Loves Me," a song everyone seemed to know.

"How's the mystery man?" Beck asked once they'd moved on to general business.

"Better," Sam reported. "His fever is gone." He looked around at the gaunt, sleepless eyes that gazed back at him. Suddenly he was transported from church to a concentration camp; the glimmer of hope that had been generated by their worship now became a cold lump of deprivation.

"When are we leaving?" Beck asked.

"I don't know," Sam replied.

Beck snorted. "I think somebody should find out what's going on down there. Where's our contact? Let's send someone down to the village to scout around."

"It's too dangerous," Amy said.

Sam smiled. "No, I think it's an excellent idea, and I want to thank Howard for volunteering to do it."

Howard spun in his chair to face Sam. "Now, wait a

minute. I didn't say *I'd* do it. I thought we could take a vote and—" Trapped, he slumped in his chair and folded his arms.

"So much for old business. Any new business?" Sam asked.

No one spoke.

Sam clasped his hands behind his back and paced around the table. By now, everyone knew that this gesture meant he had something serious to say. He slowly began. "I want to take this opportunity to curb any grumblings and rumors whispered in our midst. We are *not* going to starve to death as some would have you believe. I know we're down to some pretty skimpy meals and it is uncomfortable—"

"To say the least," Howard said.

"And you usually don't," Sam retorted. "It's uncomfortable, as I was saying, but we have to have faith that God will take care of us. Remember the other day, in one of the Gospels we read that he would never leave us or forsake us. Well, I'm kind of new to the basics of Christianity, but even a baby like me wants to take those words at face value. Unless I've got the Bible all wrong, it means what it says. I don't know how he's with us, but he is."

"He is!" Ruth added.

"So let's hang on the best we can and don't let wild fears get in the way of our faith."

"Amen," Mary said as she put her arm around a very bored Timothy.

"OK, what are we praying about this morning?" Sam asked. This was often a tough time. Beyond difficult attempts to express gratitude to God for their current safety and the more heartfelt "God help us," it was hard to know what to say.

Mary cleared her throat nervously. "I'm almost embarrassed to admit it, but I've been having trouble sleeping lately. I've been having the strangest dreams that keep waking me up." Her voice trailed off as she looked down at the knotted fingers in her lap.

Sam remembered his own dreams and shrugged them off. "It's understandable," he said. "Very often the fears we hide during our waking hours run rampant in our sleep."

"'You will keep in perfect peace all who trust in you,'" Ruth quoted from the Bible.

"I know," Mary said, "but it's the violence in my dreams that wakes me up. The running lost through the woods, the gunshots in the church, the clawing hands in the graveyard . . ."

Mary stopped suddenly and looked worried as Ruth and Amy turned to her, their eyes wide and mouths agape. Sam felt his heart throb in his ears.

"I'm sorry," Mary said. "I shouldn't have mentioned it."

"You had that dream, too?" they asked Mary, then each other, as it became clear that something very strange had happened.

"We've all had the same dream?" Amy asked. "But isn't that . . . impossible?"

"Yes, it is," Sam said.

A heavy silence hung over them for a moment. It was like someone had whispered a magic word, and they were fearfully waiting for the goblins to come and whisk them away to realms unknown.

"I didn't have a dream," Howard growled, neither disappointed nor concerned.

The silence continued, and in it Sam tried to reconcile his thoughts. He needed to say something about this. But he had nothing else to say—to Howard or anyone—about it. He simply didn't know what to make of the phenomenon. He'd have to think long and hard about it. And, even then, any guess would probably be wildly inaccurate. He was in over his head. The ache of inadequacy filled his heart like a bad toothache. "What else should we pray for?"

"Our friend," Amy said, gesturing towards the sanctuary.

"If he *is* our friend," Howard corrected her.

Amy continued, "And for Moses, Elijah, and the work of the Underground."

Sam nodded.

"Yes, yes, we must pray," Luke announced and slipped into the hallway. "I will pray for the stranger."

Sam watched him go, then mumbled apologetically, "He won't do any harm."

"We'll see about that," Howard said.

Ruth suddenly laughed. "When I listen to our prayer requests now, I remember back at my home church when we prayed for things like guidance with the color of our choir robes or the upcoming potluck dinner or Miss Claudia's sick cat; we prayed with all the fervor of Moses before the Red Sea."

"We didn't know what precious little time we had left," Mary said wistfully.

"Let's pray," Sam said.

CHAPTER 14

HE was running, running hard, aimlessly, though his fevered mind had forgotten why. He just had to keep moving, keep climbing. Something beckoned him like a siren's song that drew him upward into the mountain. Exhaustion was near, however, and he fell. His mind screamed at him to get up, but his body refused.

He lay there in the damp leaves listening to the songs of the birds and the shallow sound of his own breathing. He thought back to when he had lain on a bed in his grandparents' guest room listening to birds outside the window. That was another life, a real bed. Nothing was soft like that anymore.

He opened his eyes, and suddenly he wasn't in the woods anymore. Dim lights flickered somewhere through a haze. *I see people. They look like trees walking,* the blind man once said. Why had he thought of that? The lights, that was it. They twinkled in a strange unsettled way. A flame? Candles? He couldn't tell. Everything was still too blurry.

He pressed his palms against his eyes. Had he gone blind? Why couldn't he see where he was? He'd been running in the woods and now . . . now he felt very clammy and damp.

A hand touched him, gentle and soothing. Normally he would have reacted, sprung into a defensive position to protect himself. But the touch of this hand wasn't threatening at all. It rested on his forehead, then his eyes, and the blurriness fell away in patches, like scales. He blinked. Above him stood an old man with wild white hair and a beard. He'd seen him somewhere before. He looked like a Sunday school rendition of John the Baptist. Was this some kind of vision? The old man looked kind and patient but exuded an air of unpredictability. He wore an expression of disapproval.

"Stand up," the old man said.

"I can't. I can't seem to move. Who are you?"

The old man smiled wearily. "Why have you been running? You were not called to run. You were called to more important things."

"I know, but—"

"All things work together according to God's purpose, and though you run, you still have a place in his purpose."

"But I can't."

"You will."

The old man was gone in a flash, and with him went the clearness of sight. Darkness fell on the stranger like a thick blanket. He struggled against it, pushing upwards hard, getting to his knees and pushing, pushing. It gave away enough for him to think he could get out from under it. So he pushed up and up until he was standing on very shaky legs, the weakness threatening to drop him to the ground again. Then the blackness turned to a dull gray light.

This helped his determination to get out from under the veil. If it was a dream, then he wanted to wake up. If it wasn't a dream, then he wanted to break out somehow. Either way, it was time to open his eyes and see clearly where he was.

With all of his might, he struggled toward awareness.

❋

Sam and the fugitives were still bowed in prayer when Luke declared, "He is risen!"

"Amen," Ruth said as if to affirm Luke's declaration of praise. Otherwise, they ignored him and continued to pray.

Sam started to pray about their food shortage and their hope for the contact to come very soon.

Suddenly Tim called out, "Hey! Look!"

As Sam lifted his head to see what made Tim so excited, Mary screamed.

They were both gesturing to the doorway just beyond Sam's shoulder. Ruth's, Amy's, and Howard's eyes were fixed on the same point. Sam turned around and first saw Luke's expression of delirious amazement. Luke stepped aside, and Sam saw the stranger, carelessly wrapped in a torn blanket, looking like Lazarus unbound and standing on his own two feet.

CHAPTER 15

WITH great restraint the fugitives kept quiet while the stranger drank his coffee. But they assaulted him with their eyes—scrutinizing his every gesture, searching for unspoken clues. Even Howard waited patiently. Sam was slightly amused to see them treat this awakened stranger like a visitation from the heavens. *Deus ex machina*—and their fates were in his hands.

The stranger looked small and shriveled under the bulky blanket that still draped his shoulders. His patchy beard, sun-baked skin, and matted hair made him look like a field-worker. The coffee cup shook unsteadily as he raised it to his lips. Before drinking, he glanced up self-consciously at the seven sets of eyes staring at him. "Am I holding my cup wrong?" he asked.

The spell broken, the eyes diverted to other places.

"How do you feel?" Ruth asked.

"Compared to what?"

Ruth chuckled. "Compared to how you've felt on other days."

"Compared to other days, I feel terrific," he replied. "This is a church of some sort, right?"

"Yes, it is," Sam said.

Howard snapped, "Sam! Don't tell him anything until we know more about him."

As much as Sam hated to agree with Howard about anything, he nodded and looked solemnly at the stranger. "Before we say anything else, you'll have to answer some questions."

The stranger rubbed his forehead wearily. "I will if you promise to keep them easy."

"Fair enough," Sam said.

"What's your name?" Howard asked.

"Smith," he answered. "James Smith."

"Sounds fake," Howard snorted. "Who were your parents—John and Pocahontas?"

"Howard!" Amy cried out.

"Actually, I'm the son of John and Patricia," Smith answered unflinchingly as he took another drink of coffee. "Next question?"

"What are you doing up here, Mr. Smith?" Amy asked.

"Would you believe me if I said I got lost while taking a long walk?"

"No," Amy replied.

"Taking a long walk from where?" Howard asked.

Smith looked at Howard thoughtfully, then looked from face to face as if he'd just realized something. "You don't have to be afraid of me. I'm a Christian."

"Thank God," Mary whispered. There was a silent sigh of relief around the room.

Howard didn't take the news so readily. "What makes you so sure we're Christians? How do you know we won't turn you in?"

"You are, and you won't," Smith said. "You're Christians in hiding."

"Where's your identification?" Howard persisted.

"My—?"

"We looked through your knapsack, and you don't have anything—no papers, cards, or scanning codes," Howard said.

Smith looked down at his coffee cup. He slumped just a little in his chair, and what little color had been in his face drained away. "I'm on the run. I'd be a fool to carry an ID."

"Maybe we should save the rest of our questions for later," Sam suggested.

Smith lifted his hand. "It's all right. I can answer your questions. I don't want to return your kindness by being rude." He tried on a smile. "It must have been a shock finding me out in the woods."

"It certainly was," Howard said. "Carrying you back was no picnic, either."

"Then I have you to thank."

"You do."

"And Peter," Amy interjected. "He's sleeping right now. He stayed up with you all night."

"Oh—then thanks to you both," Smith said.

Sam hedged for a moment, then asked, "Mr. Smith, are you our contact?"

Smith looked surprised by the question, then answered uneasily, "No, I'm not."

Disappointment blew through the room like an icy wind. Sam felt his heart slide.

"How long have you been hiding up here?" Smith asked sympathetically.

"Almost a month," Ruth said.

Smith slowly shook his head. "I'm sorry to bring bad news, but there'll be no contact for a while. The Underground has been . . . disrupted."

Disappointment gave way to a muted alarm that manifested itself in worried looks among them all.

"What happened?" Amy asked softly.

"Captain Slater," Smith began. Realizing that the name meant nothing to them, he explained. "He is in charge of breaking up the Underground—capturing Moses and Elijah. Everybody is lying low until a new strategy can be formed."

"But when will that be?" Mary asked with an undisguised pleading in her voice. "Winter's coming. We'll never survive."

"Not so fast, Mary. We'll survive," Sam said, knowing it was time to stop this conversation until he could talk to Smith alone. "We should get Mr. Smith some solid food. He must be hungry."

Ruth nodded. "That's right. I'll take care of it."

"The rest of us can leave him alone," Sam said and shooed everyone but Ruth toward the door.

Smith said quietly, "Again, thank you for taking care of me."

"Think nothing of it," Sam said.

"Think *plenty* of it," Howard corrected him. "I must have carried you two miles."

Smith forced a smile. "As I said before, thank you."

In the hallway, Howard cornered Sam. "So you're giving him our food?"

"Hard for him to eat anything else," Sam said.

"I don't trust him," Howard said. "I think we should keep an eye on him."

"Do you want to go back in the kitchen?"

"Well—"

"Go ahead, Howard." Sam smirked. "He might beat up Ruth and run off with our blanket. And you better check his luggage just to make sure he doesn't steal any of our soap and towels."

Howard frowned at him. "Never mind, if you're going to be like that." He marched off to his room.

Luke stood against the wall and stared at his hands. Sam was reminded that Luke had been the one to pray for the stranger and, so it would seem, had brought him back from his illness. Or perhaps it was just a coincidence. "Good work, Luke," Sam said and patted him on the arm.

Luke smiled.

"Did Luke *really* wake Mr. Smith up?" Timothy, unseen until that moment, asked excitedly.

"Maybe he did," Sam answered honestly.

"Wow," the boy said and wandered off with amazement shining from his face.

Sam looked back at Luke again. Still staring at his hands, there was a knowing look in Luke's eyes.

CHAPTER 16

JAKE Janovitch stared silently out of his apartment window with his good eye—the one that hadn't swollen shut. Since he was swimming in painkillers, the afternoon moved in slow motion for him. In the train yard below, a blue-uniformed railway clerk took tickets from the three waiting passengers. They stood on the station platform with their collars turned up and their hats pulled down to protect themselves from the biting wind. The 2:45 Express was due any minute. Jake dreamily followed the rail until it disappeared behind the utility building near the bend. That was the building where Jake worked.

It looked to Jake as if it might snow at any minute. But it had looked like this for three or four days now. They were geared up for it at the utility company; extra circuits had been rerouted to accommodate the sudden surge of power from heat being turned on full blast. His thick lid closed over his eye. He was drifting.

The 2:45 Express arrived on time, its long blue-and-silver body obscuring his view of the station. The angle was just right for him to see the reflection of his building in its windows. Terry, Jake's coworker, would be fixing his afternoon cup of coffee. He always did just as the 2:45 Express went through. Jake could see him standing at the window now, cup in hand, stirring absentmindedly while the train rattled past.

Jake sat up in spite of his three broken ribs and reached for the phone. The neck brace creaked. A sharp pain went like lightning through his left shoulder. He winced, but continued anyway. With the receiver in hand, he said "Work," and the phone—responding to his command—dialed his office. Brenda, their secretary, answered the phone and after asking the obligatory questions, put him through to Terry.

"Hiya, bud, how're you doing?" Terry asked cheerfully, the sound of his spoon banging against a mug filling the background.

"Not bad," Jake mumbled. His jaw was very nearly broken, and it hurt to talk. "I need a favor."

"Name it," Terry said.

"The Hunts up on Pine Ridge," Jake said slowly with just enough slur to make him sound drunk. "They're two months behind. I want you to pull their power."

"Now, Jake. This isn't you getting revenge because Clay beat you up last night, is it?"

"Who said Clay beat me up? I never said it was Clay!" Jake protested, then winced again as another pain shot through his jaw.

Terry chuckled. "Johnny was at the other end of the bar last night. He saw you two get into an argument and leave."

"Tell Johnny he didn't see anything." Jake made a mental note to have a little chat with Johnny as soon as he was able to have little chats again. "Now, will you cut their power?"

There was a loud clicking as Terry punched at his computer. "Let me get them up on the screen here," he said, then hummed for a moment. The computer whirred, and then he said, "Aha. Here they are." More humming. "Not a chance."

"Why not?"

"They're on the old system. I'll have to go up to their house to turn it off."

Jake put his head back wearily. "So?"

"You think I'm going to drive all the way up there just to get chased off by Dale or Clay? They still own guns you know."

"I know. You can do it. They won't hurt you."

"Like Clay didn't hurt you? No way, Jake. This is a score you'll have to settle yourself."

"Wait a minute; hold on," Jake said, his dull brain on the edge of another idea. "Bring up the grid for the area."

"The grid? OK." Terry tapped away at the keyboard, and the computer whirred again. "Got it. What do you want to know?"

"Who do they share with? Anybody else in the grid?"

"It covers a large area. Let me see. There are the Hunts and the Lollar farm—"

"Burnt down last year," Jake said.

"Right, I see that."

"Anything else?"

"A building—code 4K. What's that?"

Jake struggled to remember. "Code 4K means . . . it's obsolete. Must be an old school or a church."

"It's a church. I remember now. Used to go past it when we went fishing." Terry paused, then grunted. "Strange, but there's power running at that site."

"Must be vagrants. So, is that it?"

"Uh-huh. Why?"

"You can save yourself a trip to the Hunts' place and turn off the entire grid. That'll cut their power."

"Good point. OK." Terry banged away at the computer for another minute. "Grid for Zone 12 is now powerless." He accented the last word with a punch of a button.

"Thanks," Jake said and wanted to let the phone slip from his fingers.

"Are you sure you want to make Clay mad again? He's an animal. Sounds like he tore you apart last night," Terry said.

Jake grabbed the bottle of painkillers to see if it was too soon to take another one. "Don't worry about me. Clay can't do anything when he's in a poverty camp."

He hung up and, in trying to smile, let out a howl of pain.

CHAPTER 17

AMY rinsed the last of her laundry in the cold clear water that ran past her indifferently. The weather had turned colder in the last couple of hours. She looked up at the woods and the mountains beyond. A flannel shirt dripped heavily in her hand, but she forgot about it for the moment. The mountains looked so large and impenetrable. Would they ever get away? Could they escape before the snow came? *Heavenly Father, what are we going to do?*

It was a halfhearted prayer—as prayers often are when the one praying already knows the answer.

She thought of Mr. Smith and dropped the shirt into an old plastic basket. She sighed for the sixth time in less than a minute. It was a sigh from her heart. This wasn't the future she had had in mind for herself. A stray lock of hair fell into her face. She pushed it back, and the gesture, so simple in and of itself, took on a vain significance. She wanted to look pretty again. Was it so wrong? Closing her eyes, she touched her face; it was dry and hard. Not the face of a young girl but of an old woman. Her hands were sturdy and manlike. What had become of her youth? It was gone, taken away from her by a cruel kidnapper who hadn't even bothered to leave a ransom note. Who could stay young when her parents had been taken away as mental incompetents, leaving her to take care of her younger brother and sister? Who could keep the lines from forming on the face when the sister had died in a State-run children's home? Who could secure innocence of heart when her younger brother—the new model citizen—had betrayed her faith to the authorities? Experience stole her youth for the cruel pleasure of it. It gave her nothing in return except the certainty that you must doubt everything in this life—family ties, the future, even love. There was one thing, though, that she didn't doubt: loneliness. It was undeniable. It clung to her like a suit of wet clothes that would never dry.

So there she stood at the edge of a cold mountain creek, doing the chores and feeling sorry for herself. She was Cinderella without a fairy godmother. In her rugged hiking clothes covering her boyish body underneath, she was unredeemably plain. Would someone like Mr. Smith even look twice at her? No, why should he? All she had to commend herself was a knack for survival. In the end, what had she survived for?

No, this wasn't the future she'd expected for herself. At first she craved normality—to grow up with normal experiences, to meet a normal man, marry, then have normal children. But the revolution was a fickle interloper. Normality was a caterpillar that could never get out of its cocoon. So she improvised. When the persecution against the faithful started, she determined that her future would be one of heroic resistance. She would stand firm and die if she had to, like a modern Joan of Arc. She and Christians everywhere would be beacons of light, knights in the whole armor of God. Moses and Elijah, as leaders of the Underground, seemed to exemplify the idea. They inspired all believers to a gallant and courageous ideal. She wanted to be part of it, to play her part with radiant dignity.

That vision faded with time as the reality of life under an iron hand took hold. The heroic faith she'd hoped to see in herself and in other Christians seemed permanently disguised by the basic need to survive. People died for the faith, she supposed, but most were thrown into camps or shocked until they were reduced to drooling idiots. Where was the gallantry in that? Where was the dignity in being old before her time, helpless and undernourished, washing clothes in a mountain stream with little chance of . . . of what? Love?

She put her hands on her hips and forced back the burning tears in her eyes. It was pointless to feel sorry for oneself. Why was she feeling this way now? Was it because of Mr. Smith? Obviously there was something about him that touched her deeply. What was it? Maybe it was the suddenness of a new kind of hope, something she hadn't realized she was missing until he arrived. It might even have been a strange kind of crush, such as someone on a deserted island might have for the sea captain of a rescue boat. Maybe it was a schoolgirl fantasy that he was the white knight she'd given up on, now come to rescue them all. She couldn't be certain what it was. She knew only that whatever had stirred inside her had stirred up *everything*. With hope came a deepening expectation that might not be fulfilled. With a heightened sense of faith came a heightened sense of doubt. It was too confusing.

Impatiently, she grabbed the basket by its two loose handles and headed back to the church.

She told herself—willed it—that by the time she reached the door to the church, she would no longer feel sorry for herself or indulge in vain romantics. She should be looking to God for answers, she reminded herself, and not look to some stranger they'd found in the woods.

✺

Sam and Peter looked at the fuse box. It was a tangle of exposed wires and odd-looking switches. "It doesn't look like anything's wrong," Peter said.

"So why did the power go off?" Sam asked. Inside, his stomach was churning. They had plenty of candles and fuel-powered lamps, but this problem was significant in a vague way he couldn't quite grasp.

Peter wielded a screwdriver like a small switchblade and pointed to the box. "I'm no electrician, Sam. I don't know what the problem is."

Sam was suddenly aware of Ruth at his elbow. "Well? Did we blow a fuse somehow?" she asked.

"No idea," Sam said.

"It's amazing timing," Ruth said. "Just when I was wondering what else could go wrong, *poof.*"

"Then *you're* to blame for this," Peter said playfully.

Sam chewed at his lower lip thoughtfully. "The stove and the furnace are gas—"

"I checked," Ruth said. "They're off, too. They must have electric starters."

Peter frowned. "Why would they suddenly turn it all off now? Do you think they know we're up here?"

Sam shook his head. "If they knew for sure we were here, I think we'd be surrounded by now. It must be something else. Any ideas, Ruth?"

"I guess we'll have to go primitive," Ruth said. "There's the old woodstove in the kitchen and the other in your room. We can make fires for food and warmth. Otherwise, we'll have to bundle up tonight."

"I'll start collecting wood when I check my traps," Peter said.

"Thank you," Sam said.

"This won't help morale much, you know," Ruth observed.

"I know. It may be just the thing to force us out of here," Sam said. "How's Smith?"

"Sleeping, last I checked," she replied.

Peter leaned against the church wall and spun the screwdriver between his fingers. "So he hasn't said anything else about the Underground?"

"Nope."

"I can't believe it's been destroyed," Peter said.

"Not destroyed," Sam corrected him. "He said it's been disrupted."

"What's the difference? Both mean we're stuck up here longer." He hit the side of the church with his hand. "I don't understand it. I've heard so much about Moses and Elijah— the way they've evaded the police, escaped under impossible circumstances. I've even heard talk of miracles. So how could God let two of his prophets be . . . be *disrupted?*"

"Be careful with that prophet talk," Ruth warned.

"OK, forget Moses and Elijah for a minute," Peter conceded. "What's that stranger doing up here?"

Sam shrugged. "We know no more now than we did when he first woke up. He's very clever about how he answers questions."

"What's everybody else think?" Peter asked.

Sam looked to Ruth for an answer; she knew better what everyone's true feelings were. She was their mother hen, their sounding board. "Well," she began, "Luke is off praying somewhere because he's convinced he healed Smith, and it's some kind of sign."

"Maybe it is," Sam suggested.

Ruth went on. "Howard said he doesn't trust Smith and took a walk. Mary is disappointed that he isn't our contact. Tim thinks he has a new playmate. And Amy—" She stopped and gave Peter a coy look. "She didn't say anything and went to wash some of his clothes."

"She's doing Smith's laundry?" Peter asked, annoyed.

Ruth nodded.

"What about you?" Sam asked her.

"I don't know what to make of him. He seems nice enough, but he's quiet. Maybe too quiet. I never could trust quiet men."

"I have the same problem with talkative women," Sam said.

"Are you trying to tell me something, Sam?"

"Not at all." Sam smiled.

"What do *you* think, Sam?" Peter asked.

Sam chose his words carefully. "It's hard to say. For the most part, I want to believe he's legitimate—a Christian, I mean. Why pretend? The only thing I can't figure out is why he was lying unconscious in the woods."

The thought faded into silence.

"Has the jury reached a verdict?" Smith asked from the back door of the church.

✳

Howard Beck steadied himself against a tree and tried to get his breath back. It hadn't been that long since he was playing tennis at the club, had it? Why was he so out of shape? He yanked a handkerchief out of his coat pocket and dabbed at his forehead. The altitude, that was it. He was at a higher altitude with less oxygen.

Squinting his already narrow brown eyes, he scanned the area for landmarks. Nothing but trees and leaves. Well, what did he expect in the woods? But he had hoped for some kind of clue—one of Peter's traps or something the alleged Mr. Smith had left behind. It shouldn't be that hard to find the spot again. But the forest was enshrouded in gray, and he couldn't see anything from yesterday's outing that looked familiar.

He turned slowly around and tried to guess how far from the church he had walked. A mile? Two miles? Carrying Smith yesterday, it had felt like a hundred. How far had they really gone? He banged his foot against a large tree root and cursed it for being in the way. Nature responded with a loud squawk from a blackbird above. Beck jumped at the sound and cursed the bird. The bird cursed him back. He grabbed a small branch and threw it at the bird. The bird rose and settled in another tree farther away. Though unsuccessful, the act of defiance made Beck feel better.

He imagined the bird plucked, basted, and ready for eating until it looked more like a Thanksgiving turkey than a blackbird.

His stomach growled, and he mused that issues of philosophy and faith rarely stood the test of starvation. The heart truly goes where the hungry stomach is. *Blast them and their rations,* he thought. They can suffer and commend themselves for having faith in God, but he was a practical man, a man of action. He was going to survive. He refused to starve to death in a run-down church while waiting for a contact who would never come.

He stopped in his tracks and looked around. Something *was* familiar about this area of the woods. There was a tree with a tear-shaped knot in the side. Didn't he see it yesterday? He looked in one direction, then another, and mentally retraced his steps with Peter the day before. He scouted toward the east and felt confident that it was the way they had gone and, ultimately, found Smith. Beck smiled.

Now all he had to do was think of a plan.

※

Smith pulled the blanket around his shoulders and gingerly stepped down from the back door of the church to face Sam, Peter, and Ruth. "Do you find the defendant guilty or not guilty?" he asked.

Sam dismissed his own embarrassment with a quick answer. "We're still reviewing the case."

"May a witness take the stand?"

"Of course."

Smith sat down on the far end of a battered picnic bench and folded his hands in front of him. It looked like he was in prayer. "I know you're suspicious, and I don't blame you. I'm inclined to be cautious myself."

"So I've noticed," Ruth said.

Smith acknowledged the comment with a flicker of a smile. "Don't be afraid of me. I'm harmless. I don't plan on staying here too long."

"It's not your staying that I'm worried about," Sam said. "You're more than welcome here. It's your *leaving* that's been on my mind." He watched Smith's face closely, looking for anything that might help him understand more about the stranger's intentions. Smith was expressionless.

"I suppose I'll head farther into the mountains and make my way to the border."

Peter stepped forward, brandishing the screwdriver like an instrument of torture. "Are you going to another hiding place—another stop in the Underground?"

Smith looked at Peter uncomfortably. "Look, I told you. I'm not your contact."

"Then what are you doing here? Why are we—?"

Sam held up his hand. "Peter, slow down."

"But, Sam—"

Sam motioned him back and sat down opposite Smith. The bench groaned. "Mr. Smith, I'm at a loss here. I'm a college professor, not an expert in wilderness survival. You see our situation; our food is almost gone. Peter hunts and fishes but so far it's yielded very little. It'll get worse when the snow comes." Sam paused for a breath. Smith waited without betraying any emotion. "I believe God will take care of us, but I doubt he'll drop manna from heaven. Somewhere there's a line between the faith to wait and the faith to take action. Right now, I'm not sure on which side of the line we should be."

"I understand," Smith said.

"We're growing desperate, Mr. Smith," Sam said. He opened his mouth to say more, then realized there was no more to say.

Smith kept his gaze firmly fixed on Sam. "I don't know what you want me to do."

"You seem to know about the Underground, what's happening down there—"

"No, I don't know."

Sam persisted. "There must be some way to contact them, some way of telling them we're here and waiting, to find out when they're regrouped."

"Maybe, I'm not sure."

"Then if you'd give me a hint about how to get in touch, who to talk to."

Smith pressed his hands against the tabletop as if it were all he could do to keep from picking the thing up and throwing it at Sam. "I would if I could, but it isn't that easy."

"Then I have to ask you, or beg you, whichever would be more effective."

Smith looked at him apprehensively.

Sam glanced at Peter and Ruth, saw their brows knitted in anxiety, and tried to speak as directly as he could. "Mr. Smith, please take us with you."

Smith sat upright, his eyes darting from one face to another. "All of you? It's impossible. You don't know what you're asking."

"I do," Sam said. "It's unreasonable, I know."

"It's more than unreasonable, it's—" Smith suddenly stopped himself, then sighed as if all his resistance passed away from him like a vapor. "Give me time to think about it."

"Pray about it," Ruth added.

Smith didn't respond.

CHAPTER 18

THE room was no more than eight feet by eight feet and pale green from top to bottom. The plaster had cracks like roads to some strange land on a map. In the center was a scarred metal table surrounded by beaten and bent metal chairs. A small mirror was firmly fixed to the wall next to the soundproofed door—a camera behind it, no doubt. With the knuckles of both forefingers, Ben lightly brushed his thick walrus mustache. He then rested his large hands on the edge of the table and drummed lightly. If they were watching him, he wanted to look nonchalant. But he didn't want to look unnatural about it. Who in his right mind wouldn't act a little agitated when dragged by the police to the local station without charges, accusations, or a simple word of explanation? So he needed to look innocent while, at the same time, looking concerned about being in the interrogation room. He leaned back and folded his arms for effect. A hint of annoyance for leaving him sit there for an hour couldn't hurt.

If he offered a prayer now, would he look as if he were praying? He never had reason to think about it before. What did he look like when he was praying? He would have to ask his wife when he got home.

He couldn't help but wonder why they wanted to talk to him. For that matter, he wondered *who* wanted to talk to him.

He'd been so very careful—except for that ridiculous bootleg-ging accusation—and was above reproach.

The trick, Ben thought, was to forget everything he knew. They couldn't catch him at anything if his mind was a blank. It was something he had learned while studying drama at the art college: *be* your character, believe who you are, shut off your imagination to everything else. He was a delivery driver for Maidstone Bakeries. That was all. He'd never heard of the Underground or anything to do with smuggling people out of the country—except for the warnings about it in the State newspaper, of course. Otherwise, he was a simple man with a simple life.

The latch on the door clicked, and Ben's eyes darted to the knob against his will. Perhaps he was a little more nervous than he thought. He hoped the camera didn't catch it. The door opened and two men, engaged in a conversation about a horse race, walked in. They weren't local enforcers, that was certain. Their clothes were of the fine fabric and good make of a city tailor. That knowledge alone made him uneasy. Somebody from the city wanted to talk to him. Why?

The first man was average in height and slender with wavy red hair and a tight unpleasant face. It was so tight, in fact, that Ben thought he'd had some kind of surgery done to it or had been scarred in an accident. It gave him no consolation to realize that nothing was wrong, that it was just how the man looked.

The second man was tall and muscular with an open, friendly face—the kind of guy you could have over for dinner or go bowling with. His brown hair looked freshly combed, giving him a fresh, just-graduated-from-college look. A rookie, Ben thought. The new kid on the force. He's probably being trained by the redhead.

"Ben Greene, right?" the redhead asked.

Ben nodded. "That's me."

"Good. It's embarrassing when we bring in the wrong people." The redhead smiled, his thin lips cutting a gash in his tight face. "I'm Captain Robert Slater of—well, let's say a special division of the police. This is my assistant, Officer Williams."

"Hi," Ben said.

Williams nodded and stood against the wall.

"I'm sure you're wondering what's going on here," Slater said as he sat down across from Ben.

"I sure am. I was in the middle of lunch when—"

Slater held up his hand. "I know it was inconvenient, so the sooner you answer our questions, the sooner you can get back to your lunch."

"Sure. What questions?"

"How long have you been transporting insurrectionists in the back of your truck?" Slater asked.

Ben felt like someone had taken one of the chairs and hit him in the teeth with it. "What?"

"Maybe I didn't speak clearly enough," Slater said. "I asked you, how long—"

"I'm sorry, but I don't know what you're talking about. I deliver products for Maidstone Bakeries and—"

"Mr. Greene . . ." Slater spoke wearily, then looked up at Williams. There was communication in their look, but Ben had no idea what it was. "It will save us all time if we just get to the facts. While you were sitting here trying to look at ease with our little camera behind the mirror, we did a thorough search of your van. We found the fake floor; we tested the bay underneath and were amazed to find a variety of human fingerprints, human sweat, bits of human hair, and fabric from human clothing."

Ben held up his hands. "Hey, it's a *working* van. Lots of

delivery guys are in and out of there." His mouth had gone dry. He wished he had a glass of water.

"Giving you the benefit of the doubt, we decided to check some of the fingerprints against a few of the people you work with. Strangely enough, none of them matched. Even stranger was that no one at the plant knew the vans had false floors. That's mostly because they don't. Yours is the only one." Slater leaned forward. "I can't wait to hear your explanation for that."

Ben worked hard to look nonplussed. "It's *my* van—I'm contracted out—so I customized it to make more room for product. I figured if it worked and the company liked it, they might pay me for the design. But I had to test it first."

Slater looked at Williams again. "He's clever, isn't he?"

"What do you want me to say?" Ben asked, his voice sounding a little more shrill than he meant it to.

"The truth would be helpful. You Christians are big on the truth, aren't you? 'And you will know the truth, and the truth will set you free,' right?"

To hear Scripture spoken so coldly by Slater made Ben's skin crawl. It was like perfume on a snake. His mind spun on raw wheels. Maybe he should cut his losses and try a different tactic to divert away from the evidence. "Look, I don't know what you're talking about, but . . ."

"But what?"

"OK, I admit that I've used my truck for some extra deliveries—you know, to ship packages and boxes for certain clients," Ben said.

Slater rubbed his chin and repeated mechanically, "Certain clients. What kind of clients?"

"You know, clients who want to ship cigarettes and alcohol without paying the tariffs."

"*You* do that?" Slater was incredulous. "A good Christian man like you? I'm having a hard time believing it."

Ben shrugged. "Why would I lie? Admitting it will get me in a lot of trouble."

Slater waved a finger at Ben like an angry librarian. "Ah, but you see, I know what you're thinking. You're thinking that if you admit to some frivolous bootlegging, we'll be side-tracked from the more important questions. You're thinking that we won't ask you about your Christianity or the Underground or how you transport your fellow believers. That's what you're thinking, isn't it, Mr. Greene?"

"I'm thinking that you're barking up the wrong tree," Ben said.

Slater gazed at him a moment. "Are you a strong man, Mr. Greene?"

"I beg your pardon?"

"It's one of the fascinating things about Christianity—all the contradictions and deceits. Strength concealed as weakness; weakness concealed as strength. It's maddening for those of us who like plain speaking." Slater stood up. "Are you a strong man?"

Ben tried to imagine what answer would be correct in this verbal chess game. "I suppose I'm fairly strong—physically, if that's what you're asking."

Slater shook his head. "Physical strength doesn't interest me as much as strength of will. Do you have strength of will?"

Ben looked at him blankly. "I don't know what you're getting at."

"For example—" Slater spun one of the chairs around backwards and sat down again—"if I told you that your wife was in one of the other interrogation rooms—"

Ben sat up, alarmed. "My wife?"

"Yes," Slater continued. "And that Officer Williams here is an expert at the art of physical persuasion. . . ."

Ben shifted in his chair, ready to leap to his feet. "Look, I told you—"

"Steady, Mr. Greene," Williams said softly and shifted his position just enough for Ben to see the gun in his shoulder holster.

Ben relaxed. "My wife has nothing to do with this."

"With what? The bootlegging or the transportation of Christians?"

"Just leave her out of it."

"I'm dealing in a hypothetical situation, Mr. Greene. A little game of What If? Whatever you're *not* prepared to tell us, I think Officer Williams will get your wife to say."

Ben looked at Williams. Williams didn't look like the type who could torture a woman, but the modern-day masks created by this new regime concealed ruthless killers. "But there's nothing for her to say," Ben insisted.

Slater smiled. "I might be lying, too. Hypothetically, Williams might have already interrogated your wife, and she might have confessed everything—the way you brought renegade Christians to your home, put them in the bottom of the van, transported them out of town to various points in the country or in the mountains near the border. . . ."

Ben didn't believe him. "You're bluffing. This is a trick to get me to admit to something I haven't done."

"Haven't you?" Slater began to dig in his jacket pocket. "I think you have. Under the circumstances, I don't think your wife was in a position to lie."

"You didn't do it. You never talked to her," Ben said, his hands curling into hard fists.

Slater found what he was looking for in his jacket pocket and pulled it out. He laid it on the table, a handkerchief spotted with red, and carefully unfolded it. "Your wife's necklace?"

Ben stared at the thin gold chain with the small cross at the center of the link. It was his wife's, a gift from Ben that she wore under all her clothes. No one had ever seen it but him. He felt his jaw moving up and down, but without the intention of producing words.

"Sorry about the bloodstains," Slater said.

Ben let out a shout and sprang to his feet. But Williams was quick and had the gun out of his holster in an instant. Williams pointed at him and fired. The gun's electric pulse sent him sideways against the opposite wall, where he slumped to the hard, coffee-stained floor. He was dazed but still conscious.

Slater leaned next to him. "I hope you're impressed with what we're prepared to do to get the truth out of you. Your wife isn't hurt, apart from the embarrassment we caused when searching her. But your wife *will* be hurt, Mr. Greene, if you don't cooperate." Slater adjusted himself on his haunches. "Now, the effects of the gun will wear off in about two minutes. In that time, I'll expect you to have made a sensible decision."

Ben groaned. Even in the numbness, he felt foolish and definitely weak. But this wasn't the kind of weakness that produced the strength of God, not the way the Bible talked about it. This weakness was very human. It was defeat. The answer to Slater's earlier question was "No, I am not a man of strong will." For his own sake, Ben thought he could withstand anything they might do to him. But for his wife's sake, he would give up anything. And the realization brought a profound sense of loss, not only to his faith but also to a heart that wanted to cry for those he was about to betray. He turned his head to the wall and looked upon the shadow of Judas. "All right."

"Good for you," Slater said. "A wise decision."

Ben felt Williams's hands under his arms, pulling him back toward the chair.

"By the way," Slater said from the table, "the blood was mine—a nosebleed from the other day."

CHAPTER 19

You want to know what I think about death, huh? I don't know. I've been so busy trying to stay alive that I haven't really thought about it. I just hope that when it comes for me, it'll be quick. Fast. I'm not very patient, and when it's time to do something, I like to do it and get it over with. I guess I feel the same about death. I wouldn't want it to drag out . . . not like it did for my parents. No—I would want it fast and painless.

—Peter, as quoted in *The Posthumous Papers of Samuel T. Johnson*

❋

CLAY stood in the kitchen of the farmhouse, a ramshackle collection of decaying wood, drafty windows, and peeling wallpaper. It was the place of his birth, the place of his younger brother's birth and death from leukemia ten years after that, the place where his mother spent the "best years of her life" until her suicide last year, the place where his father insisted they stay and work until they, in turn, returned to the dirt from which they'd all come. Clay hated it. It was an ongoing symbol of his oppression from poverty. One way or another he would escape from this mountain. And he'd long passed the point of worrying about how his father would fend for himself alone. It didn't matter anymore. Let the man return to the dirt if that's what he had his heart set on.

Clay spat in the sink and turned the handle to the faucet. The pipes groaned and spat dramatically, but the expected spray of water didn't come. He flipped the light switch nearby and watched to see if any juice went to the bare bulb hanging from a wire overhead. It didn't. He turned it off and on, off and on, just in case. Nothing happened. He glanced at the clock. It had stopped at 2:56—just a half hour ago.

He hoped that Jake had the good sense to leave town because he was a dead man otherwise.

Tapping the side of the coffeepot, he was relieved that it was still warm. He needed some coffee this afternoon, even the lukewarm kind. His mouth felt like he'd been sucking on old gym socks all night. His head throbbed from a hangover. He poured himself a cup and spat in the sink again as if he could get rid of his anger one mouthful at a time.

He had to get away somehow. There must be a plan, a scheme, to get off of the mountain that he hadn't thought of yet. He wasn't a particularly bright boy, he knew that, but he was sure he had the minimal intelligence to escape. That he hadn't succeeded yet didn't daunt him. Sure, a lot of schemes had come and gone over the past couple of years. Some faded from lack of planning, some from lack of spirit—back then he had his mother to think of—while some were blatant failures born from an uneducated mind, nurtured by an obscure fantasy, and killed by cruel reality. It seemed unfair that determination alone wouldn't do the trick. Circumstances worked against him. He needed a lucky break.

He needed money, that was what he needed. He wouldn't survive long without money.

He gulped his drink and, realizing that lukewarm coffee

wasn't acceptable after all, pushed it away. Maybe he should just have another drink from his stash in the bedroom. The hair of the dog.

He spat again and looked out the window at the dull scene—the dull brown yard leading to the dull brown fence and the dull brown fields and barn beyond. His father stood at the fence, hunched over like the old man he was, and talked to a stranger. The stranger was well dressed, though the clothes were a little worn and dirty (he could see it even from the window). Now what would a well-dressed stranger be doing up here? Was it the police? Did Jake have the nerve to report what had happened last night?

Clay's father gestured to the stranger to wait and turned to come back to the house. The stranger didn't move, but looked cautiously around. He had an expression of smugness and expectation that annoyed Clay. It was the kind of face Clay wanted to punch. He heard his father's footsteps on the gravel just outside the door, the two steps up, the screen door wrench open. Then the inside door opened, a burst of cool air coming in with his father.

"What's up, Pop?"

His father darted a disgusted look at him. "So you're finally up." He went straight to the pantry and started to gather up some boxes of dry goods.

"Who's the man?"

"Somebody who needs help, that's all. Not your concern."

Clay watched as his father picked through the cans and boxes. "You're giving him our food?"

"A little. Not much."

"We don't *have* a little, Pop. What are you doing? Did you know the utilities are off?"

His father stopped to look directly at Clay. "I know it. Are you surprised? I'm not, certainly not after that stunt you pulled last night. What did you think Jake would do? Or didn't you think at all?"

"Jake? Jake who?" Clay asked innocently. How did he find out about this stuff? Who did he talk to?

"Never mind," his father said impatiently and went back to stockpiling the food. "I'm sure you'll be happy when we wind up at the poverty camp. It won't be long now."

You might go to the poverty camp, but I never will, Clay thought. "So why are we giving our hard-earned food away to some stranger?"

"Because for the time being, he needs it even worse than we do."

"Why doesn't he sell off that nice coat or those fancy shoes and buy his own food?"

"He can't."

"He's on the run, huh?"

"Just forget about it."

"Might be a—what do they call them?—insurrectionist. Maybe we should call the police."

"On what? You managed to get the phone turned off," his father scowled.

"Even so—"

"Forget about it, Clay. These insurrectionists—if that's what they are—are people who believe like your mother did. Can you remember that far back on what brain cells you have left? I won't turn him away empty-handed, if only for your mother's sake." His father headed back across the chipped linoleum to the door. "Get to your chores."

The door slammed, the windows rattled, and Clay watched the scene from behind the torn curtains. The stranger was visibly delighted with the food and stumbled all over himself with gratitude. Clay couldn't help but be delighted, too. He'd heard the reports on the radio about the insurrectionists. There were rewards for them.

If it all worked out the way he thought it would, he and Bobby could be off the mountain within the next couple of days. All thanks to a well-dressed stranger.

He spat again and pulled his coat from the hook next to the door. *Chores can wait,* he thought. *I'm going hunting.*

CHAPTER 20

"THEY were here all along," Williams whispered to Slater. "Right under our noses."

"What did you expect?" Slater asked as he lifted the night glasses to his eyes again. They were posted in a brick doorway of an alley not two blocks from Central. Apart from the sound of late-night traffic on the main road three blocks away, all was silent. A black rat hunched and sniffed along the step, looked up at the two men to see if they were of any particular importance, then moved on without hurrying. "Well?" Slater asked again. "What did you expect?"

Williams squinted against the drizzling rain that the wind occasionally sprayed into the arched doorway. The yellow glow of the streetlight had a Dickensian appearance as it fell against the black driveway that led to the tall steel warehouse door they were watching. "I expected our surveillance cameras to see them. They're *two flipping blocks away* from our office!" he complained. His harsh whisper reverberated in the doorway and sounded like someone had let the air out of the building.

"They're roaches," Slater said. "I told you. Our surveillance cameras pick up human beings in this city. If there's a pickpocket in Longmont Square, we've got him. But roaches—not a chance. That's why they can operate two blocks away from us. That's why they're probably operating right inside our building, using our phones, eating our lunches. Y'know, somebody stole my lunch out of the refrigerator just last week and—"

Slater's and Williams's headsets buzzed softly. "Someone's coming," Wilson, who was stationed on the roof, reported. They pushed back into the darkness until Williams's back was pressed against the old factory door. The rivets poked at him, even through his coat.

Footfalls clicked on the pavement down the alleyway. The walker had a rhythm worthy of a metronome—perfectly purposeful. "It's a policeman," Williams whispered just before the cop entered their view.

"Let's see if he notices us," Slater said with a malicious tone.

The officer, dressed in standard-issue black, strolled past without noticing that two men were in the doorway or that another dozen men were positioned all around the area.

"I want someone to grab him as soon as he clears the alley," Slater said into his headset. "Get his name and badge number."

A voice asked, "Any particular reason?"

"Yes!" Slater snapped. "I want to know why he didn't see us! What kind of policeman is he when he's surrounded by half the force, and he doesn't notice?"

Williams grunted. "That explains why the roaches can operate two blocks from our office."

But the officer didn't follow the alleyway to the other end. Instead, he turned down the driveway to the steel garage door. He glanced around quickly, then pushed a button pad next to a small entrance. The door clicked and opened. The officer ducked in and closed the door behind him.

"Maybe we should go in now," Williams suggested.

Slater shook his head. "No. Not until they open the garage

door, which they will if Mr. Greene's information was correct."

The mention of the name sent Williams's memory back to the interrogation room and the image of that big man with his walrus mustache weeping uncontrollably on the floor. It was hard to tell what affected Greene the most—the thought of going to a rehabilitation center or having betrayed his co-conspirators. It seemed to Williams like a waste of tears in either case since he hanged himself in his cell two hours later.

Slater asked, "What time is it?"

"Nine-thirty," Williams replied.

"The checkpoints will be changing their shifts now. If they're going, this is the time."

As if Slater's words had acted like an open sesame, the warehouse door mechanically lurched upward.

"All right, when it's three-quarters up, move in," Slater said into his headset. "And remember: I want them alive."

The opening door revealed two delivery vans inside, their engines running, and Williams could see at least one person through the windshield of each van. The alleyway suddenly came alive. Officers quickly appeared from all sides with silent precision, their guns poised. They danced like violent shadows through the yellow mist. The reaction inside the garage was instantaneous. Figures scrambled inside the vans. The doors were thrown open as people leapt out to make a run for it—not only men, but women and children. It was like a mad marathon where the rules allowed the runners to go in whatever direction they chose.

"How many of them can they fit in those vans?" Slater asked himself, surprised.

The officers on the force were efficient and quickly headed off the fugitives like cowboys herding cattle. A shot was fired, and a man went down hard on the floor.

"No!" Slater shouted and sprinted toward the garage.

The man in the police uniform who'd walked past them earlier appeared from the back of the van and held up his hands. "Stop! Stop! Don't fire!"

"I said not to shoot!" Slater shouted into his headset as he ran.

Williams followed with his gun drawn, down the alley and into the fluorescent light of the garage. It smelled of sweat and exhaust and made Williams cough as soon as he crossed the threshold. The Christians, who were now assembled in the center of a circle of officers, were told to drop to their knees with their hands behind their heads. A man lay whimpering off to the side.

"Is he all right?" Slater shouted.

The officer nearest the whimperer reported that the man hadn't been shot, but had fallen from fright at the gunshot sound.

"Who fired the shot?" Slater asked.

Reluctantly, a young officer—one of the new recruits— raised his hand. "I did, sir."

Slater marched over to him. "Why?"

"I thought I saw him draw a gun," the young officer replied nervously.

Slater reached down to the whimperer and grabbed his hands. He jerked one, then the other. In it was a small black Bible. Slater plucked it from his hand and threw it at the officer. "There's your gun." He scowled. "Consider yourself on probation for disobeying orders."

The young officer's face fell. "Yes, sir."

Slater spun dramatically to the trembling group on the floor and paced around them like a caged lion. "Empty the vans," he shouted to the officers. Several harnessed their guns and jumped into the storage areas. Knapsacks, bags, and boxes of food were systematically brought out. Slater watched silently. All in all, it looked like a refugee camp.

Williams scanned the group of Christians closely for any suspicious moves. He knew that they were generally peaceful, but it took only one fanatic to decide to pull a knife or a gun to defend their cause. No one gave a hint of that kind of passion. They looked like scared sheep. Even more, Williams was struck by their ordinariness—people in plain clothing who looked like they'd been out for a day of shopping. They were quite a contrast to the stark black-dressed officers who surrounded them with weapons drawn.

"Who's in charge of this outfit?" Slater asked after the vans had been cleared out and nothing of interest had been found.

No one answered. All eyes were leveled at the ground.

"Save yourselves a lot of pain and just tell me who's the leader here," Slater said impatiently.

Again, a martyred silence.

"Look, I'm not asking you to divulge secret codes or give up the names of your children's pet dogs. Someone is in charge here, and I want to talk to that person."

When no one replied, Slater pulled out his gun and carelessly waved it around the nearest child—a girl about five years old with ponytails and big green eyes. "Do I have to ask again?"

"I guess I'm in charge," the man in the police uniform said.

"Yes, Officer, of course you are," Slater said. "Nice outfit, by the way. Later I want to hear all about how you got it. But right now—"

Slater was interrupted by another officer who leaned into his ear and whispered something Williams couldn't hear. Slater looked at him with an expression of deep interest.

Williams moved closer to his boss.

"Do you have the folder?" Slater asked Williams.

Williams nodded, reached into the inner pocket of his jacket, and pulled out a billfold. It was stuffed with information and profiles of suspected Christians. He handed it to Slater.

Flipping through the pages, Slater said, "Officer McKenna here thinks our policeman friend looks familiar."

Williams glanced down at the man in question. He had a narrow face with jet black hair and beard. The penetrating blue eyes were the most remarkable thing about him; they looked as if they could cut into the soul like a scalpel might cut into the heart.

"There," Officer McKenna said and pointed to one of the pages.

Slater looked at the page, down at the prisoner, then back at the page again. "Good work, McKenna." Slater passed the billfold back to Williams. With a quick look, he knew they had the same man who appeared in the stark Population ID photo.

"You're Brad Nichols." Slater smiled.

Brad Nichols turned his penetrating eyes on Slater and held them there without speaking.

Slater was unaffected. "You don't have to say anything. But it is nice to meet you after all this time, *Moses.*"

CHAPTER 21

THE clouds never broke, so it seemed as if night had merely soaked the morning with its blackness, like ink seeping into an old cotton swab. The forest took on the look of burnt matches. Ruth and Amy prepared a modest meal of canned vegetables and beans—the smallest portions possible—which everyone ate in a dislocated silence. Since the utilities were still not on, they started a fire in the old potbelly stove in the kitchen, a holdover from days long gone. It gave the normally drab room a pleasant warmth that invited an uncharacteristic peace.

Ruth and Peter reminisced about Ruth's sister—Peter's mother—and Ruth told him stories of when they were young girls. Amy listened and noted that Peter's mother seemed as strong-willed and defiant as her son had turned out to be. They laughed over the memories, something Amy didn't think Peter could do anymore. Maybe he took their conversation last night to heart. He glanced at her, and she was reminded of the *other* part of their talk, the part where he had hinted at his feelings for her. She'd thought about it since and hoped it wouldn't generate any awkwardness between them. He was a nice-looking boy, but she felt no more for him than she would have felt toward a young friend from school.

Apart from Ruth's and Peter's exchange, everyone else sat

quietly nearby, lost in thought, subdued by memories. Amy expected that from Mr. Smith, who was now clean shaven and sat staring at the fire intently. He was disclosing no secrets, and the rest had given up hoping for them. Abruptly, he bid everyone good night and slipped away to the sanctuary.

Sam was preoccupied with writing in his journal. The sound of the nib of his pen scratching against the paper weaved in and out of the hiss and crackle of the fire in the stove.

Luke sat closest to the orange glow of the stove reading Sam's Bible. His lips moved, and every now and then he would roll his eyes upward like a Shakespearian actor who'd just come across his favorite soliloquy from *Hamlet*.

Howard Beck, who normally had plenty to complain about, held his tongue, too. He didn't seem contented tonight, just quiet. That puzzled Amy, and, for no reason that she could put her finger on, it made her suspicious.

Even Tim, who normally put up a fight about bedtime, conceded the debate and went off with his mother quietly.

All in all, it seemed as if something very strange was happening to them, like some unidentified virus was working its way through their systems without their knowing it.

Amy sat and watched them all for a moment, then said good night and walked down the hall to her room. She paused at the door and battled the conflicting emotions inside her. She shrugged them off and went inside. It was already chilled; she knew she'd have to sleep in her clothes until Sam and Peter could figure out what went wrong with their power. Shoving her hands deep within her jean pockets, she paced around the room with the same expectancy as someone who had an important errand to run. She stopped suddenly and knelt next to her cot. No words would come, so she prayed the Lord's Prayer. Just as suddenly as she had knelt, she stood up and paced around the room again. She searched her memory for a psalm or a verse, something that would clear her mind so she could sleep. It was useless. She sat on the edge of her cot, ran her fingers through her hair, and groaned.

Should she check to make sure Mr. Smith was comfortable? Did he have everything he needed for the night? Ruth had probably asked already. But maybe she didn't. It wouldn't hurt to make sure. She got up and moved slowly to the door. Why was she struggling so hard over this? She only wanted to talk to him, that's all. Would it be so wrong?

Stepping into the hallway again, she looked toward the kitchen at the far end. The orange glow held steady; shadows stretched against the wall. Peter said something that made Ruth laugh again. Walking as quietly as she could, Amy headed to the sanctuary. She stopped at the doorway and felt foolish—even childish—for being there. She nearly turned to sneak away but saw Smith near his bed talking earnestly with Luke. It was an odd scene; she had never seen Luke talking seriously to anyone.

Amy heard Smith say, "So you don't remember?"

Luke shook his head firmly. "My memory isn't what it once was."

Smith nodded; then his eye caught Amy, and he turned to her. "Is something wrong?"

Luke looked over at Amy and smiled. "Hello. Would you like to have a Bible study with me?"

"Not tonight," Amy said as she walked into the room. She spied the water pitcher on Sam's table and went to it like a needle to a magnet. "I was just checking to see if there was anything you needed. Fresh water for the pitcher? Ruth said you need to drink a lot of liquids. I brought several buckets up from the stream since the tap was turned off. It's better water anyway."

"I think the pitcher is full."

"God keep us safe this night," Luke announced as a benediction and then walked out.

Smith watched him go. "Do you know anything about him?"

"Only a little bit," Amy answered. "He was declared mentally insane because he was a preacher. So they gave him shock treatments until he . . . well, you see how he is. Though Sam thinks he's improving."

"That would be optimistic."

"Yes, it would be."

They stood wordless for a moment, and Amy realized she was still standing there with the pitcher in her hands. "Oh, it's full." She set it back down on the table and felt his eyes on her. "I filled it up earlier."

Another pause. He wasn't going to make this easy for her. "Is it snowing yet?" she asked.

He looked around at the boarded-up windows. "Hard to tell from here."

"When I was younger I used to love it when it snowed. For some reason it made me feel warm and alive." She avoided his gaze and picked up the pitcher again, remembered it was still full, and put it down. "Mr. Smith, I'm glad you're here."

Smith cocked his eyebrow. "Are you?"

"Yes," she said self-consciously. "You have given me—us all—a new sense of hope."

"I don't know why. I didn't bring any hope with me; I forgot to pack it. That's always the way, isn't it?"

His smile caught her off guard. It was the first time she'd seen anything other than a stern expression, and it made her heart spin as if she'd been bestowed a very special and secret honor. He had a dimple just to the right of his mouth. With growing confidence she ventured on. "You're such a mystery, though. No one knows what to make of you. They're afraid to ask you any specific questions, and I've noticed the way you evade the ones they *do* ask."

"I've never thought of myself as mysterious," he said and held her gaze. "Do *you* think I'm mysterious?"

She hoped that his prolonged look meant something and said playfully, "There's a lot you're not telling us. I just can't figure out what."

He kept his eyes on her, and then a shadow seemed to cross them—a sudden doubt or self-reproach. Something had changed. "Don't go figuring too hard. You may find something you'd rather not know," he said disdainfully.

"See? You're being mysterious again." She didn't want to lose the moment.

He shrugged. "Maybe I am."

A stiff silence returned, but she was so convinced that they were establishing some kind of bond that she pressed on. "Peter is so excited about you being part of the Underground. He wants to join." Why was she talking about Peter?

"Right now there isn't anything to join." He knelt next to his knapsack and began to rearrange its contents.

She wondered if his sharp, jerky movements were his normal habit or if he was getting impatient with her. "He wants to join the Underground so he can fight with you, to help put an end to this insanity. They killed his parents, you know."

Smith stopped for a fraction of a second, then continued his work. "I'm sorry. I didn't know."

"Each of us would sound like an obituary page if . . . well, we've all lost loved ones. We're all familiar with that knock on the door in the middle of the night and the fear of wondering who they'd take next. Then comes the real torture of not knowing what happened to them, whether they're dead or still alive suffering in some rotten cell or work camp. Rarely do we find out." The flood of words brought a wave of anger and sadness. She felt like a small boat in a gale and clung to the table for support.

Smith was on his feet and looked as if he might move to her. He took one step and stopped. "Amy . . ."

If he had taken her in his arms to comfort her, she might not have felt so bad. But he had stopped, and she stood alone with her embarrassment. "I'm sorry. I'm being childish."

"There's nothing childish about crying," he said softly.

She wiped her eyes with the back of her hand. "All I wanted to say was that Peter wants to join and fight. What moves me to tears moves him to action."

"There's no fighting," Smith said as he returned to his knapsack and whatever it was he hoped to accomplish there. "We're not revolutionaries. We're—we *were* just trying to help our brothers and sisters in Christ. That's all."

"But what about Moses and Elijah—the miracles they've performed? I heard about the time they struck an entire regiment blind while they—"

"You can't believe everything you hear," he said curtly.

"If I can't believe that, then what can I believe?"

Smith shrugged. "Good question. When you find an answer, let me know."

This pricked Amy, and she wondered where the conversation had gone wrong. She was bewildered by his cynicism. "What does that mean?"

"It means that I can't help you. Now, are we through with this interview, or are you here to guard me for the night?" He didn't look at her.

She felt as if someone had injected ice water into her veins and stammered, "I didn't mean to . . . I mean, I didn't come here to . . . Obviously I made a mistake."

From his crouched position next to the knapsack, he turned

his head to look at her. "Sometimes I think we all made a mistake."

She didn't know what he meant by his remark, nor did she care to stay to find out. She pushed herself from the table and walked out of the sanctuary. When she reached the door to her room she saw Peter down the hall, watching her from the doorway to the kitchen. She ignored him and went straight to bed.

✳

Sam was sure he hadn't fallen asleep. He had lain awake thinking how cursed he was with observation. He had seen Luke go into the sanctuary after Smith said good night. That wasn't a big worry; he doubted that the conversation consisted of more than Luke's joy over having "healed" Smith. What kept him awake was Amy. She'd been acting strange since Smith arrived, and he knew she had slipped in to talk to him. Sam was worried for her without having any concrete cause to be worried. He lay with his arm tucked behind his head and thought he was staring at the ceiling, but a noise from the hallway made him realize he'd dozed off—and his arm had fallen asleep with him. Pins and needles worked their way up to his elbow as he gingerly slipped his legs off the sofa and crept to the door. He heard what sounded like a broom against cement for only an instant, then the soft padding of footsteps toward the kitchen. Beck wouldn't be trying to sneak a midnight snack, would he? He would, but he wasn't doing so tonight. Those weren't Beck's footsteps. They were unfamiliar.

He opened the door and was grateful the hinges didn't squeak. Down the hall, a dark figure had just slipped into the kitchen. Sam quickly followed and, fumbling in his pocket for a match, had just reached the doorway as the figure was about to open the back door.

"Who's there?" Sam asked.

The figure stopped. "It's me, Smith."

A packet of matches in hand, Sam lit one and held it up. Smith stood by the door with his coat on and the knapsack slung over his shoulder. Sam moved to the lamp on the table and lit it. "Was it something we said?" he asked.

Smith stepped toward the table. "It's better this way."

"That remains to be seen," Sam said. "Everyone will be disappointed. They thought—" He corrected himself. "*I* thought you'd help us get out of here."

Smith frowned, the creases on his brow made more intense by the lamplight. "Well, I can't help what they or you thought. You don't know anything about me or what I've been through. For three years I've been—" He stopped, his eyes diverting from whatever memory had leapt to his mind. "You don't know the responsibility I've had, and I don't want it anymore. If your people want a leader, why don't *you* lead them?"

"I wouldn't know where to take them."

"Pick a hole, any hole. The mountain is full of places to hide. But I'll give you this advice: Slater's a bloodhound, and it's just a matter of time before he and his men find this place. Get out before the snow comes and you find yourselves trapped."

Sam watched helplessly as Smith turned to the door again. He paused with his hand on the knob as if he expected Sam to say something to stop him.

Sam obliged. "Why are you running, Mr. Smith?"

"We're all running, remember?"

Sam shook his head sadly. "Not like you. *We're* running from the police. You seem to be running from something more."

Smith shrugged his shoulders to adjust the knapsack better. "I'm just trying to escape."

"So was Jonah," Sam said caustically. "I just hope this mountain doesn't become the belly of the whale."

Smith looked as though he might say something but thought better of it. He opened the door to a biting wind and seemed to throw himself into it. The door banged closed behind him.

"He's gone?" Ruth asked from the passage into the hall.

Sam grunted. "Yeah, he's gone."

"You said he would leave," Ruth observed as if being right should give Sam some degree of comfort. She wrapped her arms around herself for warmth against the night chill. "How did you know?"

"Because it's what *I'd* like to do," Sam replied.

CHAPTER 22

I've been thinking a lot about death lately. I don't know why except that I've been thinking about my family and—I know this sounds strange—but death is the only way I'll get to see them again. I believe I will, too. They all—except for my little brother—knew Jesus Christ and loved him very much. So I picture that one day we'll have this great reunion in heaven, where we'll sit down at a gigantic picnic table and eat potato salad and barbecue and hot dogs and . . . angel food cake, I guess. And since we'll have heavenly bodies, we can eat all we want and not have to worry about calories.

—Amy, as quoted in *The Posthumous Papers of Samuel T. Johnson*

❈

SAM wasn't so new to Christianity that the ironies of Christian behavior—his own in particular—hadn't escaped him. After Smith left, Sam went back to his room to read his mother's Bible and pray. It was a vigil unlike anything he'd experienced before. So why did it take a crisis like this to drive him to his knees in prayer? Why did it take someone like Smith to show him how fragile his faith really was? What did he expect from Smith anyway?

The answer was obvious: for Smith to lead them to the promised land. Sam was so hungry, so desperate for someone else to take on the burden of responsibility for the group that he was willing to entrust their lives to a complete stranger.

One thing he believed was that they needed to move on *quickly*.

As dawn crept over the mountains, Sam began to pore over some maps he'd found in a drawer in the pastor's desk, tossed there like old brochures in a cheap motel. They didn't dare take a main road, but there were several hiking paths that looked as if they might eventually lead them to the border. He was disheartened, though, to estimate that it would take three days of rigorous walking to get there. And once they arrived, he had no idea what they'd find—a giant wall, armed guards? They could go all that way just to get caught and dragged back again.

Assembled in the kitchen for their morning get-together, Sam told his fellow fugitives that Smith had left, what Smith had advised, and what he himself thought they should do.

"Why should we listen to anything that man had to say?" Amy said scornfully. "He was unreliable and—"

"An ingrate," Howard added. "I told you we should have left him in the woods."

"Howard!" Ruth snapped.

They voted on Sam's suggestion that they pack up whatever they could carry and make their way toward the border. Peter agreed enthusiastically. Amy conceded that it was the only option they had. Ruth also voted yes. Luke said that the Lord would go before them into parts unknown, but where he was taking them would require neither staff nor sandals. Sam took that as a yes. Tim had been sick with an upset stomach all night—he was still in bed even then—so Mary was anxious about how they would survive a three-day hike. Sam had to admit that he didn't know. Mary said that she would vote to go, providing Tim got over his flu in time.

Ruth asked, "What do you think he has? A twenty-four-hour bug?"

Mary nodded, then turned to Sam. "When are you planning to leave?"

"Right away," Sam said. "I woke up to a dusting of snow this morning, and I think it's going to come down solidly very soon."

"Oh, dear," Mary said.

Sam spread his hands in resignation. "We'll see how he feels a little later and pray that whatever he has will go away. Howard, what about you?"

Howard grunted. "You want us to pack everything up and follow you into the woods when you don't know where you're taking us? It's absurd."

"You could stay behind if you want," Peter said.

Howard looked indignant. "You'd like that, wouldn't you? You'd *all* like that—to leave me behind to starve."

"I have a hard time envisioning you starving," Peter said.

"Just as I have a hard time envisioning you with your mouth shut," Howard retorted. "I suppose you must be feeling foolish now that your hero has abandoned us."

"I'm sure he had his reasons."

Howard sneered. "Most cowards do."

"He's more of a man than you'll ever be," Peter shouted.

"Children," Sam pleaded, "we don't have time."

Howard stood up, knocking his chair over behind him, "You're right. I don't have time for this juvenile delinquent's insolence. Let me know what you decide—*if* you can ever decide anything!" He marched out.

"Howard, don't leave!" Sam called out. The footsteps down the hall didn't falter until Howard reached his room, presumably grabbed his coat, then continued on into the sanctuary and out the front door.

Sam turned on Peter. "Just what was that all about?"

"I'm sorry, Sam," Peter said, lowering his head.

"It's important that we get out of here as soon as we can. You know that."

Peter looked up and said defensively, "I know it, but he's up to something. He's been taking long walks and . . . I don't trust him."

"It doesn't matter. We have a lot to go through together, and it's not going to be easy. You have to try to get along with him. We're the closest thing to family any of us have left."

"He's not my family," Peter said with childish defiance.

"That's not what my Bible says," Sam returned. "Now, go apologize and bring him back."

"But, Sam—"

"Peter, *please.*"

He stood up reluctantly, like a chastised schoolboy being sent to the corner. "Yes, sir."

Sam scrubbed his hands over his face as Peter left. Ruth said affectionately, "It's taken me a long time to figure out who he takes after more, his mother or father. *That's* his mother, most definitely. She was more stubborn than any of us and used to—"

"Forgive me, Ruth," Sam interjected, "but we don't have time. Now, let's get started with our packing. Remember to keep it light, just what you can carry. Just the clothes on our backs if that's what it takes."

The group scattered.

❋

Mary stepped quietly into her room and peered into the dim light. The shapeless bundle on the cot didn't stir. *My baby,* she thought with a stifled sob. She hadn't told Sam or the rest how sick Timothy really was. She was afraid to. She knew that they considered her a constant worrier, a fragile woman who might break at any moment. It's the way people had treated her her entire life. As a child she was the frail and sickly one in her family. She had missed a lot of school, missed friends, missed everything because of colds, flu, pneumonia, infections. It set her apart, alienated her from the normal world. The ravages of adolescence made it worse. She never quite fit in, and in the tiny bubble that became her world, she found plenty to worry about in her health and circumstances.

"Tim? Sweetheart?" She moved to him though an unmistakable smell nearly drove her back. She put her hand to her nose and went over to the wall where a bucket sat beneath the fractured blackboard and torn drawings that hung limply from a chipped corkboard. They were of Jesus on the Sea of Galilee, Jesus feeding the five thousand, Jesus teaching in the temple, and Jesus hugging a group of small children. These were the remnants of the Sunday school classroom it had once been. The bucket Mary was looking for had been filled with melted crayons when they arrived but now served as a chamber pot for middle-of-the-night uses. It was empty. But that smell—

"Tim, it's snowing outside. Did you know that?" She put on her singsongy voice that she often used with him when she was deeply worried.

He groaned from somewhere under the blankets.

"What's wrong, Tim? Are you still feeling sick?" She paused to look at his face. At certain angles, he was the image of his father as a child, even as a young man back when they first met in high school. She had given up by then, resigned to a life without companionship except from her parents and those at church who felt obligated. So when Robert had first asked her out, she was more surprised than anyone. She thought it was a cruel joke. He was the quarterback on the football team, after all. But her pride was not so strong—or weak—that she didn't allow herself to get caught up in the hope of the moment to say yes. She held on to the belief that the rumors about his being a Christian were true. He wouldn't have asked her out as a joke, not if he were a *real* Christian.

That's what made Robert so exceptional. Christianity by that time—not outlawed yet—was reserved for people like her: misfits, the socially retarded, the ones with nowhere else to go for friendship. It was a refuge, a crutch. And people like Robert didn't need it because they had everything else.

He took her to a social program at his church. He introduced her around as she smiled crookedly and tugged nervously at her stringy brown hair. That night every awkward movement, every misplaced comment, every spot and blemish seemed magnified a hundred times for her. She spilled her punch. She fell off her chair. She ran to her front door at the end of the night, tearful and humiliated, sure that the punch line to the joke was coming. He patiently followed her, not for a good-night kiss, but to ask her out again. She couldn't answer him and practically slammed the door in his face. Once inside the safety of her front hall, she stood in the half-light and cried for an hour.

But he persistently sought her out for more dates. Then came their prom. Then a summer missionary program together. And they continued on into college with Mary slowly metamorphosing from the proverbial ugly duckling into the beautiful swan. He did that for her effortlessly. If he was motivated by a deep sympathy or an act of penance, he never let on. He cherished her; she worshiped him.

She remembered those days now like a dream. Timothy was her only reminder of their reality, bringing with him a dull ache that sometimes made it hard for her to look at him.

Robert had asked her to marry him two years into college. He had studied law while she dropped out to work, be a wife and, within a year, become a mother. Their family seemed so complete, so perfect. He was the hardworking student, faithful husband, and dedicated father. She was the doting wife. He had passed the bar with honors. She had tried to give him a home of which he could be proud.

She had gotten pregnant again a couple years later, but miscarried because of complications. That had been the beginning of the nightmare, she reflected. It had been a foreshadowing, the first crack in a perfect surface. Though she had recovered sufficiently from her loss, the world had become damaged in other, more fatal ways. The revolution had come without a fight, then the persecution which Robert used all of his legal prowess to fight, then the arrest—

Mary clenched her eyes shut. She'd drawn a mental line in the sand of time—and this was it. Across that line were the details and the pain of absolute desolation. Her life source had been cut off from her. She was a beaten swan turned once again into an ugly duckling. Her god was gone and had left her with the real God whom she didn't know anymore.

That's why she seemed so frail now. Rebuilding her life—her faith—took more out of her than she dared to think about. But she could be strong again, she believed. She had to be. For her son. How did Sam, Ruth, and the rest think she survived through the horror of her husband's murder? It was for Timothy. When she was at the very brink of madness, she had clung to her wits for her son's sake. He remained her link to reality. Whatever was wrong with him now, they'd get through it. They wouldn't be a burden.

And though sometimes in the deepest part of her heart she worried that she had replaced the god of Robert with the god of her son, she felt confident that the real God would understand. In the rebuilding of her faith, the God she hoped to know better *had* to understand. It was part of an unspoken deal.

Mary pushed back the stiff lick of hair on her son's forehead and felt for a fever. He was cool. It perplexed her, and she went through her mental checklist of his symptoms: no fever; stomach cramps in the night, but no vomiting or diarrhea; no energy. "Guess what, darling? We might take a long walk today, if you feel better. Would you like to take a long walk and leave this place?"

"Are we leaving?" he asked weakly without opening his eyes.

In the dim light, she could see how pale he was. She lifted the blankets to tuck them under his chin, and the smell assaulted her again. "Tim!" she cried out and tossed them aside.

He opened his eyes lazily. "What's wrong?"

"You went to the bathroom in your bed. Didn't you know?" She pulled him out carefully and tried to get him to stand up. He did on wobbly legs. "Oh, what a mess. Sam is going to be angry with us if we don't get you better. We have to leave today."

"Mom, can I bring Joshua with us? I don't think he'll—" Tim choked in midsentence, gasped for air, then began to vomit.

Mary screamed.

❋

Standing in the center of the sanctuary, Sam looked down at his solitary knapsack on the floor. So far, he was the only one who'd packed for their escape. Peter and Howard were still gone, and he wondered how it could take so long for Peter to apologize. Something was wrong, he knew, but didn't have the inclination to guess what it was. One crisis was enough. Ruth and Amy were helping Mary with Tim.

"What about you?" Sam had asked Luke.

"We bring nothing into the world, and we take nothing with us when we go," Luke announced, then strolled away, hands clasped behind his back.

Sam was tempted to laugh, not at Luke, but at the entire situation. It had turned into a farce. Circumstances seemed to be conspiring to keep them at the church. Then he wondered, circumstances, or God?

He heard footsteps in the hall and looked up hopefully. Ruth walked in with a dour expression.

"How is he?" Sam asked.

Ruth spoke softly, "Not very well. Mary's almost hysterical. Amy's with them now. I can't figure it out. He doesn't have a fever. His breathing is shallow. His stomach is upset. He finds it hard to swallow, and he says his vision is blurred."

"Do you think it's some kind of virus?"

"I don't know."

"Could it be rabies? He plays with that chipmunk."

Ruth shook her head. "I don't think so. But what do I know? Nobody told me to take a nursing course before running from the law, Sam."

Sam smiled sympathetically. "I think I'll look around the church—some of the places Tim likes to play. Maybe I'll find something."

Ruth rested her hand on Sam's arm, and her expression asked him the question her lips wouldn't form.

"Pray that we don't have to take him to a doctor in the village," Sam answered her and wished he hadn't. It felt as if the very thought was now loose in the air and might land on them as a prophecy.

Ruth sighed and turned away. "I'll go pack."

After a comprehensive search of the main floor of the church, Sam ventured out into the featherlike snow. It helped ease his mind; it was too pretty to pose a substantial threat. He wandered aimlessly, his head down and eyes moving, like a man who'd lost a valuable heirloom. In his case, though, the heirloom was an unknown clue that might help him identify what was wrong with Tim. He had a vague notion that if he could see the chipmunk, it would put to rest their worry about rabies—or confirm it. It's amazing they all hadn't been sick by now, he thought.

The wind suddenly kicked up and sent a wet chill through Sam's frame. If it was too cold for him, it was too cold for a chipmunk, so he made a hasty retreat back into the church. Once inside the sanctuary again, he glanced at his lone knapsack on the floor, a comical prop like a showman's cane or a villain's false mustache. Women's voices echoed somewhere down the hall. His mind went back to his mission to investigate the areas where Tim liked to play. There weren't many in a hideout like this. He had a nagging feeling that he'd forgotten a likely place and slowly turned in a circle in the hope that he'd see something that would jog his memory. He did. He spotted the door to the choir room and remembered that, beyond, there was another door to the cellar. Tim occasionally went down there when he felt brave enough to risk his mother's wrath.

Lighting one of the lamps, Sam descended the stairs to the cellar. The wooden steps groaned and creaked in protest. The smell of mildew assaulted his senses, and he stopped halfway down to look around. It was a clutter of boxes, garbage, the old coal furnace (disconnected years ago and useless to them), and shelves filled with worthless odds and ends. He wondered why Tim was so fascinated with playing down here and then remembered that a child's curiosity transcended adult reasoning and logic. It turned sticks into swords, empty boxes into mansions, junk into treasure troves. For a moment, Sam envied Tim his youth, wishing he could have once again a renewed sense of wonder and excitement about the world: a belief in miracles.

He lifted the lamp higher and continued on. Somewhere off to his right two rats—he *assumed* they were rats—scuffled. He hated rats and hoped to God one wouldn't brush up against his leg. He'd scream and might never stop.

Over his head, he heard muffled voices through the ceiling. One was high and shrill: Mary's voice, he knew, speaking in a rapid flow of words that ran close to hysteria. Ruth and Amy were with her; maybe they could calm her down. He doubted it. But how could any of them expect comfort at a time like this?

Sam reached the bottom of the stairs and paused again as helplessness embraced him like an old friend. Everything was going wrong. They had to leave, but he didn't know where to take them. They needed food, but he didn't know where to get any. They needed help, but he didn't know where to find it. He trembled with anger. Why was he in charge? Who put this responsibility on his shoulders? He wanted to do his best for God, but what if his best wasn't good enough—what if he didn't have the equipment?

"I'm not Moses or Elijah, you know," Sam said.

He slumped down onto the bottom step and felt like the disciple who'd dared to step out on the storm-tossed sea with Jesus. There was nowhere to go but down.

"Lord, save me," Sam whispered, praying for a hard grace, a grace that wouldn't be too presumptuous. He had no aspirations to great miracles, merely something to get them out of the church safely. Maybe that was too much to ask.

The lamplight reflected off something shiny just beyond a group of cardboard boxes ahead. Whatever it was winked at him like a signal from a sinking ship.

CHAPTER 23

Death? I don't think I know what that is.

—Timothy, as quoted in *The Posthumous Papers of Samuel T. Johnson*

✳

"WHAT'S going on in here?" Amy asked urgently as she rushed into the sanctuary. She had been in with Ruth and Mary tending to Timothy when she heard doors slam and Peter shouting angrily. Fearful that Timothy might awaken, she ran to investigate.

"Sit down," Peter ordered, roughly pushing Howard toward Sam's worktable. Amy had never seen Peter so angry. His fury was thick and tangible, something that could be bottled—and the cork was ready to blow off. To Amy's surprise, Howard obeyed silently and sat on the wooden chair that was too small for him.

"Peter, what—"

"Where's Sam?" Peter snapped.

Startled, she said quickly, "I don't know—around somewhere—why? What—"

"Just find him," Peter said, then turned on Howard. "How many times did you go there?"

Beck looked at his fingernails. "I don't have to answer your questions."

Peter jerked toward Howard like a lion before leaping and roared. "How many times?"

"A couple of times. I didn't keep count," Beck replied.

"Peter, what's wrong with you? What happened?" Amy insisted.

Peter looked at her as if she were a stranger asking stupid questions at a road accident. "What?"

She spoke firmly. "Calm down and tell me what happened."

"I discovered our good friend Mr. Beck making a deal with a farmer a couple of miles from here," Peter explained. "It obviously didn't matter to him that he might get caught or that the farmer might follow him back to us."

Amy was dumbfounded. "Is that true?"

Beck looked at her impatiently. "We were running out of food. I had to take a chance. Getting caught has to be better than starving."

"After all we've been through—," Peter began, then stopped, speechless in his anger. In two quick steps he had Beck by the lapels and yanked him to his feet. "Do you have any idea what they'd do to us in prison? Do you? Torture, insanity, death!"

"Peter!" Amy cried out and tried unsuccessfully to pull him away. "Let go of him!"

Peter pushed Beck down again. Beck staggered like a drunken man, banging the chair and nearly falling to the ground. He grabbed the table just in time.

"Does the farmer know where you came from?" Amy asked him.

"No," Beck puffed, struggling for his composure. "I was sneaky."

"You sure are," Amy agreed.

Peter paced, as if it were the only way to restrain himself. "I don't believe you. You told him we're here, didn't you?"

Beck looked away.

Peter moved toward him again. "Didn't you?"

"Yes! It was the only way I could get more food."

"*More* food?" Amy asked.

"I told him how many of us there were so he'd give me more food to bring back."

Amy was puzzled. "But you haven't brought any food back here for us."

A new realization struck, and Amy looked to Peter, whose expression confirmed it. She glared at Beck and wondered what his heart was made of.

"You risked our lives to fill your stomach," Peter said.

"You don't understand," Howard complained, his voice taking on a childish whine. "I don't want to be a martyr. I don't believe in all that hogwash about being privileged to suffer for my faith. I'm afraid of pain . . . of death. I want to survive. I don't even know what I'm doing here."

"Neither do I," Peter spat. "You're pathetic."

The three of them turned as the choir door opened and Sam came in. His face was marred with soot and dirt, giving him the look of a clown who had misapplied his makeup. His eyes were swollen and red. In his hands he held an empty can and what looked to Amy like Tim's Swiss army knife.

"Sam, you won't believe what Howard—" Peter froze mid-sentence. Sam looked so strange, so distant, and his walk was dirgelike. "What's wrong?"

Sam shook his head. "I don't know what we're going to do."

"Do?" Amy asked, moving hesitantly towards him. "Do about what?"

Sam wasn't listening. "I've been surrounded by books all

my life. Academics is what I know. I've tried to base all my decisions on good sense. God knows I've tried my best. But everything we've been through defies all knowledge and reason. You don't know how hard this has been for me, trying to guide this group, to do the right thing. But *this*—this is beyond me."

"Sam, what are you talking about?" Peter pleaded, his voice full of alarm over this Sam he'd never seen before.

"Don't you see?" Sam held out the can and the knife. "I found this in the cellar. The boy ate what was in this can, in a lot of cans. God knows how long he's been doing it. His symptoms . . . I know what they are now. . . ."

They waited, the truth moving across them like the shadow of a fast eclipse.

Sam looked down helplessly at his hands. "He has botulism."

CHAPTER 24

MARY?" Ruth knocked softly on the door. She didn't hear an answer but opened the door slowly anyway. Enough light squeezed through the boards on the room's single window that everything looked like it had been covered with a dark gray veil. Ruth could see Mary keeping vigil over her son. Ruth whispered "Mary" again. She had news and didn't know how to break it.

"He looks so fragile," Mary said as she knelt next to Tim's cot. "I keep waiting for him to open his eyes and say 'boo' like he sometimes does when he wants to scare me. He thinks scaring me is so funny. But you're not trying to scare me now, are you, Tim?" She caressed his face and caught a sob in her throat.

Ruth put her arm around the weeping woman. "I know, Mary."

"I've tried and I've tried, but I can't understand why God is putting us through this nightmare. He's my son, Ruth. He's all I have." She wrung her hands. "Hard as it is, I can accept God's will in the world, in our society, but not with my son. He's sick, and I want him better."

Ruth held Mary close and waited. The words wouldn't form. In the silence of the room, it was easy to forget her sense of urgency. But the shuffle of feet in the hallway reminded her.

That would be Peter and Sam, she knew. They were going to carry Tim to the village doctor in the tiny hope that it would save the boy's life. There was nothing else for them to do. A killer had been let loose inside Tim's body, and no one there could stop it.

Mary clutched Ruth's hand suddenly. "Pray with me, Ruth."

"Mary—"

"No, don't say anything. We have to pray. God must be merciful. If he really loves me, he'll make my son well again."

Ruth held her breath. "No, Mary, that's not true. You can't use Tim as a test of God's love. He knows—"

"He's using Tim to test *my* love, isn't he?"

"I don't know," Ruth said. "No one knows. God sees and does things so much differently than we do."

"Let's pray, Ruth."

Ruth shook her head. "We can pray, Mary, but there's something I have to tell you."

Mary looked at her with wet, suspicious eyes.

How much more can she take? Ruth wondered. *How much more can any of us take?* "Mary, how would you like to take your son out of all this? How would you like for him to escape now?"

"Why are you asking me a question like that? You know something."

Undaunted, Ruth continued. "If you could spare him from all the violence and suffering we might face ahead, wouldn't you?"

"Yes! Of course I would! But why are you asking me that? What's wrong, Ruth? What's wrong with Tim? You're not telling me something."

"Sam and Peter are in the hall. They want to take Tim to a doctor."

"A doctor in the village? Is it that serious?"

"Yes."

"But they'll be caught; we all will. We can't take him to the village. The police'll take him away from me!"

"You may lose him anyway, Mary."

"Why?"

Ruth hesitated, her determination draining. She spoke before it all but vanished. "He has botulism."

Mary's face was blank. Ruth couldn't be sure if she didn't understand what it meant or simply refused to believe it. "Botulism?"

"Tim opened a can of beef stew in the cellar and ate it. He must've done it yesterday."

"But what does that mean?"

"If we don't take him to a doctor right away, he'll—" Ruth stopped and rephrased her thought. "The Lord will take him, Mary."

Mary's eyes widened in a frozen expression of horror. "No! God wouldn't take my baby away from me. He's all I have! You're wrong!" She put her arms over Tim. "God's not going to take him away from me!"

Sam and Peter slipped into the room and looked apologetically at the two women.

"Mary," Ruth said, signaling with her eyes her need for help. "We have to take him."

Mary held fast to her son. "No, I won't listen to you! I won't! You have no faith. If we pray, Timothy will get better. You watch!"

It was an awful moment for Ruth, one she would never forget, as she grabbed Mary's arms and Peter and Sam came forward to pull Mary's hands from Tim's blankets.

"No!" she hissed. "He'll be all right. You'll see. We don't have to take him anywhere!" She put up a fight, lashing out

189

wildly, until Ruth locked her arms around Mary's chest to restrain her.

"Mary, please," Ruth gasped and pulled back. The effort knocked them both off balance and threw them backward. Mary kicked out, catching the side of the cot with her foot and toppling it over. Tim spilled out onto the floor, lifeless.

"Timothy!" Mary screamed when she realized what she'd done and, breaking free from Ruth, scrambled on all fours to get to him. Sam and Peter were instantly on their knees next to the boy to make sure he was all right. His unseeing eyes told them otherwise.

"Oh, God," Peter said, turning away to cry.

"Timothy!" Mary cried.

Sam's legs gave out, and he collapsed on the floor.

"Is he . . . ?" Ruth asked breathlessly.

Sam nodded and buried his face in his hands.

Mary wailed her son's name again and again as she pulled his limp body into her arms.

CHAPTER 25

Why in the world are you asking me about death? I'd rather not think about it. No, I don't want to think about it at all.

—Mary, as quoted in *The Posthumous Papers of Samuel T. Johnson*

✳

MARY wept over Timothy for two hours. Ruth and Amy alternately held her and prayed for her until they could ease her away from his still body. She kissed him, then gave him up.

"Mary, I'm sorry," Sam said, his voice trembling slightly. "But we have to bury him now so we can leave soon. We're running out of daylight, and the snow is falling heavily." Sam adjusted the blanket that covered the boy.

"No! Don't put the blanket over his face!" Mary commanded.

"But, Mary—"

"He's afraid of the dark. Leave him alone! Don't you touch him."

Peter stepped forward and said gently, "I'm going to bury him, Mary. Will you give me the honor? Do you mind?"

Mary looked solemnly at Peter and slowly moved her head in a barely perceptible nod. "You loved him, Peter. You understand."

"I do. And I'll take care of him." Peter carefully wrapped the child in the blanket and felt for a moment that he was wrapping up more than just a human body. It was hope. It had hung precariously on Tim's shoulders like a target—it was the mark of all children first and foremost. But, like a target, it meant they were the first to get hit by tragedy, to suffer, to fall.

"I'll come with you," Sam said.

"No, I want to do this alone," he said softly. "Maybe you should have some kind of service while I'm gone."

Sam agreed.

Peter carried Tim to the sanctuary, where he put the body down long enough so he could get dressed for the cold afternoon. The sun was beginning its descent behind the mountains. The snow had already left a couple of inches on the ground. Digging would be hard, but he was determined to do it.

Luke suddenly appeared at his side and said, "Peter, let me have the boy."

"Why?" Peter asked more sharply than he meant to. "So you can pray for healing? So God can bring him back to life? Is that what you can do?"

"He is alive, but in a different place now," Luke said meekly as he put his hand on Peter's shoulder and looked deeply into his eyes. "You understand, don't you? We pray for help, and God in his wisdom has answered that prayer for Tim."

The statement was so simple and so coherent that Peter nearly forgot that he was talking to a man who was supposed to be insane. "But what about us?" Peter asked. "Some of us loved him."

"Time is so very short," Luke said. "Short for life, short for

192

love, and suddenly it's gone—but that isn't the end. Remember, it isn't the end."

Suddenly Luke turned his head as if something had caught his eye on one of the walls. Peter waited, thinking he might say more. He didn't. He merely stared vacantly as if the meter had suddenly run out on whatever coin had given him this moment of lucidity.

Peter zipped up his coat, grabbed the shovel Sam had found in the shed, and gazed down at the small body. He lay like an unkept promise. What was left for them? They could leave now, but could they ever really escape from this loss?

✻

Peter patted the last shovelful of dirt on the makeshift grave in the farthest edge of the church graveyard, just inside the woods. This is only an empty shell, he reminded himself, a hollow vessel. Tim is long gone. Maybe Luke was right. God had provided Tim with the best possible escape.

He stood straight, every muscle in his body aching from toiling the hard, frozen earth. He was aware of being watched by the solid angels with chipped wings and the rounded crosses in the graveyard behind him. There were vases, too, where brightly colored remembrances had once sat, but now they were empty as if life had grabbed the flowers and run away with them.

He folded his arms and offered a simple benediction. "God, bless Tim," he whispered, "and help us now." The snow, white tears from the eyes of God, fell quickly now. The wind wailed through the trees mournfully.

With a final glance down at the grave, Peter slowly turned and made his way back toward the church. He was ready to leave. The church was tainted now. It would have the memory and smell of death. None of them, especially Mary, could bear that. They had to face whatever waited for them ahead.

He blinked against the snow and could barely see beyond the tombstones to the church. At first he thought he was seeing things and then dropped behind one of the granite monuments. His mind raced to assimilate the picture ahead: There was a dirt-covered Jeep parked next to the door. Two armed men climbed out.

CHAPTER 26

WILLIAMS was having a hard time concentrating, which concerned him. His mind was usually a reliable instrument, and now it was thrown off its calibration. Moses—real name, Brad Nichols—had turned out to be a difficult interrogation. Persuasion did not affect him, which Williams expected. The mind games that comprised the second step of effective interrogation did not wear him down. The third step was old-fashioned pain applied in new technological methods—this was where Williams had the highest expectations. He was disappointed. Moses screamed, as most men did, but wouldn't yield any helpful information. When it got to be too much, he resorted to phrases like "The Lord is my light and my salvation—so why should I be afraid? The Lord protects me from danger—so why should I tremble?" (Slater later identified it as Psalm 27:1.) They'd been at it for six hours, and now Williams was losing his patience— the very thing he couldn't afford to do, the thing that wrecked his concentration. To lose one's patience meant that one was becoming emotionally involved. Emotions were a forbidden area for well-trained interrogators. It meant that control had been lost.

"Do you think man is basically good or evil?" Moses asked him, his voice hoarse from screaming. His wan face was bruised and dripping with sweat. The room smelled of it, of flesh and blood and all its in-betweens.

"I ask the questions here," Williams said as he washed his hands in the rusted basin on the far wall of the otherwise stark interrogation chamber.

"I know," Moses croaked. "You're not supposed to talk to me. Talking would make me human to you, and once you remember I'm a human, you couldn't do this, not without severing yourself from your own humanity."

"You're a roach." Williams dried his hands and casually touched a button on the control pad. It sent a signal through the wires to an electrode attached to the prisoner's cheek. The result was a stabbing sensation that went straight to the nerves of Moses' front teeth. He cried out long and hard.

"Like I said, *I* will ask the questions and direct our conversation," Williams said softly.

Moses gasped, "The Lord is my rock . . . my fortress . . . my savior. . . ."

Williams rounded the metal table Moses was strapped to. "I want to sort out the details about your transportation system."

"For God so loved the world that he gave his only Son—"

"We need names of your drivers, the kinds of trucks they drive—"

"So that everyone who believes in him will not perish—"

"Pickup and drop-off points, your contacts—"

"But have eternal life."

"John 3:16!" Slater said happily as he walked into the room. "Do I win a gold star for knowing it?"

Moses spoke through the numbing pain. "You'll win more than a star if you take it to heart."

"I'd rather have the star," Slater said, then turned to Williams. "He's a tough one, isn't he? The true martyrs always are. How's he doing?"

Williams shook his head. "He's in terrible physical shape for a man of thirty-nine. I'm afraid his body'll give out before his spirit will." They spoke as if he weren't in the room with them, as if what he knew or didn't know about their process meant nothing.

"The spirit is willing, but the body is weak," Slater said.

"I don't get enough exercise." Moses swallowed, his throat clicking as if someone had thrown a switch. "Captain, can I assume that asking for a sip of water would be inappropriate?"

"Ask away," Slater said.

"May I have a sip of water, please?"

Slater went to the basin, grabbed a small glass by the rim, and filled it up. He returned to the table and set the glass down six inches from Moses' mouth. The straps kept him from getting it. "Tell us about your partner in crime."

Moses looked at the water and licked his dry tongue across his chapped lips. A tear slid from the corner of his eye.

Slater pushed the glass a little closer to the prisoner. "Tell me about Elijah."

"Ah," Moses said, "that's a mystery."

"It is?"

Moses turned away from the water. "He has vanished. If you don't have him, then I can't tell you where he is. He simply disappeared."

"You don't expect me to believe that," Slater scoffed.

"What you believe is your business, but it's true. We thought you had him locked up somewhere."

"We did. But you helped him escape."

Moses coughed. "From the rehabilitation center, yes. But

after that, we don't know where he went. He didn't rendez-vous with us at the appointed place."

"Oh? And what appointed place was that?" Williams asked.

"God is my refuge and strength," Moses said.

"Tiresome, isn't it?" Slater asked Williams.

Williams nodded. "The tenacity of a roach after a piece of bread."

"Moses," Slater began as he sat down next to the head of the table. "What do you think happened to Elijah?"

"He was always a sensitive soul, just like his namesake. He often felt alone against the corruptions of Ahabs and Jezebels. But God will raise him up for mighty deeds. His work has not been completed."

"You're assuming he's still alive," Slater offered.

"He is. I can feel it." Moses gazed at Slater through half-lidded eyes. Williams recognized the look; he was getting close to the end.

"Then where is he?"

"In the belly of the whale."

"What?"

"Do you believe in dreams and visions?" Moses asked.

Slater smiled. "I dream of a day when our world will be rid of roaches like you."

"The people are in mourning over the death of a child—men with guns approach—while somewhere he hides. Jacob wrestled the angel and overcame him as we all wrestle the forces of light and darkness. God causes everything to work together for the good of those who love God and are called according to his purpose. . . ." His voice faded; he closed his eyes.

"What's he saying?" Williams asked his boss, as if Moses had spoken in a language that needed translating.

"Gibberish," Slater said. "Are we losing him?"

"I think so."

"We can't. There's too much we don't know yet." Slater stood up, grabbed the glass, and threw the water in Moses' face. The prisoner didn't react.

Williams moved to the door. "I'll get the doctor."

"Wait—no. He's coming around."

Moses slowly opened his eyes. "Captain, you lost this battle before you began."

"I'll be the judge of that," Slater chuckled.

"You'll be the judge of nothing," Moses whispered. "For the Lord Jesus Christ sits upon the throne to judge and to show mercy. Accept his mercy before it's too late."

"As a nonexistent entity, he has little power to offer judgment or mercy. So, let's go back to Elijah, shall we?"

Moses lifted his head, a bowling ball on a trembling stem. "'God did not send his Son into the world to condemn it, but to save it. There is no judgment awaiting those who trust him. But those who do not trust him have already been judged.' You are a condemned man, Captain. You are dead in your trespass and sins."

"This is getting us nowhere," Slater said to Williams. "I think we're being too easy on him."

Williams watched his boss slide around the table to the control panel. "Sir—"

"What?" Slater snapped as he perused the buttons.

"I'll take care of it."

"You'll take care of *what?*" Slater snarled. "You've had him for six hours, and you haven't taken care of anything!"

"Patience. Maybe we should go out in the hall for a minute."

"*You* go out in the hall if you want. I want some answers

from this roach. Whatever they taught you at college isn't doing the job."

Williams knew now that, unless he physically tackled his boss and dragged him out, there was nothing else he could do. Slater was a cat who toyed with his prey for only so long before he pounced viciously.

Moses dropped his head heavily onto the table. He said, "Captain Slater, your soul is required of you. I knew your father, you know. I remember his visits with my family when I was a boy—"

"Be quiet!"

"He was a man of faith, a soldier of righteousness—"

"That's enough!"

Williams stepped toward his boss. "He's goading you. Don't listen."

"Your father was an inspiration to me. My work with the Underground is a direct result of—"

"Shut up! Shut up!" Slater roared and dropped his fingers onto the buttons haphazardly.

Williams leapt at the control panel. "No!"

Moses howled as his body jerked and twitched like a spasmodic puppet. Only the straps kept him on the table; he would otherwise have been thrown off by the surge of energy that jolted through the electrodes and into his most tender parts. Abruptly he went limp.

"Get the doctor," ordered Slater as he collapsed into his chair. It was as if the effort of pushing a few buttons had been difficult.

Williams glared at his commander.

"Get the doctor, and then we'll start again," Slater said more firmly. "He won't forget that kind of pain. When he comes to, he'll want to tell us everything he knows."

With insubordination emanating from his every move, Williams marched over to the table and snatched up Moses' wrist to check his pulse.

The door swung open and Officer Nesbit, the interrogation monitor, ran in. "What happened in here? What did you do? His vital signs are gone."

Williams dropped the pulseless wrist. "Where's Dr. Kennedy?"

"He just went to get coffee," Nesbit said before speeding out of the door again. "I'll find him."

Slater stood up and said irritably, "You're not going to tell me he's dead."

"As good as dead," Williams said as he began lifesaving procedures on the man. It was a halfhearted attempt; he knew there was no bringing Moses back from that last trauma.

"What kind of man was he?" Slater complained.

"A man with a heart condition," answered Williams before attempting mouth-to-mouth.

CHAPTER 27

IT was the nature of grace, Sam thought, to be present when you don't think it is. Only after a crisis or a catastrophe do you suddenly realize that grace had been there all along, giving strength at the point when there was no strength left. He had come to that theory in a time of relative safety, and now he hoped to God it was more than just theory. For as he sat looking at the beaten-down group of refugees gathered among their knapsacks in the sanctuary, he knew that it would be by some supernatural means only that they could carry on. Life had been pulled out of them as if it had been wrapped up and taken away with Tim's body. Sam felt as if they were only going through the motions now; he knew it was true for him. Any leadership he asserted now was a sham. His helplessness now was complete and thorough. Whatever happened now had to come from God.

The wind rattled and swirled through the church rafters so hard that Sam imagined for a moment that he'd heard a car drive past. He dismissed the thought when Ruth asked, "Has anybody seen Howard?"

"Not since Peter dragged him back from that farmer's," Amy replied.

"He's probably pouting in his room," Ruth suggested. "I'll go get him."

Sam watched her leave and wondered how Howard would act now that their worst suspicions about him had been confirmed: He was sneaky and selfish. Once Peter had explained it all to him, Sam was ready to throw Howard out. It seemed unimaginable that he could do such a thing. But Sam realized that it *wasn't* unimaginable. It was, in fact, predictable. The essence of our human condition was self-centeredness, and it took the will to survive to draw it out and expose it for what it really was. *What Howard did, any of us are capable of doing,* Sam thought. It wasn't an excuse, just an observation. And for that reason, Sam saw no point in banishing Beck. Besides, Beck by himself was a worse danger than Beck staying with them. At least they could keep an eye on him.

Ruth returned a moment later with a drawn expression. "Most of his things are gone. He must have decided to leave without us."

"Oh no," Sam said.

"He was humiliated by what happened. He probably thought we'd throw him out anyway," Amy said.

Ruth frowned. "I could never figure him out. Something wasn't quite right about his being with us."

"We'll have to forget about him for now," Sam said. Then with a sweeping gesture, he spread the crude map he'd found onto the ground and pointed at his markings. "Here's our route out of here."

Ruth whistled through her teeth. "It's a long way."

Amy shivered. "Will we make it? It's still snowing, you know."

"God did not call us to fear or panic, but to victory through Jesus Christ," Luke announced.

"Is it still snowing?" Mary asked quietly, her face still a mask of grief.

"Yes," Sam replied.

"The ground will be cold," she said.

Sam knelt next to her and said tenderly, "Mary, I want you to know how sorry I am about Timothy. We would all like to stop and grieve with you, but we can't now. It's very urgent that we get out of here."

Mary looked at Sam sadly, then nodded.

"'Can anything ever separate us from Christ's love?'" Luke said. "'Does it mean he no longer loves us if we have trouble or calamity, or are persecuted, or are hungry or cold or in danger or threatened with death? (Even the Scriptures say, "For your sake we are killed every day; we are being slaughtered like sheep.")'"

"Luke, please," Amy entreated him.

Luke continued, "'No, despite all these things, overwhelming victory is ours through Christ, who loved us. And I am convinced that nothing can ever separate us from his love. Death can't, and life can't. The angels can't, and the demons can't. Our fears for today, our worries about tomorrow, and even the powers of hell can't keep God's love away. Whether we are high above the sky or in the deepest ocean, nothing in all creation will ever be able to separate us from the love of God that is revealed in Christ Jesus our Lord.'"

"Amen," Ruth whispered.

Sam strode to the front doors. "I'll see how Peter is doing, and then we'll go."

As he reached for the handle, the doors were abruptly yanked away from his grasp. A blast of cold air preceded the snow-blinding light, and he flinched. Squinting, he made out the silhouette of a man pointing a rifle at him. Instantaneously, Amy cried out, and Sam turned back to see a second man standing in the doorway leading to the hall.

"Freeze! Nobody move!" the second man ordered as he

crouched, holding a pistol at arm's length in standard police fashion.

The one with the rifle shouted, "Bobby, will you stop it? We're not playing cops and robbers." He gestured at Sam to move back and carefully pulled the doors closed behind him.

The one called Bobby ambled into the sanctuary and said happily, "It looks like we got us a whole flock!" He smiled like a kid who'd just discovered a secret supply of candy.

"Looks that way, don't it?" the one with the rifle said. He spotted the knapsacks and bundles on the floor. "Caught 'em on moving day, too. Guess we got here in the nick of time."

No one moved or spoke. They were frozen in a combination of shock and confusion. Sam noted that the two weren't dressed as policemen. They wore large, colorful hunting coats, thick wool caps, jeans, and boots. He guessed that they were in their late teens or early twenties and could have been students in one of his classes. The one with the rifle was tall and lean with a hard, angular face. The other—Bobby—had gentler features and friendly eyes. The pistol was out of place in his hands. He was like a kid with a toy—a *dangerous* toy.

The one with the rifle eyed the small gathering. "Funny, I don't see our friend here. Where is he?" he asked Sam.

"Who are you talking about?"

"The hoity-toity one with the silver hair. He came to my daddy's farm looking for food. I saw him from the window."

A sickening realization visibly worked its way through the group. "You must mean Howard," Sam said. "He's gone."

"Too bad," the rifleman said. "Less reward that way."

"Who are you? What do you want?" Ruth asked.

"Yeah," Sam added. "Why are you here, and why are you waving guns at us?"

"Because you're rebels."

"Rebels?" Sam asked. "What do you mean?"

"*Christians,*" the rifleman replied as if he'd just bitten into an onion and had to spit it out. "Don't try to tell me you're not."

Sam cautiously moved forward. "Look, maybe we can discuss this and—"

The kid lifted his rifle. "You can talk to Clarisse here. She's good at shooting her mouth off."

Sam backed off. "I make it a point to never argue with a loaded woman."

"Smart thinking." He turned to his partner. "Bobby, you go check for any stragglers. Then get the cops on the radio and tell them what we have."

"Snow's getting deep fast, Clay. The police probably won't make it up here on these roads."

"Then we'll have to take 'em down in the Jeep. Just get going," he said.

Bobby pocketed his pistol long enough to give his cap a good pull over his ears, then slipped out the way he'd come in. Sam and Ruth exchanged a knowing look—Peter was out there somewhere. Had he seen their visitors? Was he concocting a plan to help them? Sam was afraid because he knew Peter was reckless enough to do something foolishly heroic and get them all killed.

Clay turned the rifle on Sam again. "Why don't you sit down with the rest of them? You look like you're thinking something stupid."

"It's my usual condition," Sam said, sitting on the chair next to his table.

"What are you going to do with us?" Amy asked.

Clay's expression told Sam that it was the first time he'd noticed Amy—and he was impressed with what he saw. His tone changed noticeably. "Well, sweetie, I'm going to take you to the police and get a big fat reward for you. See, Bobby and me have been trying to get off this mountain, and you folks are going to make it possible."

"It's nice to know our lives have purpose," Sam said.

Ruth stood up. "Listen to me, young man, do you have any idea what you're doing? If you turn us in, they'll probably kill us. Is that what you want?"

Clay shrugged. "What they do with you is their business. All I know is that people like you are wanted by the government, and they're willing to pay a lot of money for you."

"But don't you care that they'll kill us?" asked Ruth.

"Just sit down, lady," Clay snapped. "This ain't no press conference, and I ain't answerin' no more questions. All of you can just shut up and wait for the police to get here."

Ruth sat down with an indignant *harrumph* and stared crossly at him. Sam knew intuitively that her scorn would have no effect on the boy. He reeked of rebellion and resentment. Whatever had happened to him on this mountain was ample preparation for dealing with a group of meek and inoffensive Christians.

The front doors exploded open—again with the bright light and cold wind that heralded someone's arrival. Peter was pushed in by Bobby, who followed close behind. Everyone leapt to their feet, but Clay swung his rifle around in case someone used the opportunity to attack. "Don't get no ideas!" he shouted.

Peter fell on all fours, coughing. A trickle of blood slipped from his lip.

"What's going on here?" Clay asked.

Bobby was breathless. He and Peter must have scuffled outside. "This one—he busted the radio, Clay!"

"What?" Clay shouted. "Aw, and I just got it paid for! Well, we'll just have to get another one with the reward. Let's pile them into the Jeep and—"

"Can't," Bobby gasped. "He flattened our tires, too. They're like pancakes."

With this announcement, Peter glanced at Sam with a wry smile.

Clay found less humor in it. With a stream of obscenities, he closed the gap between himself and Peter in a few short steps. "You'll pay for that!"

Peter was on his feet quickly, ready for whatever Clay might do. Bobby jumped between them. "Don't, Clay. You promised."

Clay tried unsuccessfully to push past Bobby. "Police don't care what kind of shape they're in when they get them."

"I do," Bobby said, holding his friend back. "No fighting. You promised."

Clay spun away angrily and pouted. "But now we're stuck here. We can't even make it back to the farm in this snow." His face flushed, and his veins bulged out of his neck as he pointed threateningly at Peter. "I oughta kill you, boy!"

"If you could." Peter smirked.

Clay started for him again. "It'd be no problem."

Bobby interceded again, pushing Clay toward the door. "Just go out and cool down, OK? Just go on."

Clay hesitated long enough to scowl at the wide eyes staring back at him. He pushed Bobby aside and stormed down the hallway. "I'm gonna go find something to eat."

"Good luck," Peter said under his breath. He sat down next to Ruth.

"Now you listen and listen good," Bobby began once he was sure Clay had gone. "Clay's got a fiery temper, and when it starts up he stops thinking. Just do what he says and don't smart him. You won't get hurt that way. Understand?"

This warning—which seemed to Sam like an attempt at reasonability—encouraged him enough to approach the boy.

"Bobby, you seem like an intelligent sort of person." He felt as if he were talking to a student about a bad grade. "You don't want to do this, do you? I mean, we're human beings just like you. You can't turn us in for money. We're *people*."

There was a second—a fraction in time—when Bobby's eyes betrayed his inner conflict. Sam knew it well; he'd been struggling internally ever since they'd arrived at the church. It was a remnant of humanity in a very inhuman circumstance.

"Come on, Bobby," entreated Sam.

Bobby shuffled his feet nervously, then looked at Sam with a hardened gaze. "It's the only way off this mountain."

Sam had no response. He thought, *This is what neutralizes humanity in the end: expediency.* In the name of expediency, souls have been lost, nations have gone to war, entire generations have been obliterated. The expediency of life is what most often takes life. Their whole society had been built on it.

"This place is a dump!" Clay announced from the hallway as he walked back in. He used the barrel of his rifle to poke at the bundles on the floor. "Where's your food?"

Everyone looked at each other awkwardly, as if drawing straws to see who would break the bad news to Clay. Sam cleared his throat and looked at him squarely. "There is no food. We ran out."

"No food? You hear that, Bobby?" He kicked one of the bundles. "And it's snowing like crazy out there. Now what are we going to do?"

Bobby held up his hands in resignation. "Don't know."

"It's all *your* fault." Clay pointed the rifle at Peter like a prosecutor's finger.

"Nobody asked you to come up here," Peter said.

"Don't rile me, boy. I'd just as soon kill you as look at you for trapping us like this."

Peter held his gaze. "Don't like the feeling do you?"

"Just shut up," Clay shouted.

"Peter," Sam said, throwing Peter a look warning him to back off.

Peter kept his eyes fixed on Clay but spoke to Sam. "I don't care. They're willing to see us die for money. I don't mind seeing them suffer a little."

"The only suffering around here will be done by you," Clay said, walking in a circle around the bundles. His eyes stayed with Peter's. They were like a couple of elks ready to lock antlers in a primitive contest of wills.

Sam looked to Bobby, hoping he would do something, say something. Bobby watched with an apprehensive expression. This wasn't new to him, Sam thought. He'd seen it before. "Look, you two." Sam stood up and slowly made his way toward them. "Let's calm down before something happens we'll all regret. Count to ten, Peter."

Clay laughed. "Yeah, Peter, listen to your daddy. Count to ten."

"I'll bet it's more than you can do," Peter snipped.

"Peter, please stop," Ruth said firmly. "This isn't a friendly tussle in the locker room at high school. For our sakes . . ."

Peter broke his gaze away from Clay. "You're right," he said quietly.

Clay continued to prowl around the group as if the animal had been stirred up and needed somewhere to go. "That's right; you be a mama's boy and listen to what she says. 'Cause you'll get hurt otherwise."

"I'm not his mother," Ruth said.

"You're not? Then who are you?"

"His aunt."

Clay turned to Sam. "You his uncle?"

"No," Sam replied. "Just a friend."

"And who are you?" Clay asked Luke.

"A humble servant," came the answer.

Clay pointed at Mary. "*You* must be his mother. You've got the look of a mother."

Mary simply shook her head.

"Can't you be quiet?" Amy asked impatiently. "Take us prisoner if that's what you want to do, but just be quiet."

Clay looked at Amy with wonderment, then crouched down next to her. "You know, for Christians, you're a spunky bunch. Most people would be quivering in their boots at a couple of guys like us with guns. But not you. The fact is, I like spunky . . . in women."

"Clay," Bobby groaned.

Clay ignored him. "You're a pretty thing. I'll bet we could make good use of our time together, y'know, while we're stuck here."

Amy watched him with a shriveling coldness. The rest of the group visibly tensed and watched. Sam rested his hand on his chair, ready to use it to clobber Clay if he had to. He'd read about turning the other cheek, but he wasn't sure how it applied to this situation.

Undaunted, Clay reached out and stroked her hair. "You'd like me a lot, I'll bet. Be nice, and maybe I won't take you in."

"Don't touch me," she said through clenched teeth.

"I could be the best thing that ever happened to you."

"Stop it," Peter said in a low voice.

"What's your name?" Clay asked, his smile vindictive, his strokes harder.

Amy swiped her arm at him. "Leave me alone."

Peter stood up. "Keep your hands off her."

"Stay back," Bobby said to Peter, his pistol waving shakily in the air as if it hung by a loose string. His eyes darted around the room, sizing up the situation.

"I think we're getting a little overheated here," Sam said.

"Oh, yeah," Clay cooed to Amy. "Let's get a little over-heated."

Peter took a step toward Clay, but Clay was instantly on his feet, his rifle aimed at Peter. "Not another move, boy. You can't do anything, you understand? You're my prisoner, and you can't do *nothing!*"

"Yeah, you're tough."

"I can do whatever I want. You're nothing but trash. The government won't care what I do with you!"

"Clay, come here," Bobby shouted, but it was a feeble command.

"I can do whatever I want," Clay said again.

"You might try," Peter sneered.

The vindictive smile returned to Clay's face. "I can do more than try." Bending over, he grabbed Amy's jaw and kissed her hard on the mouth. She tried to pull away, but his grip was firm. Suddenly he cried out and staggered back, his hand to his mouth. "You bit me! I'll teach you—"

He made for her again, but Peter leapt at him. Skillfully, Clay jerked aside while swinging the butt of the gun around, hitting Peter on the side of the head. Peter fell to his knees, a trickle of blood at his ear.

They all moved forward until Bobby stepped in with his gun nervously trained on them. "Stay back! I mean it!"

Ruth cried out, "Stop it!"

Mary began to whimper.

Clay leveled the rifle at Peter. "Just the way it should be, boy. On your knees."

"Not for you," Peter said and lunged at him again, wrapping his arms around Clay's waist and driving him backward to the wall.

Clay used both hands to bring the rifle butt down onto Peter's back. Peter went down again.

Clay shouted, "I'm sick of you, boy. You're a real pest." He kicked out at Peter and caught him in the ribs.

"That's enough, Clay!" Bobby yelled.

"You're a punk," Peter wheezed. "The worst kind."

"You wanna step outside? Let's step outside," Clay said and grabbed the back of Peter's jacket. Sam was startled by Clay's strength as he hoisted Peter to his feet. Clay gave him a hard shove to the door. Peter stumbled, then collapsed against the wall.

"No, don't," Ruth pleaded.

Sam called out, desperate to say something that would diffuse the situation. "Clay—"

"Shut up! All of you!" Clay screamed. The rifle now shook in his hand, but it was anger not fear that made him tremble. He was red faced; his nostrils flared like those of a charging bull. He said to Peter in a cruel whisper, "I'll show you what's what for breaking my radio and flattening my tires and bein' such a smart mouth. And then I'll have your girlfriend, and you won't be able to do a thing about it."

It was as if the seconds spun away, flying loose from the wheel of time, disjointed and fragmented. Sam thought that movies made moments like this happen in slow motion. It wasn't slow; it was an eternity that he would play over and over again in his mind.

Peter roared as he pushed away from the wall and spun toward Clay with both fists.

Clay lurched back, the rifle drifting up until it was level with Peter's chest. He pulled the trigger.

The Path

CHAPTER 28

THE village was called Hopewell, a fact Howard Beck had missed somewhere along the way. It was the quintessential one-horse town, with a row of innocuous shops selling everything from dry goods to rank imitations of the latest fashions to feed and fertilizer. A large tin shack, a holdover from the more prosperous coal-mining days, had been converted into a bar imaginatively called Hank's 2. Beck needed only to look across the street at another bar set in a log-cabin frame to find the original Hank's Place. A blue-and-green neon light displayed the name of a beer through smoky brown glass—the same beer advertised in the window across the street. It was a cheap, government-sanctioned brand. He pondered the building like a vulture on a rooftop. The street was empty except for the whipping snow and a pickup truck waiting patiently at the single intersection for a light that refused to change.

Beck limped in the direction of Hank's Place. His feet were cold and ached from the long trek down the mountain. The snow had reached his ankles and occasionally blew in over the tops of his boots. His hands, though gloved, felt numb. His shoulders ached from carrying the knapsack he'd shoved his few belongings into. He knew he had to keep a low profile, but the wall of snow and the weariness from the walk gave him a feeling of recklessness, as if no one could make him suffer any more than he'd already suffered. He had a sense of safety born out of the anonymity of the village; no one would care about him here. It was time to duck out of the white deluge and indulge in something that would warm his belly. He thought a whisky would be nice; better yet, a brandy. He pushed open the solid wooden door that said Hank's in chipped letters and stepped inside. He blinked at the darkness, needing a moment for his eyes to adjust. The place smelled of beer, sweat, and cigarette smoke. The combination made Beck feel slightly euphoric. It was a hint of civilization and normality after the church. He felt like a prisoner who'd been released from solitary confinement. Guilt was not an issue; being free was everything.

The interior of the bar was true to the cabin motif established outside. Large wooden beams crisscrossed overhead. The walls were rough and poster-packed with ads for beer and whisky featuring scantily clad women in provocative poses. Logs also comprised the foundation of the large rectangular bar in the center of the room. Small round tables and uncomfortable-looking chairs dotted what was left of the floor space. The bartender, a burly bald man in a white shirt—presumably the Hank of legend—leaned against the counter reading a newspaper. He looked to Beck like a heavenly messenger standing amid the sparkling glasses and multicolored bottles within arm's reach above him. A few stools down, an old man sat hunched over a drink. Beck gasped, his heart jumping—the man looked exactly like Luke. Beck collected himself and shrugged it off. Of course, anyone with wild white hair and beard would remind him of Luke.

Neither of the men looked up at him. Somewhere a jukebox played an old song, the thumping bass being the only thing Howard could hear. He strolled to the bar and slid onto a stool. Dropping his knapsack on the floor next to him, he folded both hands in front of him like a man in prayer. And in a perverse way, he felt like praying—thanking God for deliverance from the mountain, thanking him for bars and stale cigarettes and bad music and liquor. Mostly liquor. It was exactly what he needed to break from the past, to insert a wedge between him and what he had left behind at the church.

He wondered why he hadn't run away before. Why hadn't he escaped and come to the village sooner? He knew the answer to the question but purposefully avoided it. There was no point in dealing with realities now. He was momentarily free and knew he had to enjoy it while he could. Now was the time to consider his options for the future.

The bartender suddenly looked up and eyed him suspiciously. "What can I get you?"

"Brandy," Beck said.

"You have money?"

"Of course I do," Howard said indignantly.

"Let's see it," the bartender said.

Howard frowned at the man. When the bartender didn't move, Howard yanked off his gloves, jerked open his coat, and dug into his back pocket for his wallet. Finding it, he produced a gold credit card. It was enough to satisfy the bartender's concerns.

"It says they executed him," the old man on the other stool said through a toothless mouth. Howard realized they were talking about something from the newspaper. The headline gloated that one of the leaders of the Christian insurrectionists had been caught.

"Executed him?" the bartender repeated from where he poured Howard's drink. "Well, it makes sense that they would. They need to be put down."

The old man grunted. "I wonder why they didn't show it on

television—the execution, I mean. Nothing better than executions, except maybe wrestling."

"I'll bet they say because of security reasons." The bartender put a glass of brandy in front of Howard and grabbed his card. "You want a running tab?"

Howard nodded, then rested the brim of the glass next to his lips, savoring the heady smell, building anticipation of the nearly forgotten taste. He sipped the drink and closed his eyes as the warmth filled his mouth and then worked its way down his throat. He wanted to drown in it.

The old man pointed at the page. "Yep, right there. They executed him quickly for security reasons. Says he ran a significant risk. The other insurrectionists might have resorted to terrorism to free him."

Beck stifled a laugh, but it caught the ears of both men.

"Something funny?" the bartender asked, clearly bothered that the laugh might be connected to the drink.

Beck held up a hand. "No, no. It's that line about terrorism. What kind of terrorism would they resort to? Wave a cross at the building, call down fire from heaven?"

"It's happened." The old man scowled.

The bartender waved a finger. "That's right. You remember the fire two years ago. Where was it?"

"The Committee Building," the old man said.

"That's right. They said Moses and Elijah caused that."

"Burnt the thing to the ground without any kind of those whatchamacallits."

"Incendiary devices," the bartender helped.

"That's right. Nobody can figure out how they did it."

"They didn't do it by praying, that's for sure," Howard said as he took another drink. This was just like the old days at The Inn, around the corner from his office. Talk about the latest business, the latest gossip. Howard knew that the fire at the

Committee Building was a frame to stir up public hatred against the Christians. Making them look like fanatics with supernatural powers gave everyone the desire—and the license—to kill them on sight. It created another violent purge.

"What are you, some kind of expert?" the bartender asked snippily.

"I used to work three blocks from the building," Howard said proudly. The local yokels would be impressed by that piece of information. Here was a big-city boy in their midst.

The bartender's bald head folded into creases between his eyes. "What are you doing here, then?"

"Oh, I'm just passing through," he replied and took another sip of his brandy. It was doing wonders for him already. The snow, the church, the events up there were blurring quickly.

The bartender and the old man eyed him skeptically. He glanced down at the worn sleeves of his coat and suspected that his face looked worse. When did he last shave? They no more believed that he was a big-city businessman than they believed he was the man in the moon. But Howard didn't care. Let them think what they wanted so long as he got another drink. He pushed the empty glass toward the bartender.

"You can have another when I've checked your card," the bartender said and slipped over to the processing machine. He ran the number through for a check to make sure it was still good. The digitized display indicated that it was.

"Satisfied?" Howard asked.

The bartender brought him another drink.

This is the way to go, Howard thought. A single night in oblivion would make all the difference for him. Then he could ignore the feelings that nibbled at the edge of his conscience like rats on the other side of a wall. Those rats had to be fought. They had to be exterminated with lots of drinks. They carried with them the diseases of guilt and remorse, two things

Howard had been fighting for years. They weren't practical. They got in the way of thinking clearly about his options.

"Do you have rooms in this town?" Howard asked.

"What kind of rooms?"

"A place to sleep if I decide to . . ." *Drink too much* was the finish of that sentence, but he left it alone.

"I've got rooms upstairs," the bartender said. "You can stay in one for a fee. You can even have someone to go with it, if you want."

Howard chuckled. "That depends on how drunk I get."

❋

Central's Data Department hummed with life every day and night, twenty-four hours a day, seven days a week. The men and women who worked there wore glasses and white lab coats, blending in perfectly with the thick computer monitors and giant white mainframes. They liked to think that they were the brains of the Security Forces. They monitored and distributed the information that streamed in from all parts of the world. Police reports, tax returns, confidential memos—they had it all. If you wanted to know what so-and-so paid on his November electric bill three years ago, they could call it up with just a few keystrokes. Need to know when the mayor last had the oil checked on his car? It was there. Data had it. They were to be honored and feared.

At least, that's how Brewster saw his job. Who needed political power or position when he had information? The keeper of the secrets would win in the end—and he had them all right here at his fingertips. He was manager of the evening shift.

Maggie, his assistant, popped up over the wall of her cubicle next to his. "A 971 just came in."

"So?" Brewster said. He was sitting with his feet up on his desk, twirling a pencil in his fingers. "Give it to Alex."

"I thought you'd be interested in this one," she said.

"Why?"

"It's not your usual bad-check writer or late-on-alimony payments. Take a look."

He sighed and leaned forward to his keyboard. With a rapid-fire sound, he keyed in the report. It told him that at 7:33 P.M., Howard Thomas Beck had used his credit card at Hank's Place in Hopewell. From that point, Brewster could have gone in any direction—a complete history of Hank's Place, its owners, its yearly grosses, how much food and beverage it had purchased in the past day; nothing was withheld. But Beck's name was flashing, an alert that something was fishy about the man.

"See?" Maggie said. She had moved around the cubicle wall and stood behind his right shoulder. He could smell her perfume and the starch she had used that afternoon on her lab coat. The sound of her breathing excited him. He wished he'd been given an enclosed office.

He zeroed in on Beck and let the information pour forth. "OK, Howard T. Beck, what have you been up to?"

Maggie pointed to the screen. "There."

Beyond Beck's life history, description, photos, and pertinent government numbers, the screen said that he'd been wanted for questioning regarding the First National Investment Company bankruptcy; specifically, there had been allegations of embezzlement, misuse of funds, fraud, et cetera. Beck had disappeared from their monitoring six weeks ago.

"Interesting," Brewster said. Highlighting Hopewell for a moment, Brewster pinpointed it on a detailed map and saw that it was a tiny village in an obscure mountain region near the northern border.

"I wonder what Beck's doing in a tiny town like Hopewell," Maggie mused.

"A tiny town like Hopewell, so near the border." Brewster said with an insipid smile. "We better notify the boys downstairs."

He returned to the main screen about Beck and began a more detailed review of the man. Within an hour, he knew more about Beck's history than Beck probably did. He then clicked over to a collection of surveillance photographs. This was the fun area for Brewster. Here he might find some sordid pictures of his man in compromising positions. The government wasn't beyond blackmail. Neither was Brewster.

For the most part, though, the assemblage of high resolution color photos was boring—taken while Beck was being investigated for his shady investments. There was Beck sitting in a restaurant talking to an investor, Beck meeting in a hotel lobby with the CEO of a big corporation, Beck shaking hands with a local politician, Beck wheeling and dealing, Beck trying to be discreet in sunglasses while negotiating with some other unsuspecting clown in a parking lot. The faces and names of all Beck's contacts popped up for further cross-referencing if Brewster felt so inclined. He didn't. He forwarded to the last photo they had of Beck. He was standing in a crowded thoroughfare talking to a man with a mustache. The man's name flashed: Ben Greene.

Maggie returned with a cup of coffee for Brewster. "Well, Detective? Have you found anything interesting?"

"Maybe," he said and viewed the report about Mr. Greene. Apparently the significance of Ben Greene was that he was a Christian insurrectionist who'd recently been arrested and was later found hanging in his cell after an extensive interrogation by the head of Special Forces, Captain Slater.

"What's this?" Maggie asked, leaning forward again so her face was near his. She was teasing him, he knew.

"Tell me something. Why would an embezzler like Beck have secret meetings with a Christian like Greene?"

Maggie shrugged. "I haven't a clue."

"Forget the regular routine," Brewster said. "We should get this report directly to Captain Slater."

It was nearly nine o'clock.

❋

As the night wore on, Beck learned that Hank's Place was where the village's old sour-faced drinkers gathered, while Hank's 2 was a dance hall for younger and more energetic drinkers. Tonight, however, there wouldn't be too many people in either.

"It's a blizzard out there," one old local announced when he came in. "Nobody'll be going anywhere for a while."

Beck's hope that the drinking would keep his mind focused on his options was misguided. He kept slipping from what he needed to do to what he'd already done. His conscience wouldn't be kept at bay. He found himself wallowing in self-pity, a back door to the conscience. He fought the feelings with as much effect as a single man holding the door against an invading army. Why shouldn't he feel sorry for himself? He wasn't like the rest of them at the church. Suffering was an ugly and cruel thing to be avoided at all costs, not embraced for some bizarre redemption or a mythical crown. Let the saints and the martyrs suffer. He was neither.

He thought of the boy. No doubt the martyrs at the church thought Tim's death was in some way his fault. If he had taken food back to share, Tim wouldn't have eaten from the cans in the basement. That's what they would say. But how could they be so sure? He didn't know much about botulism, but he knew enough to argue that it couldn't have come on so fast unless the boy had been eating from the cans for days. So it wasn't his fault. They had no right to think that it was. Since when was he responsible to them—to anybody other than himself—anyway?

The thumping of the jukebox's bass pounded in his ears, and he wished it would stop. "Can you turn that thing down?" he slurred at the bartender.

"Turn *what* down?" baldy asked.

"The jukebox."

"It isn't on, you moron," he said. The two other men at the bar laughed; the old man's was a high cackle.

Beck slumped over his drink and followed the scars in the counter with his finger. Where would the road take him now? Where could he go? He was a man without a community. He couldn't go back to the city; they'd catch him quickly if he did. Where did he belong? Nowhere. He was disenfranchised, a true alien in his own country. Regret welled up in him like a backed-up sewer. He had weighed his options carefully and made his choices. But now he suspected that they hadn't been the right ones. Maybe he should have made a deal with the lawyers and trusted his luck. If everything had hit just right, he would have done some community service for a while. But what if things hadn't hit exactly right? He couldn't bear the thought of prison. Not even for a couple of years. He had had to escape. But how? By then they had revoked his traveling pass. He had no way out of the city.

He remembered it clearly now. Not even the drink could dull the memory of that night when he had stumbled into the alley and seen the tiny group slip into the doorway. He had thought it was an illegal bar, the kind with potent drinks, not the watered-down stuff they served in joints like Hank's or even The Inn. He had followed them in and had been amazed to find himself in a secret gathering of Christians. It had been a worship service played out with softly glowing candles, a whispered liturgy, and tearful prayers. Why they hadn't suspected him or raised an alarm at his presence he didn't know. They had welcomed him, in fact, and when he had heard them speak of the Underground, his mind had weaved a plan for escape. He had enough Christianity in his background to say the right words and fake the prayers. All he had to do was deceive them long enough to get away.

His conscience had pricked him even then. He had been used to fighting in a wolf's lair where sticking it to your neighbor, lying to get ahead, deceiving your own mother to line your pocket was standard fare. Doing it to these sheep was a different matter. He hadn't been so severed from his conscience that he didn't feel guilty . . . for a while. But a conscience ignored is a conscience controlled. He had mastered the feelings, considered his options, and embarked on yet another deal with his god. After all, his god had been made in his own image and liked to make deals just like he did. With a wink and a handshake, he and his god plotted together. Howard was certain that he could succeed in his plan.

His lawyers had stalled the legal system long enough for him to wire what was left of his money across the border and secure his place on the next truck out. It was so easy. Yes, he had disliked the squalor of their meeting place, the indignity of hiding in a stinking truck with people who gave every appearance of being Christians because they had nothing else to do with their lives, but it had served his purpose. They got him out of the city.

The jukebox continued to thump in his head as he finished his drink. He hit the glass hard against the counter and wiped his mouth. Leaning heavily on his propped-up fist, he fiddled with the glass with his free hand, and some brandy spilled out.

The glass was filled up again. Hadn't he just finished it? He didn't question the blessing, but simply took another sip. The taste went sour in his mouth. His enjoyment of it was gone. The bartender was probably giving him the bad stuff.

That was the problem with life, wasn't it? No matter what he did, he wound up with the bad stuff. He had married a beautiful woman—Louise—who turned into a wrinkled, sickly hag. He had made shrewd business investments that brought him accusations of embezzlement. He had made a deal with his god, and his god had gone back on his word. He was supposed to make it across the border, not get stranded at the church. He was supposed to travel with reasonable comfort, not wind up hungry and cold.

Well, what else was he supposed to do except check his options? Going to the farmer for food had made good sense. Sam and Peter and the rest were being ridiculous in believing that it would all work out, that God would take care of them. He hadn't, had he? He'd double-crossed Howard, and he would double-cross them eventually. After all, what kind of God would let the boy die like that? Even Howard wouldn't have been so heartless. Or would he?

He looked with unfixed eyes across the counter and saw the old man still there. He was the spitting image of Luke now. A chill shot up and down his spine. It *was* Luke. "How did you get here?" Howard demanded to know.

"What?"

"How did you get down from the church? Did you follow me?"

"I don't know what you're talking about," the old man answered.

Howard was suddenly aware that all the people gathered around the bar turned to look at him. He wondered how it got so crowded when the weather was so bad. There were only a couple of them there a minute ago. He turned his gaze to see who his new drinking companions were. A woman whose face was in a half-shadow peered at him self-consciously. It was his dead wife, Louise. She smiled at him in that crooked way he once found so odd. Next to her sat Tim, his face white, his eyes encased in dark circles. Next to Tim was Peter in a blood-soaked shirt. Sam held a pen made of a skeleton's finger. Ruth, Mary, and Amy were adorned in linked dandelions, and even Ben, the truck driver, was there dressed in an apron made of a square of sod. They were all clearly dead and unhappy to be so.

"What do you want?"

The bartender leaned next to him, his teeth green and his breath smelling of old earth. "What kind of God kills children? The kind of god made in *your* image," he said.

Howard refused to yield to this bizarre incarnation. "We had a deal."

"Your deal was with the wrong god," Sam said. "My God keeps his promises. Your god is just like you—a liar and a thief."

Howard tried to stand to leave, but his legs were immovable.

Louise said sweetly, "You are your god, my love. You can't pretend you didn't know it." He was not aware that she had moved from her stool, but suddenly she was sitting next to him, her decaying face next to his. "Daddy always said you were a confused man. You confused strength with weakness, courage with cowardice. Every time you said you were being practical, I knew you were trying to take the easy way out. But I loved you for it. I really did. I thought your weakness was a virtue."

"No. You loved me for my strength. You thought I was clever."

"Oh, Howard," she said sadly.

"Do you have any idea how many people you hurt with your cowardice?" Peter asked.

"You're a walking curse. Everything you touch is cursed," Amy said.

"You bear the mark of Cain," the rest of them said like a Greek chorus.

"You're a condemned man, Howard," the bartender added pleasantly.

"I was being practical," Howard moped. "It's not my fault how it worked out."

Tim pointed at him. "It's your fault. It's all your fault."

"It's all your fault," the entire bar chanted along over and over again.

He opened his eyes without realizing they had been closed. A cracked ceiling was the first thing he saw. He traced it over and down to the peeling wallpaper that looked as if someone had pulled the corners away to see what was underneath. Light streamed through the floral pattern on the loosely hung, threadbare curtains. The place smelled of moldy linen. He was lying on a bed.

Where was he? He swung his legs off the sinking mattress— he was still fully dressed—and battled a wave of nausea. He was in a rough way. How did he get here? On shaky legs, he crossed to the window and peeked out. Frost edged its way around the glass, intensifying the brightness of the snow on the street below and the roof directly across, the tin roof of Hank's 2. Had he drunk so much that they had to carry him up and put him to bed? He supposed so. The last thing he remembered was encountering an entourage of ghouls at the bar. What an awful dream. The feelings it conjured hung on him like the taste of brandy and vomit. He'd been sick in more ways than one.

Collapsing on the bed again, he tried to muster the will to ward off his feelings of guilt. He needed the strength to set things right again, to reestablish his normal, practical perspective. But he didn't have strength, did he? How could he? He was a coward. That much he could no longer deny. How could he ever use the word *practical* again without hearing Louise's words? *You're a weak man. You're a coward.* It's what she had said to him the night before she died. She had begged to be taken off her medication, not to ease her pain but to ease his inconvenience. And he had accepted her offer. She was no longer practical, and he hadn't had the strength to stay with her.

The reality poured over him like hot tar, and he spun over on the mattress just quickly enough to vomit in the trash can nearby.

He had just finished and rolled back onto his back when someone pounded on the door. "What do you want?" Beck called out miserably.

The pounding continued. His annoyance turned to dread as he realized that whoever it was wasn't pounding on the door as much as kicking at it. He sat up, not sure of what to do. "Who is it? I can open the door if you'll give me a second."

It was too late. The door wrenched from the lock, splintered the jam, and then flew open. "What's the matter with you?" Beck cried out as two men marched into the room with their guns drawn.

"Howard Beck?" a man with red hair asked.

"Yes! What do you want?"

The red-haired man glanced at his partner, a tall dark-haired and congenial-looking fellow. A hint of a smile worked across his lips. He holstered his gun. "We're going to have a little chat."

CHAPTER 29

COMFORT *is the enemy of faith,* Smith thought with chagrin as he poked at the roaring fire. He sat back, nestling into a thick-cushioned wing chair, and surveyed the small, cozy cabin. It glowed red and orange from the fire. The single window shone like a white easel, the high snowdrift just outside its strokes of paint. On one wall, nearest the makeshift kitchen, the shelves were thoroughly stocked with boxes of dry goods—cereal, rice, flour, sugar, anything that wouldn't spoil—and canned fruits, vegetables, soups, jams, milk, and biscuits. It was like an old-fashioned grocery store. On another wall were entertainments: books, music, and films. The third wall was covered with framed paintings by the masters (copies, of course). The fourth wall held the large oak door and window. Whoever had chosen this cabin and stocked it did an excellent job. If Smith were allowed to choose his heaven, this would be it. He had everything he needed—and no responsibility. There wasn't a soul to be found for miles. Alone, he relished the chance to think clearly.

The cabin was one of only four structures in a deserted mining camp—apart from the tin huts that littered the mountainside. There was a large square building that had once been a hotel or a brothel, he wasn't sure which. A small wooden shack served as the general store. Next to that was the post and telegraph office. Then, away from the rest like a shunned runt, this cabin sat. It was the last stop on the Underground Railroad before reaching the border. Smith had arrived here from the church—when was it? Yesterday? The day before? He'd lost track. A restful abode defied the movement of time. He would stay here awhile. There was no reason to rush for the border when the accommodations here were so good.

He had also harbored a hope that the refugees he'd left behind might suddenly show up. It was a contradiction, he knew, and he selfishly kept it hidden in the recesses of his mind, never actually giving it form in words. He wanted to be let off the hook for refusing to help them. Their appearance would give him that much. But when the snow shook from the sky in a blizzard, he tucked the hope further away, knowing that they'd never make it until things thawed out.

He sipped his coffee, the steam curling around his nose, and picked up the book of poetry he'd pulled from the shelf. He resumed his reading with "Uncertain Light," a poem in German by someone named J. C. v. Zedlitz. Smith had studied German in college and read aloud:

> *Without wood or path, man scales the rocks, a*
>   *wanderer:*
> *Rushing streams, surging rivers, windswept woods,*
>   *nothing halts his stride!*
> *The darkly massing clouds billow over his head;*
> *Rolling thunder, streaming rain, a starless night,*
>   *nothing halts his stride!*
> *At last, at last, a distant light glimmers!*
> *Is it a will-o'-the-wisp, is it a star?*
> *Ha! how friendly is its gleam; how it entices and*
>   *beckons me!*

The wanderer hastens swiftly through the night, drawn
towards the light.
Is it fire or the light of dawn?
Is it love, is it death?

He felt a stab of sadness. Not that the poem had immediate relevance, but it reminded him that he once thought he had a poet's heart like this. There had been a time when the world seemed colorful and alive; his head had been filled with visions of beauty and a longing for words to describe them. It had been so long ago, long before the world turned black and white with heavy black shadows and thick grays and empty white pages. His poet's heart had been stolen and replaced with a machine that pumped blood into his being. It was a functional organ that allowed him to do his work—no, *God's work.*

Why did it seem as if those who responded to God's call often found themselves lost in a colorless world? Was it the realization that beauty was an illusion, the top of the rock that merely disguised the earth, worms, and decay underneath? God's call got your hands dirty; it put you face-to-face with the ugliness of the world, its lack of peace, its futile happiness. But where did that leave the one who had answered the call? How was he expected to cope with visions of brutality day after day? Smith couldn't. It was unfair of God to expect him to. He saw that clearly now, like a man who sees the horror of war only after he's returned home to the comfort of his bed. The human capacity to adjust to the worst possible conditions was enormous. For years now he had been in a mode to survive; now he wanted to live. In this cabin he felt what he thought was the pull of life—in a full stomach, a warm fire, books of poetry. Perhaps he could immerse himself further in it once he crossed the border and could work with his hands again. Maybe his poet's heart would break through the machine.

He turned the pages of the book and his eye caught a combination of words that drew him in. It was another German poem, by Paul Heyse:

> If you go over to the churchyard,
> you will find a fresh grave;
> there they tearfully buried a dear heart.
> And if you ask what it died of, the gravestone gives no
>   answer;
> but the winds whisper,
> it loved too much.

He thought instantly of the church, how it had stood like a large tombstone on the mountainside. He had an image—call it a vision—of the people he'd left behind buried there alive. He saw the boy encased in dirt and the others walking like the living dead. He looked down at the book of poetry and flung it away, as if it had accused him of something. It had: of deserting his true love.

Standing up, he scowled at the fire and then paced angrily around the small room. The snow still fell outside, carried by a wind that howled and whistled down the chimney of the potbelly stove in the corner. He didn't want peace—his expectations weren't that high—but he might at least be allowed to enjoy some quiet. How could he silence the voice that spoke deep within? It wasn't even his voice. It was Sam's.

The mountain was the belly of the whale. That's what the voice said repeatedly.

"God, if you have something to say to me, say it directly," Smith said. "Let's stop playing around."

The fire spat and sparked at him indignantly, as if to pour

scorn on his request. It was an act of pride, he recognized. Making demands of God showed his attitude for what it was. Giving up was never an act of humility. It was useless to pretend otherwise. The source of his despair was pure selfishness: He'd had enough and wanted out. There was nothing noble or sacrificial about that. Where was the mortification in abandoning those strangers back at the church? Where was faith to be found in this cozy little cabin?

Comfort is the enemy of faith. It was his father who used to say that. Our faith is never so neutralized as when it is withdrawn from the hard edge of life.

But why? Why? Smith continued to pace, his hands knotting and unknotting in front of him. Why did it have to be this way?

It was an unanswerable question. That was the trick he'd taught himself over the past few weeks: keep the questions so abstract that they couldn't be answered. A vague notion went a long way in helping to avoid hard answers because hard answers went hand in hand with taking action, and taking action created responsibilities, and responsibilities were the things he wanted most to avoid.

So there was a truth to chew on. Even if God spoke to him directly, he wouldn't want to hear what God had to say. The questions would be too direct. The answers would be too hard.

He returned to the wing chair and slumped into it. His whole line of thinking was spoiling the place. It was like trying to enjoy a meal with starving children watching from the windows.

Again, he saw an image of Tim encased in the earth. *They tearfully buried a dear heart.* What did it mean?

> *but the winds whisper,*
> *it loved too much.*

He scrubbed his hands over his face. That was the question: What did he love? What was he willing to die for? It had always been the Call. He loved the Call and was never afraid to die for it, though, in truth, he never believed he would have to. The Call made him feel secure, invincible. How could one be on a quest for God and not feel safe?

Was it coincidence that he decided to run away just when his work was becoming more difficult—less secure, less invincible? They'd had so many setbacks. The risks increased regularly. Betrayal lurked around every corner. He was never consciously afraid—his passion more than covered fear—but what had happened when the passion ran out? He had decided to escape.

What was it he loved? Perhaps he loved the Call more than he loved God.

> The wanderer hastens . . . drawn towards the light.
> Is it fire or the light of dawn?
> Is it love, is it death?

A tree branch tapped at the window like a specter wanting an invitation to come in. For a second he thought that maybe *they'd* come. Smith watched the branch wave at him with a sense of disappointment. It wasn't them. It couldn't be. They were stuck where he was meant to be. But he had escaped—or tried to. Into the belly of the whale he went.

He reached for the Bible on the bookshelf. Even before his fingers touched the binding, the words leapt to his mind: *I can never escape from your spirit! I can never get away from your presence! If I go up to heaven, you are there; if I go down to the place of the dead, you are there. If I ride the wings of the morning, if I dwell by the farthest oceans, even there your hand will guide me, and your strength will support me.*

"God," Smith cried out, "why don't you just let me go? I'm not worth holding on to. I'm useless to you now, don't you see that? *I am driven away from your sight; how can I ever look upon your holy place again?"*

The branch banged frantically against the window, and the entire cabin shook as if it might be lifted from its foundations and thrown aside. Suddenly the door blew open, and the snow swirled in like searching spirits. Smith sprang from the chair and, with all his might, slammed the door shut. His heart raced as he fell back against the wall and slumped to the floor. The branch clawed at the window until the glass cracked and shattered, allowing the branch to poke inside. It pointed and shook at him like a long accusing finger.

He was afraid now, afraid that he had become addicted to his despair, that his heart could no longer be moved by the truth, by Scripture, by guilt, or by love. Worse than losing the passion of faith, he was afraid he'd lost the habit of faith. And he wept with tears that felt hot and thick—as thick as blood.

CHAPTER 30

When I was a young girl, I used to love playing in my grandfather's bedroom. It was a world unto itself with a big feather bed and knickknacks . . . oh, those knickknacks. He had so many personal trinkets and mementos . . . each one with a different story about his life. It was a treasure chest of memories, an escape to a different place and time.

As he got older he would say, "Rutherford—" which is what he used to call me because I think he wanted me to be a boy—"Rutherford, one day I'm going to die, but don't you be afraid or sad because death is just a doorway. Just like the doorway that leads into this bedroom.

He died peacefully in his sleep in that big feather bed of his. But they wouldn't let me in to see him. And after he was buried, they locked the door to his bedroom, and I never went in again.

That's what death is to me. A locked door. But one day I'll get through, and it'll be just like playing in my grandfather's bedroom again.

—Ruth, as quoted in *The Posthumous Papers of Samuel T. Johnson*

✳

ON the morning of their third day with Clay, Sam grabbed the bucket of melted snow and, under the scowling eye of Clay, passed it around for everyone to drink. They had all huddled to sleep around the stove in the kitchen, and the uncontrollable heat—alternating between stifling and nonexistent—dried out their throats. He pondered them all sadly and wondered how they had endured the past couple of days together, trapped by the snow, choked in a vacuum of anger, hunger, and despair. The small group's unified will had been broken. Each person's faith stood alone—quiet—left to the individual's watchful gaze. They had been cast adrift on a lifeboat and now looked at each other through the dark, sleepless eyes of people who suspected they wouldn't be rescued by any human effort.

Peter was dead. He'd been killed instantly by the blast from Clay's rifle and even now lay wrapped in tarps in the cellar; the snow was too deep and the ground too frozen to bury him. Ruth wept at first but then seemed to call on an inner strength that Sam couldn't help but covet. Amy and Mary were inconsolable. Luke prayed silently through moving lips.

Though Clay was obviously shaken by what he'd done, he was determined to hold them all hostage in the hope that the snow would stop and he could take them to the police for the reward. Bobby seemed dazed by Peter's death and caught between his revulsion of what his friend had done and his fear that it might happen again if he didn't play mediator.

Meanwhile, the snow piled up around the church like layers of blankets sealing them in. If the group had felt claustrophobic before, it was intensified tenfold now. Their captors escorted them to the toilet, berated them for not having any food left, and occasionally knocked them around when Clay had had too much to drink from a supply of whiskey he'd kept in the back of his Jeep.

Clay and Bobby took shifts watching their captives and sleeping, but the result was that neither of them looked rested.

As Clay took a drink, Luke said, "Jesus said to drink from the well that ends all thirst."

"Shut up," Clay growled. "Three days. Three *lousy* days, and I'm sick of this. When it isn't snowing, the wind is blowing, and when the wind isn't blowing, it's too dark to travel. I never thought I'd see the day when my stomach would feel like this."

Sam was the last to drink from the bucket and felt as if they'd just taken Communion together. *The body and blood of our Lord Jesus Christ keep you in everlasting life.* But it was only water, and they had no bread.

This is life as it really is, he very nearly said out loud. Sam scanned the emaciated group and considered that maybe he'd had it all wrong. His experience until now had been based on a false premise—that life was meant to be peaceful and safe. It was what he'd worked toward for years in his career with that mistress of his, Academia. That was his mistake. Peace and safety were illusions in this world. *This* was real life, this huddled group, this church. Here was a microcosm of the living world; here was the struggle to know faith, to keep hold amidst suffering, to see death face-to-face and know what it is to live. God cannot meet man in comfort because man won't answer him there. God has to meet man at that place where everything has been stripped away, where life is raw and sweaty, where the sinews are stretched and the blood runs dark red. God does not rest on cushions but on a cross. Life is found only there. Once that is found, then maybe peace will follow.

"Mind if I go get my journal from the sanctuary?" Sam asked, wanting to write down his thoughts.

"Yes, I mind," Clay replied.

Bobby, who'd gone off to the bathroom, returned with a strangely animated look on his face. "Clay, it's stopped snowing. It looks like the sky's clearing. It'll be hard, but I think we can make it back to your farm!"

Clay leapt to his feet and tried to look out the window in the back door. The drift obscured any possible view.

"The front door," Bobby said. "Go look."

Clay marched off to the sanctuary to see for himself.

Everyone looked at Bobby expectantly. "Are we really going with you?" Amy asked.

"I guess."

"Can we take care of Peter's body before we leave?" asked Ruth.

Bobby frowned. It was the first time anyone had mentioned Peter for quite a while. "I don't see why not. If Clay makes a fuss, well, I'll . . ." He looked away from them, as if he were suddenly ashamed. He spoke gently. "I'm sorry about what Clay did. He's never done anything like that before. I know it's hard for you to believe, but it's true."

Sam glanced uncomfortably at Ruth. Her expression was sadly compassionate, and he wondered if it was another kind of grace at work in her life that allowed her to forgive something so brutal. If so, he didn't have it. He imagined that Bobby had been an accessory to Clay's violence for years—and had done nothing to stop it.

Bobby continued, speaking directly to Ruth. "I know you were his kin, and I'm really sorry. If I thought there was something I could do—"

"Let us go," Ruth said.

Clay was back before Bobby could answer her. Clay's wan

face was oddly alight with a newfound cheer, as if someone had painted a smile on a death mask. "Let's get 'em together, Bobby. We'll take 'em to my place, then make our way to the village from there. Looks like we'll get our reward after all."

Bobby looked as if he might challenge Clay. His expression betrayed his inner turmoil about whether or not to insist on letting the hostages go. But he said nothing. Sam knew that such an act of intervention would have to come from a strength that Bobby didn't have.

Slowly, like mourners in a funeral march, they made their way from the kitchen to the sanctuary, where they picked through their belongings and made ready for the long walk to Clay's farm.

Sam was just about to walk over to the table to retrieve his journal when a new voice rang through the sanctuary. "Going somewhere?" it asked.

Everyone jumped in surprise, and Clay and Bobby immediately swung around with their guns poised to fire. But the voice had echoed from no single place, and they couldn't pinpoint where it had come from.

One of the front doors creaked open, and everyone spun to look, but no one was there. A sliver of light poured in with the crisp morning air. The voice then came from behind them. "It's not the best of days for a walk." The voice's owner stepped out of a shadowed pocket near the choir loft.

"Smith!" Amy exclaimed.

Smith didn't respond; it was as if he didn't see them. His eyes were fixed on Clay. "Why don't you put your toy away before you do any more damage?"

Clay stiffened, still shocked. "Who are you?"

"The name's Smith. Sorry we don't have time to chat, but we have to leave before it starts snowing again." He turned to the rest of the group with complete disregard for Clay or Bobby. "Get your things together."

No one moved. Clay and Bobby were dumbfounded by the nerve of this stranger.

"We don't have time to waste. Sam, tell everyone to get moving!"

Sam looked from Smith to Clay and back again. "I would, but I'm afraid Clarisse will start shooting her mouth off again."

Smith sounded exasperated. "Just move!"

With watchful eyes on Clay, they began to put on their coats.

Their action snapped Clay out of his stupor, and he stepped closer with his gun raised. "Now hold on just a minute. I don't mean to interrupt your big heroic entrance, but these folks are coming with me. As a matter of fact, you're coming with me, too."

Smith smiled indulgently. "Clay, why don't you and Bobby get home? Your daddy hasn't seen you in a couple of days, and he's worried."

"I don't know you from a hole in the ground!" Clay gripped the rifle more firmly. "Now get on over and join the rest of these folks. We're going back to my farm, getting the truck, and taking a ride down to the village. Got it?"

"But if we wait much longer, some of the people from the village are going to meet us here. I'd like to avoid that if at all possible," Smith said in a voice so calm that Sam found it almost maniacal.

"You think you're tough, don't you?" Clay sneered.

"Clay—"

"Stop calling me that!" Clay screamed at Smith. "I don't know you!"

"Maybe we should wait outside until you decide what you want to do," Sam said.

Clay jerked the rifle at them as if he were spraying them with a hose. "Nobody move. I swear I'll start shooting. You know what happened to that other smart mouth."

"Give me the rifle," Smith said, holding out his hand like a father to a disobedient son. "Come on."

Smith's eyes seemed to burn into Clay and for a moment's hesitation, Clay seemed transfixed by them. Then he said in a low growl, "Buddy, you've got five seconds to get over with the rest of them. That's all I'm giving you." He lifted the rifle and placed its butt against his shoulder. It was pointed at Smith's face. "One . . ."

Smith moved toward Clay, his hand still outstretched. Sam clenched his fists. He had stood by helplessly when Peter got shot, but this time he was ready to throw himself at Clay, come whatever.

"Get back, mister. He's not bluffing," Bobby said.

"Two . . ."

Mary began to weep. "No, please not again!" The air didn't move, as if the entire church were holding its breath.

"Three . . ."

"Clay, don't do it. I can't handle this," Bobby cried out. "I give up. See? It's not worth it."

Smith said, "Clay—"

"Four . . ."

Sam readied himself to lunge, but Bobby stepped in the way, his pistol held high—at Clay. "Clay, stop! I'll shoot you, man. I swear I will. Now put the gun down, and let's get out of here."

Clay glanced at Bobby out of the corner of his eye. "Don't be stupid."

"I mean it," Bobby said, the pistol trembling and sweat

beading on his flushed face. "I'll shoot you before I let you kill anybody else. Understand? I'm done with this!"

The three-way confrontation was silent for a moment. Sam had no idea what would happen next.

"Are you gonna move or what?" Clay shouted at Smith, but his tone was less convincing.

Smith shook his head. "It's finished, Clay. Listen to Bobby. Get out of here."

Bobby cocked his pistol. "Let's go."

"I'll never forgive you for this, Bobby," Clay said softly as he lowered his rifle. Without another word he spun on his heels and marched out of the church. He pushed both doors open wide as he went, the white light flooding in with waves of snow.

Bobby exhaled loudly and stiffly dropped his arms as if the muscles might have stayed in that position forever. He uncocked the pistol and turned to the group, his eyes resting on each face in turn.

"Well done, Bobby," Sam said.

Bobby moved his mouth as if his courage had left a bitter taste there. He simply nodded to them silently and followed Clay out. He pulled the doors closed behind him.

Visible relief swept through the group. Mary buried her head in Ruth's shoulder. Amy slumped to the ground. And Luke, who had been staring at the scene mutely, said, "Not at their hands . . ." Sam leaned against his table, the adrenaline still surging through his body, his head throbbing. It didn't seem possible that they'd reached the end of it.

"Take only what you can carry," Smith suddenly shouted, startling them all. "Hurry."

They moved sluggishly at first, then more quickly as the reason to move filled them with hope. Once again this man, this stranger, had appeared. This time it looked as if he might really lead them to the promised land.

"This is going to be a long and difficult journey. I hope you're up to it," Smith announced.

"Anything to get out of here," Amy said.

Sam felt a twinge of doubt. He couldn't believe they were really going to leave. Somewhere in the last three days he'd resigned himself to the idea that they would never get out of the church—not through Clay or Bobby, and not through Smith. He grabbed his knapsack and checked to see what he was missing.

Smith was at his elbow and said softly, "I saw Peter's body in the basement. We don't have time to take care of it. I'm sorry. Where's Howard?"

"Gone."

"And Timothy?"

"He died. Food poisoning."

Smith nodded as if he knew it was an inevitability.

"I have a lot of questions for you," Sam said.

"I'm sure you do," Smith replied. "But don't get your hopes up that I have any answers."

Coats were pulled on, knapsacks hoisted, final necessities taken care of, and they were ready to leave.

"Let's go," Smith said.

They hesitated, surveying the sanctuary one last time. Sam wondered if other fugitives and hostages developed a twisted affection for their places of captivity like he had for this church. It seemed as if it had been all he ever knew. His time at the school, his apartment, all the other components of his previous life had been washed away by the baptism of suffering he'd experienced here. It was as if he had died at home, been buried in this church, and would now walk through the front doors into a light-filled new beginning—death leading to a new life.

"Let us pray for guidance and strength!" Luke called out in a loud voice that sounded like he was speaking to a large group. Sam looked to see if others had joined them. Perhaps others had; perhaps they'd been there all along. The sanctuary might be filled with a congregation only Luke could see. The communion of the saints.

Smith conceded. "All right."

They bowed their heads.

Luke raised his hands. "Father, we thank you for your love and the peace you offer us through Jesus Christ, your Son. . . ."

There was a sound, barely discernible to Sam's ear but niggling there like a gnat. It was low and mechanical.

"We thank you for this means of escape that comes to us even now," Luke continued.

Sam peeked up and saw that Smith was already looking around, tilting his head like a dog, trying to get a fix on the noise. One by one, Amy, Ruth, and Mary also lifted their heads. Luke was the only one who seemed oblivious to what was happening. "Be with us in the journey you're about to set us upon. . . ."

"We may be too late," Sam whispered and knew it was true. Somehow it had always been true.

The sound, unmistakable now in the way it whipped the air in short, low blasts, shook the church. The snow blew and billowed outside. A different sound faded in, too—a buzzing as if someone had started a chain saw in the graveyard. But it wasn't a single chain saw. A chorus surrounded the church. It grew in Sam's ears as fear grew in his chest.

No one ran or moved, though Sam was certain that every fiber in their beings told them to run. They merely stood there, mesmerized by the cacophony of sound that penetrated the accustomed silence. It was like a brass band suddenly tuning up in a mortuary.

The front doors flew open, and a stark shadow framed itself in the doorway. It was spectral and otherworldly as the light exploded furiously around it. Other shadows appeared, and the group shielded their eyes to see who or what it was.

The shadow stepped in and became a man—tall, lean, redheaded, with catlike eyes and a thin, sharp mouth. "I am Captain Slater with the Committee's Special Forces. You are all under arrest."

CHAPTER 31

VARIOUS men dressed in the government's distinct brown uniforms burst through every doorway and took position around the group, guns held securely. Instinctively, the group huddled together like frightened sheep. Sam noticed that Smith had positioned himself in the center, his head bowed down and turned away. Slater paraded ceremoniously before them and spoke as if he were admiring his personal trophies. "This is a fine catch."

"What's this all about? What's the meaning of bursting in here like this?" Sam asked, putting on confidence he didn't feel. He had tried this same indignation with Clay and Bobby. It hadn't worked then either.

"Be patient," Slater said.

Another man appeared in the doorway; he was in plain clothes, taller than Slater, and had a pleasant face and curly hair.

"Ah, Williams!" Slater called out as if he were seeing his assistant for the first time in ages. "Bring our friend in. No sense keeping him away from the rest of his family."

Williams nodded and signaled someone out of sight. Howard Beck was pushed into view like a child who wasn't quite ready for his part in the school play. Williams took Beck's arm firmly and pointed him toward the group. Howard, hands clasped in front, walked slowly toward them, his head hung low, his eyes avoiding theirs. He had the stricken look of someone who had been in a dungeon—dark eyes and an expression fixed with pain. They had tortured him, Sam knew and hoped optimistically that that was the only reason Howard led them to the church.

"Thank you for all your help," Slater said to Howard. "We couldn't have done it without you."

"I didn't—," Howard started to say but changed his mind and fell silent.

"Howard," Amy said scornfully. "I should have known."

Slater circled the group, carefully eying each member. His cool gaze disturbed Sam. His expression held the smug satisfaction of a successful hunter inspecting his prey, taking in every detail, ready to put a few more notches in a belt already full of dead men's dreams. He paused when he saw Luke, his look changing to a question mark. "Haven't I seen you somewhere before?"

Luke stared back at him without a hint of recognition.

Slater dismissed the moment, then announced, "I'm here because you're accused of being insurrectionists. I doubt you'll deny it, and I'm hoping that through you, I'll be able to—"

Slater stopped midsentence. His eyes lit up over his surprised, gaping mouth. "It isn't possible. I couldn't be so lucky." He pushed past Sam, Amy, and Luke to face Smith. He smiled cruelly. "Finally."

Smith looked back at him indifferently.

"I didn't expect to find you here," Slater said happily, as if welcoming an old friend. He turned to Howard. "You lied to us, Mr. Beck."

"I didn't!" Howard cried out defensively "He left. I told you!"

All eyes went to Smith, and Sam felt the significance of the moment. Truth should always be accompanied by a feeling of significance, he thought, and this truth was about to change them.

Mary asked, "Is he someone important?"

Slater laughed and turned to Williams. "Did you hear that?"

Williams smiled politely.

Slater leaned closer to his assistant. "Signal the helicopters to get some Jeeps up here as soon as they can get the roads cleared. The snowmobiles will be useless. Until then, I'll have to do everything here. I don't want to take any chances."

Williams nodded and left.

"What are you going to do with us?" Ruth asked.

"Administer a little justice," Slater replied.

"Justice? Here?" Sam asked. "You mean you're not taking us back for a trial?"

Slater said impatiently, "The trial will take place here."

"But you can't!" Ruth insisted.

"I can, and I will." Slater scowled, then pointed at Smith. "I can't take the chance of losing this man. I lost him once, and I won't lose him again."

"Why? What makes him so special?" Ruth asked for all of them.

Slater rolled his eyes. "You really don't know?" Then he asked Smith, "You didn't do any magic tricks to impress these people? No miracles? No prophecies out of a hat?"

Smith stared him down as a reply.

"Ah, just like the Master before Pilate." To the group Slater said, "I'm surprised you don't know who you've had in your midst. To have been so honored and you didn't realize it."

He paused dramatically for effect, then gestured grandly to Smith. "Meet Elijah."

Everyone but Sam turned to Smith with a dumbfounded look. Sam had already guessed it the night Smith left. Who but Elijah or Moses could have been so bowed under the weight of lives other than his own? But the revelation wasn't lost on him now. It reinforced his growing belief that in this play he and the rest were supporting characters now relegated to mere spectators. A battle was coming between the titans, and mere mortals like Sam wouldn't decide its outcome one way or another. It struck him that this was true of life itself. The illusion of control was maintained only by fools and imbeciles.

"God have mercy," Ruth said.

Smith kept his eyes on Slater without expression.

Slater rubbed his hands together briskly, like a man about to set upon a meal. "Let's get this over with. There are too many of you roaches for me to remain idle. We got Moses, you know," Slater said to Smith. "He said he didn't know what had become of you. I didn't believe him, but now—well, it's obvious he was telling the truth. It's a shame, because he died for it."

Smith tensed but didn't move or say anything.

Again the cruel, taunting smile flashed as Slater asked, "What happened, Elijah? Did the responsibility of so many souls become too much for you? Maybe you thought you'd take a little vacation from it all? Or maybe the cowardice that is inherent in your faith overwhelmed you, and you decided to run away."

Smith shook his head. "You're wasting your time, Slater. Remember? I know your psychological games."

Slater turned on the whole group and said firmly, "Here's the deal, plain and simple: Renounce your faith, and I'll let you go."

"You're a liar," Smith said.

Slater continued, "Keep your faith and lose your lives."

"You call that a deal?" Sam asked.

"It's the best you're going to get," Slater answered, then smiled again. "It should be easy for you. I know you Christians, and you love this—all of it. From the beginning you have thrived on being persecuted, whether real or imagined. You enjoy running and hiding and having your secret meetings. You crave the opportunity to suffer for your Master. Oh, the honor of it all. Nothing unifies you people more than to be attacked and pursued. If my superiors would listen to me, there'd be no persecution. I'd let you have whatever you want so you'd get fat, lazy, and complacent. You'd fight among yourselves and devour your own beliefs. You're your own worst enemies when you aren't hunted. But my superiors won't listen. They command me to offer you a choice." He said this last part with a deep, dejected sigh.

"Sorry to cause you such inconvenience," Smith said.

Slater gazed at him with undisguised loathing. "I've given you the offer. It's up to you. I'll leave you to give it some thought." He motioned to an officer who obediently stepped forward. "Watch them."

The officer saluted, and Slater walked out, his long coat flying behind him like the robes of the Grim Reaper.

The fugitives stood around like mourners at a funeral, an invisible casket before them. Smith remained in the center with his arms folded.

"The infamous Elijah. So it was you they were after," Howard said with a hint of his former self. No amount of torture could have snuffed it out.

"It appears so."

"I'm disappointed."

"You wouldn't be the first."

"They kept at me for three days. I couldn't figure out what

they wanted." He spread his hands in appeal to the group. "I held out as long as I could. I thought you'd be gone by now."

No one believed him. The unspoken suspicion was that he told Slater everything he knew at the first sign of pain.

"We tried to leave, but couldn't seem to get past the door. Timothy and Peter are the only ones who made it out," Sam said.

"Peter?" Howard asked. "Where did he go?"

"He's in the basement," Ruth said.

Howard's eyes grew wide. "How?"

"The son of the farmer shot him," Amy said venomously. "You remember, the farmer who gave *you* food. His son followed you back."

Howard slowly sat down as if someone had hit him in the stomach.

"Why did you come back?" Sam asked Smith.

"It seemed like a good idea at the time," he replied. Even now, he wasn't telling them anything.

"You're all Peter talked about," Amy said, her anger still seething. "You and Moses. He believed in you completely. It's a shame he didn't know that Smith the deserter was the same as Elijah the savior."

"Amy—," Sam entreated her.

"It's all right, Sam," Smith said, then turned to her directly. "Forgive me for not living up to your expectations. I'm sorry if I don't have long white hair, a beard, and a staff that brings lightning from heaven. I never claimed to be more than I am. If you put your faith in God and not in imaginary heroes, you wouldn't be so disappointed."

Amy held his stare for a moment, then turned away. "I'm sorry. I'm sorry for all of us," she said.

"My name *is* James Smith," he explained. "We chose biblical names for our work in the Underground. I spent years working with it until a few months ago. . . ." A strained silence followed as Smith stumbled for the words to continue. "I decided to give it up. I couldn't go on with the work. You were right, Sam. I was running away from more than I thought."

"We can't run and hide from God," Luke interjected.

"Will Slater really kill us?" Ruth asked.

"He's insane," Smith said. "He will if that's what he wants to do."

Howard looked up. "But it's *you* he wants. Maybe he'll let the rest of us go. Maybe we can make a deal. . . ."

"What kind of a deal, Howard?" Sam asked, annoyed.

"Smith in exchange for our freedom."

"Listen to yourself!" Ruth cried out, throwing her arms up.

"Well, he *is* responsible for putting us in this situation. The police wouldn't be here if they hadn't been looking for *him*. They don't really care about us. He should talk to them, make some sort of arrangement."

Sam grabbed Howard's arm. "Stop it, Howard. He wouldn't even be here if he hadn't come back to help us."

"And *we* wouldn't still be here if you hadn't been seen begging for food at the farmhouse," Amy piped in.

"And they wouldn't have known to come to the church if *you* hadn't led them," Ruth added.

Howard slumped back, visibly beaten by their accusations. "But I don't want to make this choice. I don't want to die," he said softly.

Ruth continued relentlessly. "None of us wants to die, Howard. But, in heaven's name, if we have to, then let's do it with dignity. Stop whining and cowering."

"Do not grieve as those who have no hope," Luke told them. "Our victory is in Jesus Christ and eternal life. We will die, yet we shall live again."

Howard put his hands over his ears. "No, I don't want to hear about that. I want to stay alive. We have to be able to make a deal!"

Howard had just spoken when Slater and Williams entered from the hallway. Slater smiled. "I'm truly impressed. This is the perfect hideout."

"Obviously not perfect," Sam said.

"Point taken," Slater said. "But it's remarkable nonetheless. Imagine a group of runaway Christians hiding in a church. It's so obvious that it's ingenious. You seem to have everything you need."

"Except power and food," Ruth said.

"Really? Williams, can we find them some sandwiches and drinks? There's no reason to prolong their discomfort."

Williams gestured to an officer nearby, making the suggestion a command.

"Each of you will be going to your separate rooms now," Slater declared. "I believe you'll be able to think more clearly about this matter of . . . life and death."

The officers routed them to the hallway like cows to the slaughterhouse.

Slater instructed the guards. "Don't let them talk to each other through the walls. I don't want any of their ridiculous camaraderie going on."

Back in the pastor's office, Sam pondered the darkness that rested like a scrim over his eyes. This had been his room for weeks, but now it felt as if it had been moved behind enemy lines. It felt unfamiliar to him, desecrated by Slater's corrupting presence. He didn't want to be here anymore; he didn't want to be anywhere else either. Whatever acts of violence had been committed in this place before seemed holy by comparison to what was about to happen.

Sam knelt to pray. He had once asked God for a miracle, an

escape. Now he asked for a different kind of miracle, a different kind of grace.

I'm going to die, he thought. And somehow in knowing the worst, he also knew peace.

CHAPTER 32

NOW it's just the two of us," Slater said.

"I'm thrilled."

Slater pulled a pistol from his shoulder holster and gestured to a chair. "Sit down, please."

Smith obliged him, then nodded at the pistol. "You don't really need that."

"The mind of a desperate man sometimes produces foolish actions," Slater said.

"I'm not desperate."

"You should be." Slater began a slow circle around Smith. "Jesus Christ is not returning in the nick of time to get you out of this."

"Don't be too sure about that."

Slater laughed and continued his stroll around the chair silently.

"What are you going to do, Slater?" Smith asked. "You have me. Why don't you let the rest go?"

"Not so fast. I have a better plan. You see, I've had a lot of time to think about this while chasing you all over the blasted country. You are Elijah—mover of mountains, man of miracles, leader of the Exodus—"

"Moses led the Exodus, not Elijah," Smith said.

Slater ignored the correction. "You and Moses were and are

the inspiration to Christians all over the country—Moses even more so now that he's dead. You Christians love your martyrs."

"What's your point?"

"It would do me little good to kill you since your death would fuel the fires of Christianity rather than quench them." Slater raised a finger, pleased with where his thoughts were going. "But if you openly, publicly denounced your faith—"

"Forget it."

"Not so quickly," Slater reproved him. "Consider your situation. You're a scrawny rebel trapped on this desolate mountain—and why? I know why. Because you got tired of all the heartache and the death, the constant drain of having lives depend upon your decisions. You gave up, thinking that one human being could only do so much and maybe, just maybe, your God would give you a break."

Smith was ready to argue with Slater but couldn't. It all rang true.

Slater leaned close, his voice a hissed whisper. "He's giving you a break *now*, my friend. Join me. Renounce your futile faith and call your people in. The State will take good care of them, even grant clemency, if they'll just go along with us. That doesn't sound unreasonable, does it?"

Smith didn't answer.

Slater waved his arms impatiently. "Blast it, man! Don't you see what I'm offering you? An opportunity to end the running and hiding for you and all your people. Isn't it worth a minor sacrifice on your part to do it?"

"Give it up, Slater," Smith said firmly. "It won't work."

Slater grinned, his sliver of lip stretching across his face. "You're a stubborn man. But I know your stubbornness. It has that self-righteous smell of a man who thinks he is forgiven and renewed. You ran from God but somehow, some way, you did something that you think redeems you. What was it? Was it because you came back to help the poor souls here in this church? That makes you feel strong." He chuckled. "I'm not surprised. You'd give up your life for your cause. But what about someone else's life?"

Smith looked up at him. "What are you talking about?"

"I'm adjusting the rules of our little game, Elijah. You agree to do what I say, or I'll kill your friends. One by one. It's your choice."

"You're insane," Smith said with disbelief, but knowing that Slater would do exactly what he said.

"Maybe I am." Slater called out, "Williams!"

Williams stepped in from the hallway.

"Bring in one of the women."

CHAPTER 33

RUTH sat motionless on her small cot, hands folded neatly on her lap, her mind turning her life over and over as if it were an old sympathy card. She inspected it, cherished it, regretted it. She'd had a full life—she knew that for sure—and her realm of experience covered everything she thought she would have wanted from it.

She had been born and raised with the good sense and godly faith a country girl needed to survive. When her father died, she had managed the farm and turned it into a profitable enterprise. Profitable enough that when it was sold, she made enough money to give her mother a comfortable existence for the short remainder of her life. No one in her family seemed to live past the age of fifty. Her father had had a stroke at forty-eight. Her mother had died two days short of her fifty-first birthday. The death certificate said it was from "unknown causes." Ruth was forty-nine.

She had had two children. The small boy she had named for her husband, Andrew. He had died of pneumonia when he was three. Ruth had been pregnant with her daughter when Andrew Sr. was crushed under a tractor. Her daughter, Sarah, must have sensed in the womb that her father was gone, for she declined the invitation to life and died at birth from complications.

Ruth had grieved a year for each child, living in the darkness of self-pity and black shrouds of resentment. She had been alone, isolated in the firm belief that no one could understand her feelings or pain. Friends and neighbors did their best—God bless them—but their words were only so many trite phrases and meaningless clichés. She was only twenty-five after all, and who could know what it was like to be so young and to have lost so much? That sort of tragedy was supposed to be reserved for older, more mature people who were equipped to handle it.

Yet, without realizing it until much later, those two years were for her a cocoon out of which she emerged a more mature person. For it was there that she found God. Not the God of her youth—a thunderous being of Sunday school miracles and genie-in-the-lamp prayers—but a real and living God of respect and love, compassion and chastisement, fear and power. He came to her in the darkness on a wintry night when she had been contemplating suicide. She had been asking herself, "Why should I live?" and he had said as clearly and audibly as someone standing next to her, "Because I live." He tore the mourning rags from her windows and let the day in. And she grasped life with a quiet determination and a newfound joy.

Peter had been born—her sister's son—and he was as her own. She had watched him grow as a boy, and when the persecution began, he had become a man. He had been the fulfillment of a promise God hadn't made but she believed in, a covenant for her life.

She had held Peter so close that one last time before they wrapped him in a tarp and took him to the cellar, hoping that his spirit would move through hers and touch it ever so briefly before making its way home. She was sure it had.

Someone knocked at the door gently and then opened it. The policeman called Williams stepped in.

Ruth smiled at him.

✸

"Look at her! What a fine figure of a woman," Slater exclaimed as Williams led her in.

"Mr. Smith?" Ruth asked quietly.

Slater strode with Williams toward the hallway. "I'll leave you alone for a moment to think about your future."

After they'd gone, Smith leapt to his feet and scoured the room like an animal looking for an escape.

"Mr. Smith, I've made up my mind," Ruth said. "I'm not renouncing my faith."

Smith stopped next to her and said softly, "It's not your choice anymore. If *I* don't reject Christ, he'll kill you."

Ruth touched his arm. "You won't, will you?"

"I don't know," he said as he checked the boarded windows. "If we could wrench one of these boards away quietly enough—"

"And if there isn't a guard outside," Ruth finished, as if to show how absurd the idea of escape was. "Don't worry about me. This insanity has to end somewhere, and this is as good a place as any."

Smith glanced at her as if he didn't believe her. "I appreciate your courage, but—"

"Don't patronize me," she snapped. "I mean what I say, and you mustn't compromise your faith on my behalf."

Smith impatiently grabbed his coat and threw it to her. "I don't see any guards near the front door. If you run—go straight for the cover of the graveyard—"

"Mr. Smith," Ruth began, but didn't have time to say more. Slater appeared in the doorway with his hands on his hips.

He clucked his tongue disapprovingly. "I'm disappointed in you. Now we'll have to handcuff you." He drew his pistol again and aimed it at Smith.

Williams took the cue and guided Smith back to the chair.

"You can't do this, Slater," Smith said angrily. "Kill me, but leave them out of it."

Slater shook his head. "Still trying to escape from the responsibility of making decisions. I would have thought you'd learned by now. You're no use to me dead. But these others are . . . well, they're expendable." He tipped his head towards Ruth. "Nothing personal, of course."

"It never is when people like you kill people like me," Ruth said.

"What's your decision?" Slater asked Smith.

"Keep the faith, Elijah," Ruth said.

Williams had just produced a pair of handcuffs with which to secure Smith, when Smith suddenly threw himself at Slater and put his hands around Slater's throat. They fell to the ground and struggled until Williams, more powerful than he looked, grabbed Smith and pulled him off.

"No!" Ruth cried out and, as Williams and Slater wrestled Smith back to the chair, begged them not to hurt him.

Slater clasped the handcuffs securely around Smith's wrists. "Desperate thoughts and foolish actions, my friend," Slater puffed, his tongue searching out a break in his lip where a tiny thread of blood fell. "I take that as your answer."

He signaled Williams, who took Ruth by the arm and led her through the front doors. The light was blinding compared to the relative darkness of the sanctuary. It gave the scene outside the look of an overdeveloped photo. Smith trembled and strained at the handcuffs, the cutting pain in his wrists a small token, a gift, for Ruth. "You can't do this," Smith said.

The doors banged shut, making Smith jump in his chair as

if the shot had been fired. Then the shot itself came, and Smith slumped as if he had been the one to receive the bullet.

"What a waste," Slater said with practiced sadness. "Is your faith *really* worth the lives of all these people?"

The doors opened again, and Williams returned. There was no change in his composure, as if he'd stepped outside merely to check the temperature. An unspoken signal passed between Slater and Williams, and the latter continued on into the hallway.

Smith looked at Slater and spat, "How could you do this? How could you have the flesh and blood of a human being and be so inhuman inside?"

"We'll see who is inhuman," Slater said. "The decision remains yours. You can stop this anytime you want."

Williams returned with Mary. Smith groaned and lowered his head, "Oh, Mary . . ."

"You don't have to lock us in our rooms, Captain," Mary said. "We won't try to escape."

Slater said cordially, "Your circumstance here is entirely in Elijah's hands. Talk to him about it." He and Williams stepped into the hallway again.

"I thought I heard a gunshot," Mary said.

"You did."

"Who was it?"

"Ruth."

She sighed deeply, a slight breeze from her innermost soul that echoed through Smith's with a mournful whimper.

Smith searched her face. Her red, tear-eroded eyes looked back at him, and he was struck that this must've been what the mother of Jesus looked like at his crucifixion. "Mary . . . ," he began, but didn't know how to finish it.

"Don't say anything, Mr. Smith."

"You don't understand," he said. But her eyes told him that she did.

She said, "Losing Timothy was like death for me. I was afraid then. I'm afraid now, too, but it's different somehow. Maybe it's anticipation. I have a husband and a son I'm waiting to see."

She stood erect, strong, and determined. Smith had a sense that he was seeing her true self—a person who'd been buried by circumstance and time and was now coming alive.

"Well?" Slater asked upon his return. He looked eagerly at Smith and then Mary. When neither responded, he said, "So be it."

"Come with me," Williams said and guided Mary to the front doors.

She didn't look back but held her head high, her face directed ahead into the ethereal light of day.

"The shame of it all is that no one will ever know what happened here. It will never be written or recorded and put in a Bible somewhere. It will be forgotten like the decaying bodies in this church. How does the saying go? Ashes to ashes—"

The shot rang out.

"—dust to dust?"

Smith felt the tears well up in him like a wave of nausea.

"What's it for, Elijah? For nothing."

Williams moved through the sanctuary and disappeared down the hallway again like a dark spirit.

Slater continued, ignorant of or unaware that Williams had been there at all. "You could make the difference, my friend. You can make what happens here worthwhile, meaningful. This church could become a shrine to the diplomat who made peace between two opposing factions."

Smith jerked toward him angrily, the handcuffs scraping

against the metal backing of the chair. "What is it about Christians that makes you do this? I'll tell you what it is: It's because we have something you don't. And it's eating at your insides because you can't touch it or take it away from us. No matter how hard you try, you can't smother it or stop it. You may think you know human nature, but you don't know anything about the Spirit. And it's driving you crazy because you never will!"

Slater leaned into Smith's face, his nostrils flaring, his hot breath filling the air between them. "I know a lot more than you can imagine."

"Why? Because of your father?" Smith said.

Slater flinched as if Smith had struck him.

Smith went on, pressing the nerve. "Is that what this is all about? You want to stamp out the Underground because *your father* created it?"

"Williams!" Slater called out as he stepped back. "Bring me *two* this time!"

Smith clenched his teeth. "No."

"You can't sit here and let these people die. You won't do it! No faith—not even yours—can bear the responsibility of killing your brothers and sisters. Stop it *now*, Elijah! The power to do it is in your hands!"

CHAPTER 34

ALONE with Howard Beck and Luke, Smith tried to think. Two men might have a chance to change the playing field of Slater's little game. If Howard jumped Slater and Luke could get the better of Williams . . . No, it was absurd to think about.

"I demand to know what's going on," Beck said. "I thought I heard gunshots."

Smith couldn't think clearly. Slater's constant barrage and the deaths of Ruth and Mary squeezed his brain like a vise. It was all because of him. *Because of me.* Self-reproach visited him, turning the vise tighter. What if he hadn't run away? What if he hadn't come back? What if he gave up and went along with Slater's demands now, with the hope of escaping to undo it later? What if . . . ?

"Are you listening to me?" Beck asked. "Captain Slater was ready to make a deal of some sort. So what's the problem? Do what he wants!"

"You don't get it."

"What's to get?" Beck asked. "You put us into this situation; you can get us out."

It sounded so easy, Smith thought. Why not? A simple nod from him and Slater would stop this massacre. And then what? Smith felt the cold grip of the devil's handshake and asked himself, so what if he gained the world and lost his soul?

Smith looked at Luke and was startled by the serenity on his face. Was he really oblivious to what was happening around him, or was he at peace? Luke caught Smith's gaze and smiled. This was not the dull, abstract expression he characteristically wore. He looked vibrant and alive. A fist tightened around Smith's heart.

"There was darkness in the belly of the whale," Luke said. "There was darkness in the tomb, too. But it lasted only three days. Today is your day of release."

Smith felt a warm tear gather in the corner of his eye. "Forgive me," he whispered.

"What are you talking about?" Beck demanded. "Forgive you for what? Be practical, Smith. If you go along with whatever he wants, then we're free to go, right? 'He who fights and runs away, lives to fight another day.'"

Smith spoke calmly. "If I deny Christ, then he'll let you go. Otherwise . . ."

Beck asked impatiently, "Otherwise what?"

"Those gunshots you heard were . . . he killed Ruth and Mary."

The blood drained from Beck's face. "What? No!" His eyes reflected deep panic. "What are you going to do? You're not going to let him kill me, are you?"

Slater and Williams reappeared in the doorway.

Beck rushed over to them. "Captain Slater, you can't be serious about this. It's not fair to put my life in his hands. It should be my decision. We had a deal. You said no one would get hurt if I cooperated."

"Smith?" Slater asked Smith, ignoring Beck with an expression of disgust.

Smith looked away.

"Get them out of here," Slater snapped. Williams took Beck's arm to lead him out. Luke followed peacefully, obediently, a lamb to the slaughter.

"No, please!" Beck begged as Williams pulled at him. "Just tell me what you want! Smith, please help me! This isn't fair! I'm not ready to die!"

Williams pushed him through the doors, and even after they'd been closed, Smith could hear Beck's voice outside.

"Don't do this!" he cried. "This is insane! Oh, God, forgive me."

The gunshot cut him off. Then the second.

Smith's head dropped, tears sliding down his cheeks freely.

❋

On his knees in the wet snow, Howard Beck slowly lifted his head. Williams held his gun to the sky as if he'd just signaled the start of a race.

"We said that *you* wouldn't get hurt if you cooperated," Williams explained. "Here are your coats, knapsacks, and some additional provisions. Now take your lunatic friend and run."

Beck stood up on trembling legs, the cold air jabbing at his skin like pinpricks. Luke was already standing, his expression unchanged from what it had been in the sanctuary.

"Both of us?" Beck asked, his mouth hanging open, his brain still not grasping what was happening. He looked helplessly at Williams. Having been sure of his death, he now felt an odd disappointment that he was still alive. Relief, he hoped, would come later. Or would it?

Williams jabbed a thumb at Luke. "He's useless to us. Now take him and go."

"But—where?"

"Run!" Williams commanded and turned to go back into the church.

Beck quickly grabbed the knapsacks and thrust one into Luke's arms. "Let's go, Luke," he said and tugged at Luke's sleeve.

They pushed through the snow until they found the path that took them into the mountains.

CHAPTER 35

The question I keep hearing—the one that keeps
echoing through my own mind—is "Why is this
happening to me? I'm a Christian—why are these bad
things happening to me?" But I keep coming back to
another question: "Why not?" Considering the
ongoing corruption of the world, I have to wonder
why terrible things don't happen to us more often.

—from *The Posthumous Papers of Samuel T. Johnson*

✳

S AM wondered why God seemed to speak to man only
through beauty or pain. Through the crack in the board
over his window, he could see past the patrolling guard
to the mountain beyond—the blanket of snow, the majestic
pines, and the high hills that rolled like the spine of the earth.
Deep patches of blue appeared like lakes in the sky. He hadn't
noticed the beauty of the area before; funny that he could
afford to now. It spoke to him like a gentle tap on the shoulder
and a whisper from God.

Yet it hadn't been through beauty that God got through to
Sam's heart, not before he'd become a Christian and not since.
It had been through pain—the pain of a cross, the pain of

separation, the pain of their experience in the church, and now the pain of imminent death. Pain preceded a resurrected life, a resurrected heart. Sam didn't understand why, but that's the way it was. If God's own Son had to abide by that rule, then there could be no exceptions.

Two figures moved through the trees, but Sam couldn't make out who they were. Certainly not officers—they weren't dressed right. Before he could ponder their significance, the door behind him opened. He turned, and Williams stood expectantly.

"I don't suppose you've come to play cards," Sam said.

A smile twitched at the corners of Williams's lips. Sam followed him out of the room and down the hallway. As they approached the sanctuary, he could hear Slater.

"Your heart must be completely broken by now," Slater was saying, prowling around Smith like a lion. "Surely it couldn't withstand the weight of all that has happened here. No heart could. Put an end to it."

Slater saw Sam and, as if well rehearsed, crossed the room to him as if he were about to greet an old friend. He spoke conspiratorially. "He's being stubborn. Reason with him." He then slipped into the hallway with Williams.

From the back, Smith was the picture of suffering. His arms were stretched behind him, cuffed together around the chair, and he was hunched over as if exhaustion had forced his head to his knees. Sam moved to stand next to him.

"I heard the shots," Sam began in a low tone. "It's strange. I always thought that when it was time for me to die, I'd have something significant and profound to say. I don't. Right now I feel a very quiet peace. It's the kind of thing I've prayed for—that peace—but never thought I'd experience."

Smith didn't respond. His shoulders shook slightly, and only then did Sam realize he was crying.

"Mr. Smith . . ."

Smith slowly drew his head up, his body trembling. His eyes were red and puffy; tear-stained trails crisscrossed his ruddy cheeks.

"It was important that you came back here," Sam said. "I've been thinking about it, and I believe it was intended this way. Everything that has happened over the past few weeks has pointed to this moment."

"But why?" Smith asked.

"Why not?" Sam shrugged. "We can all run like Jonah, but we must face our Golgothas like Jesus. The battle may seem lost, but we've won the war. So, in a way, it's incidental how it all plays out. We're going to die sometime."

Smith took a deep breath and closed his eyes.

"Besides, who said there can't be a happy ending in death?" Sam called out, "Slater!"

Slater looked curious as he and Williams stepped in from the hallway.

"Let's get this over with," Sam said firmly.

Slater looked disappointed, then motioned to Williams. Williams stood next to Sam, like a waiter about to show him to a table.

"Guard your faith well, Elijah," Sam said as he was led out.

Sam clasped his hands in front of him to keep them from shaking. He didn't want his reaction to the sudden cold to be mistaken for fear. He was afraid, yes, but there was no reason to show it to Williams or the guards nearby. His knees trembled.

"Would you like to remain standing or get on your knees?" Williams asked.

"My knees," Sam replied and knelt down in the snow. Not far away, he saw the small pockmarks in the snow where other knees had been placed, a spray of red dotting the soft white ground like a bad complexion. *It'll be over quick,* he thought.

"Aim well," he said to Williams.

The cocking of the gun was the last thing he heard.

CHAPTER 36

SMITH tried to pray, but Slater's voice kept cutting in. "One more, Elijah. One more life here and many more elsewhere that you can save if you so choose."

Smith was drained now. Guilt dug its talons deep into his soul. It seemed to echo throughout his inner emptiness until there was nothing left but the sound of his own heartbeat. *It's all my fault,* he thought. *This is for me.* He was beyond regrets, the *what ifs* of what he should or shouldn't have done. He had five deaths on his conscience and no time left to atone for it. *God, I hope there is a purgatory somewhere,* he thought. *Hold me accountable.*

But the sight of Amy was a blow to his determination. She was like a lost love to him, the kind of girl he had once hoped to marry and have children with. Maybe if she survived, her youth and energy might somehow save what was left of this awful world. She was a tiny ember of innocence that might start a new fire. Were there any like her left?

If he didn't agree with Slater, there wouldn't be.

"She's such a sweet thing," Slater said vociferously, like a slave auctioneer. "It would be a shame to lose her. But you haven't made up your mind, have you?"

Smith refused to look up at Slater or Amy. If he saw her eyes, he would weaken.

Slater gestured to Williams. "How about it, Williams? Do you think our young officers outside would enjoy this young girl?"

Smith's head snapped up as Williams grabbed Amy. She struggled against his grip but with no effect. "No!" she cried out again and again through clenched teeth.

"Tell them I said they can do whatever they want with her," Slater shouted.

Amy fought every inch of the way as Williams dragged her to the door.

"She's a fighter." Slater smiled. "They'll like that."

The image of Amy being brutally raped filled Smith's mind. It was worse than anything else he could have imagined. A bullet through the brain, other types of torture—he might have had the strength to withstand—but this was the rape of hope, the total corruption of innocence. The last ember would be snuffed out, and it would be his fault. He didn't know if he spoke for her sake or for his, but he was too weak to keep silent.

"All right," Smith snapped.

"Wait!" Slater called out to Williams, then turned to Smith. "What did you say?"

"Let her go," Smith said, defeated.

"You agree then?"

Smith nodded so slightly that Slater didn't seem to catch it. "You agree?"

Smith was about to say yes when Amy suddenly broke free from Williams and raced to Smith. "No!" She fell and skidded on her knees in front of him. "Don't do it. Any agreement with this man would be like making a covenant with the devil. Whatever he says he'll do is a lie. You have to know that better than I do. Please . . ."

Smith whispered despondently, "But, Amy—"

Amy locked her eyes onto his. "They can't hurt me inside
. . . not where it really matters."

Williams yanked her to her feet.

"I don't care what they do," she said.

But the tears came to her eyes in spite of her resolve, and in
them Smith felt his own heart bleed. It covered him like a
setting sun. *This is for me,* he kept thinking in his hollow,
prayerless void. The words bounced and echoed like the cry
of a small boy lost in a deep cave. *This is for me.*

Another voice entered into his darkness, not a distant echo
but a very present resonance that whispered in his ear. "This
is not for you," it said. "This is for *Me.*"

"I want your word on this," Slater said.

Smith kept his eyes on Amy's. She forced a smile through
the stream of tears. "We don't have to run ever again."

"I'm waiting!" Slater shouted, his voice betraying a crack
in his composure.

"No," Smith said as he lowered his head again.

Slater's rage blew in a volcanic explosion. "Get her out of
here! Put her with the rest!"

Williams dragged Amy away, kicking open the doors and
disappearing into the light as his boss screamed after him.

"I want the bodies hung from the trees! Do you hear me? I
want this place to be a curse to anyone who'll think of hiding
here again!"

Slater was out of control now. He lunged at Smith, pummel-
ing him with slaps and punches. Then Slater grabbed him by
the lapels and, with surprising strength, pulled him, chair and
all, to the open doors. He carelessly threw Smith down on the
threshold so that he landed partly on his knees, the chair
doubling him over so his weight also went to his shoulders.
"You are a fool!" Slater shrieked. "I want you to see what
you've done! Watch!"

Smith tried to turn away, but Slater held his face firm. Through the light he saw Amy standing in the snow. Williams pointed his pistol at her head. Smith clenched his eyes shut.

"I want you to see how her blood looks on the beautiful white snow! Look!"

The shot reverberated through the church, the countryside, and Smith's own soul. The spirit departed from her and went to a better place; her body fell in a heap.

"You are to blame," Slater gasped, collapsing on the floor next to Smith. He was expended now, the tantrum climaxed and subsided.

Still on his knees, Smith wept. What else could Slater do to him? There was nothing left that could hurt him, which is as it should be when it comes to matters of faith. With no pride to cling to, no despair to wallow in, Smith looked into the eyes of faith and saw its simplicity. *God, how loving you must be to put yourself into the fragile hearts of men.*

Slater hissed, "What do you have to say about your faith now?"

Smith's voice shook as he answered, "Jesus loves me, this I know, for the Bible tells me so. Little ones to him belong; we are weak, but he is strong."

The activity outside was electric and confused as the bodies of those who'd been shot were pulled out from under tarps and carried toward the single oak that watched over the graveyard. Williams barked out orders to the men who, with sickly expressions, tied ropes to the corpses' ankles and strung them up like so many turkeys in a butcher-shop window. *There is no dignity,* Smith thought. *Not in these bodies, not in this life—only in eternity.*

He heard the loud click of a gun being cocked behind him. It was Slater's, he had no doubt. The madman had run out of moves; there was nothing left for him to do. Smith was a useless pawn now.

"God forgive you," Smith said with the taste of dirt and snow in his mouth.

If Slater replied, he never heard it.

CHAPTER 37

S LATER staggered to the small table and leaned on it for support. He rubbed his hands over his face. Losing control like he had made him feel nauseous. It was a sign of weakness. Even Williams looked upon him with obvious disgust.

His eye caught a stack of papers near the edge of the desk, and he picked them up. *The Posthumous Papers of Samuel T. Johnson* the top page said in distinctive handwriting. He was about to hand it to Williams as evidence when the last page slipped out and fell on the floor. He retrieved it, suddenly curious about the final entry—whatever it might be.

Sam had written it the day before.

"O death, where is your victory? O death, where is your sting? How we thank God, who gives us victory over sin and death through Jesus Christ our Lord! Brothers and sisters, I want you to know what will happen to the Christians who have died so you will not be full of sorrow like people who have no hope. For since we believe that Jesus died and was raised to life again, we also believe that when Jesus comes, God will bring back with Jesus all the Christians who have died. I can tell you this directly from the Lord: We who are still living when the Lord returns will not rise to meet him ahead of those who are in their graves. For the Lord himself will come down from heaven with a commanding shout, with the call of the archangel, and with the trumpet call of God. First, all the Christians who have died will rise from their graves. Then, together with them, we who are still alive and remain on the earth will be caught up in the clouds to meet the Lord in the air and remain with him forever. He will remove all of their sorrows, and there will be no more death or sorrow or crying or pain. So comfort and encourage each other with these words."

Slater threw the papers at Williams and stormed out of the church. "Burn it," he commanded. "Burn it all."

HOWARD and Luke stood on a high ledge overlooking the valley. In the distance, Hopewell sat nestled like a toy village in plastic trees. Closer, just below them, they could see the last of the police leave the church. After a moment, smoke billowed from the sanctuary. Tiny tongues of flame appeared in the sanctuary wing, growing larger, and in no time at all engulfed the church. It went up quickly, like the kindling it was.

Luke said simply, "God have mercy."

Beck sobbed breathlessly. His eyes were already red from weeping, and they now burned from the irritation of constantly rubbing them. He wished with all his heart that Williams had killed him, if only to save him the trouble of doing the job later. It wasn't mercy that let him live. It was a curse, like the mark of Cain.

He turned away from the scene below and looked to the path ahead. It forked in two directions. He wondered which one to take. He could take the path of Judas or the path of Simon Peter. One betrayed Jesus and hanged himself; the other betrayed Jesus and found forgiveness.

Forgiveness seemed an impossibility now. He had done too much, more than God himself could accept. It would be better to kill himself, fling himself over the ledge now, and be done with it. He glanced at the drop and wondered if it would truly kill him. Cursed as he was, he might well survive it.

He was a coward, but he wasn't that much of a coward.

Luke sighed and faced Howard, his eyes brimming with tears. Did he really understand what was happening? If Howard killed himself, what would become of Luke? Maybe he was rationalizing, but he couldn't leave Luke alone in the wilderness, could he?

"What will become of you?" Howard asked.

Luke replied, "The Lord is our strength and provision."

Howard shook his head. He had betrayed the others by wanting to stay alive. Could he betray Luke now by killing himself? Perhaps Luke could be his penance, his means of redemption.

No, he abruptly thought and slumped against a large boulder. No. He was trying to negotiate another deal with God, and that was something he couldn't afford to do. Not again. Never again. At least Judas and Peter carried their betrayals to the end, to their full consequence. Howard had to do the same. He had to make up his mind. Which path should he take?

He looked one last time at the burning church and then waved at Luke. "Come on," he said.

They strolled to the fork and took the path that would lead them farther up.